WORTH THE
CHANCE

New York Times Bestseller
VI KEELAND

Worth the Chance
Edited by: Warneke Reading
Cover model: Micah Truitt, Wilhelmina Models
Photographer: Domonick Gravine
domgravinephotography.com

"Sometimes, life gives you a second chance because, just maybe, you weren't ready the first time around."
-Unknown

For Chris.
Without whom, I'd be lost.

CHAPTER 1

Vince

The pounding in my head rises from a dull base drum playing in the background to a full snare drumroll just beneath my eyelids. I'm afraid to crack one eye open, for fear that the drum playing inside my head will escape and follow me around for the rest of my life. But the god damn noise coming from that phone is too painful to ignore.

I trace the horrible music to the other side of the room in the darkness, desperate to make it stop. It's not hard to locate the intruder; it's flashing and buzzing and jumping around like a Mexican jumping bean. I pick it up and look at the picture of some girl I don't know smiling at me from the caller ID. She looks fucking annoying. It takes a few seconds for it to register that it's not my phone. Hitting REJECT on the screen, I toss the thing back on the dresser and make my way to the bathroom and back without turning on any lights. Light makes the pounding worse. I know from experience.

Ignoring the jackhammer that replaced the snare the minute my head went from horizontal to vertical, I crawl into bed, shut my eyes, and begin to drift back to sleep. Until another god damn phone starts ringing. This time it's coming from the night stand within my reach, and the ringtone is familiar. My screen flashes Elle's name and, just as I'm about to hit REJECT again, I catch sight of the time. Fuck! Nico's going to kill me this time.

"Hello." I answer trying to hide the grogginess in my voice that would give away I just woke up. I'm not too successful at it.

"Did I just wake you?" Elle's voice is full of concern. She knows Nico is looking for a reason to kick my ass out of training. Again.

"No, I'm on my way now…I got caught in traffic," I lie.

"Good, because he's already downstairs waiting for you not to show."

"I'll be there." I hang up, heave my phone across the room, and groan when I hear it hit the wall and shatter. Another fucking four hundred bucks down the toilet.

"What's the matter?" The woman's voice startles me as I'm about to get out of bed. I have ten minutes to shower and get to the gym or I'm going to be out on my ass without a trainer again. I feel a hand reach for my naked ass and pieces of last night come flooding back to me. Krissy. Shit.

"Get up. I need to be out of here in two minutes." I don't even try to be nice. I'm pissed off at myself that I brought her here. Broke my own no groupie golden rule last night because I was too drunk to shake her off.

You see, I'm a fighter. A pretty damn good one. And good ones have groupies. We call them GIMPs. Short for Groupie I Might Pound. Yeah, I know. It's not nice. But who said I was nice anyway? If a woman wants to follow me around and let me fuck her doggie style in the bathroom of a bar, who am I to say no? I'm not a dick to them. I take care of them. See to their needs before my own. Most nights, anyway. I just don't bring them home with me. Bringing them home gives them false expectations. Plus, then they know where I live.

Nico's at the entrance when I walk in. "You're late." I ignore his comment and take my place in front of the class.

Yeah, I'm late, but less than ten minutes, thanks to his wife's call. Today is my day to volunteer at the Women's Center. Yeah, right, *volunteer*. Like anyone could ever tell Nico Hunter no. Even if I weren't already one fuck up away from him dropping me as my trainer, I still wouldn't be able to get out of this. If you want to train with Nico, you do what he wants…even if he poses what he wants to you as a question. You don't really have a choice in your answer.

My stint volunteering at the Women's Center is part of my penance. Nico thinks I need to build more character, learn to respect women more. Sure, everyone should be pussy-whipped like him. He thinks I don't remember how he was before he met Elle, but I do. A different woman took the walk of shame almost every morning out the back door of the gym. I was only thirteen, but I remember. Mostly because they were all pretty fucking hot. Tits sticking out and short little skirts, who could forget seeing that shit each morning when you're thirteen? Some mornings I had to run on the treadmill with a damn hard-on. Then he met Elle and everything changed.

Don't get me wrong, Elle is the coolest chick I know. She runs interference between me and Nico when things get too heated. But this volunteer crap is their gig, not mine. Yet here I am at 10AM on a Saturday about to teach self-defense to a room full of women.

I take a quick look around the packed room and give them my best smile. The one that always helps me get away with shit when I'm in trouble. Well, at least when the trouble I'm in is with the ladies.

Nico watches from the doorway as I lead the class through a few minutes of warm up stretches. I'm relieved when he eventually disappears and I can stop pretending I'm happy to be at the head of the class this morning. I'd much rather still be in bed, lying flat on my back, *getting* head. I weave my way through the students as they begin their leg kicks. Some I help with their form, others I pass and smile at as I check them out in their skimpy, tight clothing. I'm sizing up the class, looking for my next assistant. If I have to demonstrate on someone, they might as well be worth touching, right?

Out of the corner of my eye, I catch a glimpse of a woman in the back row. She's turned around, but I already know she's going to be my assistant just from the sight of that ass. It's shaped like a perfect heart and, as she reaches up to tie her hair into a ponytail, I'm treated to a glimpse of porcelain skin beneath her shirt that I get the urge to sink my teeth into.

I walk towards her, thinking maybe this morning's gig won't be so bad after all. Hell, if the front looks half as good as the back, this class may even go long today. I make my way up the aisle to reach her, ready to turn on my charm, just as she turns my way. What I see stops me dead in my tracks. Can it really be her?

CHAPTER 2

Liv

James Hawthorne is a total sleezeball. Two minutes ago I caught him pinching his secretary's ass and now, as I graciously bend down to pick up the papers that dropped from his desk, I catch him looking down my shirt. He probably pushed them off on purpose. He doesn't even have the decency to pretend he wasn't looking. Instead, he actually smiles at me when I catch him peering over his desk. Total sleezeball.

I return the smile as I take my seat in front of his desk anyway, even though it physically pains me. I want the job that badly. Bad enough to put up with his crap for another seven weeks of my internship.

Sleezeball loses interest in me the moment my competition walks in. Summer Langley. She's tall, model thin, and her long, bleached blonde hair contrasts starkly with her olive skin. She's pretty, I don't blame him for drooling over her. But we're not in a beauty competition, we're competing for a job. And not just any job, one of the most coveted jobs in all of Chicago. And it's down to just the two of us. My only alternative position is located in New York, almost a thousand miles from my family and friends.

My resume speaks for itself. A 4.0 in college and grad school, editor of my college newspaper, and TA to a renowned English professor while working on my Masters. Summer, on the other hand, has a resume with a slight edge. She has two things I can't compete with.

Her father sits on the board of the *Daily Sun Times* and she has no problem flirting with the boss.

But I've wanted this job since high school, so I force myself to believe that the best candidate, the one who does the best work, will actually get the job when this internship is over in seven weeks. Eleven hundred people applied for these two spots. Now it's down to just the two of us. I'm so close I can taste it.

I've wanted to be a writer at the *Daily Sun Times* as long as I can remember. Writers here earn Pulitzers and chair literary guilds. I smile at Summer as she takes her seat next to me and we both wait for our new assignment from Sleezeball. She's not qualified for the job. The reality is she wouldn't even be here if her daddy didn't sit on the Board. But there's a sinking feeling in my stomach as we both receive our assignments. Summer will be interviewing a young up-and-coming entrepreneur, one who is about to take his cutting-edge internet marketing firm public. I, on the other hand, am being sent to the warehouse district to interview some troubled mixed martial arts fighter who beats the crap out of people for a living.

I smile at Sleezeball as I take the assignment sheet from his hand, pretending to not be affected by his giving Summer the better story to write.

"Thank you, James. Sounds like it could make for a very interesting story." Yeah, right. Someone shoot me now and put me out of my misery.

James smiles back at me politely, but his attention is quickly refocused on Summer. He tells her to stay so they can talk about the angle she is going to write the story from. He asks me to close the door as I leave. He falls short of telling me not to let it hit me on the ass on the way out. Barely. I wonder if he even notices the steam coming from my ears as I walk out his door.

Some quick research revealed that the fighter volunteers to teach a self-defense class for women. Maybe I can work a good guy side of a bad boy fighter angle to this story, keep people from falling asleep before they reach the end of the article.

I get lost downtown and barely make it to the gym before the class I'm scheduled to attend starts. I was hoping to get to class early to speak to the instructor and set up an appointment to interview him for my article. But I'm late and the full class is already starting. So instead I slip into the back, toss my bag behind me, and quickly tie my long auburn hair back from my face.

I hear the instructor's voice getting louder as he walks through the room in search of a volunteer to help him demonstrate moves. His voice is distracting, sexy with an edge to it, almost gravelly, like he's been yelling all night and now he's straining to have his deep voice heard. Then suddenly the voice goes quiet in mid-sentence. Finishing tying up my hair, I turn, curious to see what's quieted the sexy voice. I almost fall when all of the air in my lungs is violently sucked out of my body by the vision of the man I find standing in front of me.

CHAPTER 3

Liv – 7 ½ years earlier

He walks into the library and, unconsciously, I hold my breath. I watch as he looks around the room, knowing he is looking for me. We've been meeting here at the same time every Thursday for the last five weeks. For a second I let myself pretend he scans the room for me because he's mine. Not because Mr. Hunter is paying me to tutor him. He looks so different from the other boys, and it's not just because he's taller and wider. No, it's definitely more than that. Something about the way he carries himself sets him apart. It's hard to put into words what it is…he just has it. Strong, confident, unaffected by the normal high school stuff going on all around him.

I watch from a distance as he spots me and smiles in my direction. The way his dimples dip deep into his beautiful tan skin sends my mind racing. He makes me forget where I am. Hell, he makes me forget *who* I am with that smile. Vinny walks with purpose directly to the table I'm sitting at, completely unaware of the girls stopping in their tracks to watch him pass by.

"You okay, Liv?" I can see in his face he's concerned, but I'm not sure why.

I don't answer, but not because I don't want to. Suddenly, I physically can't respond. I'm lightheaded, the room begins to spin, and I feel as though I might pass out any second.

"Liv?" Vinny repeats himself, his voice louder, more urgent this time. It snaps me out of my daze and I realize I'm not breathing. A strong rush of air whooshes out of my lungs and I gasp to take my next breath. But the deep inhale after depriving my lungs of oxygen burns my throat, sending me into a coughing fit and I can't seem to stop myself from coughing uncontrollably. The whole library is looking at me now and I want to climb under the table and hide. Vinny is holding my hand and hovering over me. He looks genuinely concerned.

It takes me a minute, but I finally catch my breath and my coughing fit slows enough to squeak out an answer. "I'm fine. I just choked on a cough drop," I lie. I can't tell him he steals my breath away and I forget to breathe sometimes when he's around me. I'm sure he already thinks I'm a weirdo.

Vinny grabs a chair and turns it backwards to sit, his forearms leaning on the top of the chair back as he straddles it. Such a boy way to sit. "Jesus, Liv. I thought I was going to have to perform the Heimlich on you there for a minute. I was worried I might break you, you're so tiny." He leans in and whispers as he teases me with a devilish smile that makes my heart pound loudly in my chest.

"I'm fine." Luckily, my face is still red from my coughing fit, so he can't see that I'm heated from just feeling his breath on my neck as he speaks. "We better get started. We have a lot to cover today if you want to pass the English midterm next week." That, and my heart just might explode if we don't get back on track. I can't think around this boy. He makes my brain turn to mush so that I forget to breathe. Who *forgets* to breathe? I'm such a dork.

The librarian shushes us and Vinny throws his hands up in playful surrender and smiles at her. Her angry face changes when she's on the receiving end of his smile. His charm knows no age boundaries.

Eventually we fall back into our roll of student and tutor and I'm able to refocus on the reason I get to spend so much time with Vinny Stonetti. Although he's a senior and two years older, he's a year behind in English and I'm a year advanced, so we're both in the same English class. And he's in danger of failing this year. Again. Most likely it's because he doesn't spend much time in our actual class. He seems to be either out sick or suspended for fighting most of the time.

Six weeks ago when my dad told his friend that his daughter would tutor a boy who was struggling in English, it didn't seem like such a big deal. Not until I found out the boy was the same one I've had a major crush on since seventh grade. I spent three long years watching him from a distance, secretly obsessing over the way he walks, the way he sits, and even the way his full lips move as he chews when I steal glances of him in the cafeteria.

And now, here I sit. Up close and personal for three hours each week with the boy who visited my dreams on more nights than I can count. I expected him to be something very different, although I'm not sure what it was that I thought he'd be. But he's even better than I'd made up in my head. He's smart, a fast learner, and funny too. We actually have a good time while we work through the material, and I'm surprised that we've almost caught up on the full semester's work already.

"Did you figure out what comes after Juliet tells her mother about the wedding in the courtyard? I'm wondering when we're getting to the good stuff...the wedding night?" Vinny wiggles his eyebrows playfully.

I still can't believe I told him about my little geeky hobby. Ever since I was old enough to read, I've been a sucker for tragic romances. Devouring every word, I sometimes cry through the tragic beauty that sweeps me away. Then, when I'm done, I just can't help myself. I rewrite the ending. Every story deserves a happy ending in my mind.

Two weeks ago, when we were finishing up Romeo and Juliet for class, I was so caught up in the love story that I blurted out the ending I had begun writing. Embarrassed at my own admission, I wanted to crawl in a hole, but Vinny actually seemed interested. Intrigued even. Instead of finding my quirky habits odd and scaring him away, he seems to want to know more. More about what I like to do. What makes me happy.

"Actually, I think after her mother…." I'm just about to tell Vinny about the chapter I wrote over the weekend, when I'm interrupted by a voice I've come to despise.

"Well don't you and your little tutor girl look like you're having a good time?" Missy Tatum's snide voice brings me crashing back to reality. One look reminding me of everything I'm not. I'm pretty sure if she wore any less clothing she would get arrested for indecent exposure. From where I'm sitting, the underside of her full boobs are clearly visible. Her half shirt barely covers her at eye level, even less so from the view from below. Immediately I feel self-conscious about my lack of curves. She's a senior and I'm in tenth grade. A late blooming tenth grader at that. In less than thirty seconds the comfort I've felt settle in with Vinny the last few hours is gone, and I'm back to being the little girl.

"Wait outside Missy, I'll be done in a few minutes." Vinny's voice changes from the gentle and playful tone he has with me to something harsher, more controlling. For a second I think Missy is going to complain, but Vinny gives her a look daring her to respond. She pouts, but turns and walks toward the door to wait without another word.

"Sorry about that."

"It's fine."

"No, it's not. She shouldn't talk to you that way." His voice is still angry, so different than how he usually speaks to me.

"Thanks, but I'm used to it."

"What do you mean you're used to it?"

"Her crowd." I shrug, motioning with my eyes toward the door where Missy and her friends are gathered smoking cigarettes outside the library. "They just make little comments, that's all."

"Like what?" Vinny's jaw flexes and his temper flares. It's a side of him that I've seen from a distance, but never up close, never directed at me. He's scary when he's angry. His relaxed and playful demeanor is gone, replaced by clenched fists and shoulders more squared than usual.

"It's not a big deal." I feign an indifferent smile and start to pack up my books.

Vinny's quiet for a minute, but I can feel him watching me as I pile all my things back into my backpack. It makes me nervous and I feel my face heat from the intensity of his stare. I have no choice but to look up at him when I'm done, even though I'd rather crawl under the table. He doesn't say anything, but his beautiful, pale blue eyes capture my attention, and for a minute I forget who we are and surrender to his hold. But then he abruptly stands and grabs his books off the table.

"See you next week?"

I nod my head, my words stuck beneath the lump in my throat.

I watch from the table as Vinny walks out of the library. Missy wraps herself around him the minute he exits the glass door. For a second, Vinny turns back and looks at me still frozen in my seat. Then he puts his arm around Missy's shoulder and I watch as they walk off arm in arm.

CHAPTER 4

Vinny – 7 ½ years earlier

I'm still pissed about what happened with Liv when I walk into my apartment. I plan to work off the anger with Missy. She's always ready for whatever I feel like giving her. And today I think she's going to be taking a lot.

As if the day hadn't already turned to shit, my mother's passed out on the couch and two junkies are eating cereal out of the box, staring in the direction of the TV. I'm pretty sure they can't focus enough to see what's playing. It's three o'clock in the afternoon and they aren't up from the night before. I walk over to the skinny dirtbag sitting in the chair. He's so wasted he didn't even notice me come in. I kick the side of the chair he's sitting in, the chair falls over with him still in it. "Get the fuck out."

He looks up at me, seeing me for the first time. "What's your problem, man?"

"You are. Get. The. Fuck. Out. NOW." I roar, barely controlling my temper. Each word comes out growling louder than the one before.

The loser's wasted, but at least he's not stupid. He takes one look at my face and knows he's about thirty seconds away from a beating. A bad one. One I'd be more than happy to dish out. Might even help me clear my head. He grabs the other junkie and they scramble for the door quickly. Smart move. My mother doesn't even budge, even though I'm pretty sure the old lady two floors down just heard me yell. I look at her back as she lays face down on the couch. She's still breathing. I'm not sure if it makes me feel relief or regret.

I turn to the right, movement out of the corner of my eye catching my attention. Missy. I forgot she was even here. "Go in my room. Clean off the bed." She disappears quickly.

I cover up my mother and throw out the food strewn haphazardly on the table and floor. There are empty plastic containers that were once microwave dinners but have now become ashtrays with cigarette butts in the remnants of food. Great, we'll have no fucking food again this week.

Entering my room, I find the bed I'd left with crap all over it is already cleared and Missy's stripped down to her underwear.

I walk to the bed and she reaches for my hand. She wants me to make nice. To kiss her, go gentle. But that's not what I want. Not what I need. I take the hand she offers, but use it to flip her over on the bed so she's laying on her stomach. Grabbing her legs, I yank her down to the edge of the bed so she's standing with her feet on the floor, her waist bent and body face down on my bed. Her round ass is positioned high and looking at it ready to submit to me makes me hard as I unzip my pants and free myself.

I spank her ass hard a few times with an open hand. Instantly her skin turns bright pink and it makes me harder as I watch the color deepen. The condom barely settled into place, I enter her without warning, ramming myself to the hilt in one deep thrust. She's wet already, not that I cared enough to check first. She likes it when I spank her ass, punish her, show her who's in control. Missy's as fucked up as I am. I close my eyes as I pull out and slam back in. As my eyes close, the vision of Liv's sweet little face hits me hard. It's so clear, it makes it easy to pretend it's her I'm inside. I pound in and out fiercely, desperately chasing the vision in my head, hoping to scare her away, but it doesn't work. She's stuck in my head, no matter what I seem to do lately.

CHAPTER 5

Liv

My heart is racing a million miles a minute as I take in the man he's become. I'm literally frozen in place, staring at him. He looks the same, only older, sexier, if that's even possible. He was always big, but he's grown even more, filled out in all the right places. He's tall and lean, but solid muscle defines his arms. Arms that I remember wrapping around me all those years ago. Only now there is ink covering most of his smooth, tanned skin. A large cross and symbolic lettering on his left arm catch my eye as he folds his arms across his chest causing his bicep to bulge and tighten. It distracts me and I find myself tracing the path of inky patterns, curious to see the parts that are hidden underneath his shirt. I'm not sure how much time passes, but when I look up at his face he smirks knowingly. I've been caught leering at the beautiful man before me.

His smirk turns into a full-blown smile, revealing two deep creviced, knee weakening dimples. It's a confident smile, one that tells me he knows the effect it has on women. Stunning, pale blue eyes squint ever so slightly. A glimmer of amusement shines in his eyes as he cocks one eyebrow, "Miss, would you mind being my assistant for today's class? I need someone to demonstrate technique with."

I furrow my brow, confused for a moment. But then I realize he must not recognize me. He's not the only one that's changed. The last time I saw him I was just a girl. One that developed late and didn't mature into curves until later than most. My dark, shoulder length, unstyled hair from high school is gone, replaced by thick, highlighted auburn waves that I've learned to style. Glasses turned into contacts and makeup helps to bring out my naturally high cheek bones and offset my porcelain colored skin. I'm no longer stick straight. I work hard to keep my curves well defined. I've definitely changed since the last time he's seen me.

Vinny arches one eyebrow, patiently waiting for my response with a playful smile. I look past him, finding the whole class has turned around and is watching us. Waiting. "Ummm, sure."

"Great." Vinny turns and announces to the class. "We have a volunteer for today." He motions for me to follow him to the front of the room and wastes no time jumping in. The first few maneuvers he walks us through are harmless enough. He teaches the proper way for blocking a hit and protecting your head. But we quickly come to what he calls the "sneak attack" defense lesson.

Vinny motions for me to turn around and I feel his body come up close to mine from behind. Leaning his head down close to my ear he whispers. "I have to hold you tight to demonstrate this one." His low, sexy voice and hot breath on my neck sends a shiver down my spine. Slowly, he wraps his arms around my chest, his hands locking just beneath by breasts. His warm body pressed flush against my back, goosebumps prickle all over my body. I inwardly curse my body for its reaction and pray silently that he doesn't notice.

"Cold?" I hear the smile in his voice as he whispers the word in my ear. Shit.

"Ladies that are attackers, hold on as tight as you can. Ladies that are victims, try to escape the hold." Vinny speaks loudly to the class, his grip around me never loosening.

"You can try to escape now." He whispers again in my ear.

I'm suddenly reminded just how long its been since a man has had his hands on my body. More prompting. "Go ahead, struggle, try to get away from me." Too long. Definitely way too long.

Eventually my brain takes back over command from my body which had temporarily usurped control, and I try to break free of his grip. But it's no use. The more I struggle, the tighter Vinny just grips me, and the more fused our bodies become. He takes a step back, releasing his tight hold, and for a second I feel disappointed. Turning his attention to the class, he instructs the victims on how to free themselves of the hold. "Watch as we demonstrate for you."

His grip around me from behind tightens again. "Go for it."

Really? He wants me to do all the painful things that he just instructed the class? "I don't want to hurt you." I say quiet enough so only Vinny can hear me.

"Don't worry about it. I can take whatever you can give me, Liv."

"Are you su..." Wait, did he just call me Liv? "Vinny?"

"Liv?"

Bastard. He knew all along it was me and didn't say anything. I catch him by surprise, following all of his instructions to perfection and escape his hold, leaving him doubled over in pain with the last lift of my leg.

Leaning over, hands on his knees in pain, Vinny starts laughing. "Okay class, I think we're done for today."

Annoyed, I march to the back of the room to collect my bag. Women are surrounding Vinny as I make my way to the door to quietly escape. I'm glad he's distracted so I don't have to talk to him. I'm not sure what I'm going to do about the assignment, I only know I need out of here. Now.

I'm almost out the door, when I feel a long arm wrap around my waist and pull me back. "You were going to sneak out of here without even saying goodbye to me?"

"I saw you were busy and I didn't want to interrupt you." I don't turn around as I speak.

"I'd never be too busy for you." Vinny turns me around to face him, still keeping his arm tightly wrapped around my waist. His gaze sears into me.

23

"Well you looked busy." My words come out a bit more bitter than I intend. I motion to the few women still stalling at the front of the room, waiting for their chance at his attention.

"You look…" Vinny leans back to take a slow, assaulting look up my body, "…all grown up."

"Well, that happens when you don't see someone for seven years."

"My loss." Vinny's confident smile falters and he looks sincere. It makes my irritation with him fade. Just a little.

"Did you know who I was the whole time?"

"I'd know you anywhere, Liv." The words feel intimate, seductive, and I feel my guard come down just a little bit more.

"How have you been?" Now that our conversation is moving into normalcy, I become painstakingly aware he's still holding me tight. Almost like he's afraid I'll run off if he lets go of me.

"I've gotten by." Vinny lifts his hand to my face and softly pushes a loose wave of hair that escaped my ponytail during our demonstration back behind my ear. "How about you?"

"Good. I'm a writer."

Vinny smiles. It's genuine and reminds me of our time together. It seems like a lifetime ago. *Before* what happened, happened. "I knew you would be. It's what you always wanted to do." His comment is sweet, touching that he remembers me telling him my dreams. Another inch falls down off my guard.

I smile back at him and watch as his eyes drop to my mouth. His gaze darkens and the goosebumps that haven't left me since he first touched me transmit a shiver that runs through me. I feel heat scorch through my veins and everything else in the background fades away. His eyes come back to mine for a quick second and then fall back down to my mouth. He leans in and I think he's going to kiss me. But a woman's voice rips me from my temporary moment of insanity.

"Vince, are you almost done? I'm getting bored in the car."

CHAPTER 6

Vince

Fuck. I completely forgot about Krissy. I was running so late, I didn't have time to drop her home and there was no way I was leaving her alone in my apartment.

Her nasally voice goes right through me. "Go wait in the car, Krissy." She huffs, but turns around and heads back outside.

But the damage is already done. Liv's face is back to a mask, whatever emotion I saw is gone in a flash. "I need to go, I have to get back to work." Her voice is curt and businesslike. She's grown up to be a strong woman. A beautiful, strong, incredibly sexy woman. I wouldn't have expected anything less.

She reaches for the door handle and doesn't turn around as she speaks. "It was nice seeing you, Vinny. Take care of yourself."

Something hits me and panic suddenly slices through my bones. "Wait."

Liv halts, but doesn't turn around.

"Turn around, Liv." I watch her reflection in the glass door. Eyes shut, for a moment she looks conflicted. Unsure of whether to flee or not.

"Just tell me, what made you come here today?" The thought of a man putting his hands on Liv to hurt her makes me insane with anger. Why else do women come to the Women's Center for self-defense lessons? They've been attacked and are scared, or they still live with their attacker. Either way, I feel the bile rise up in my throat at the thought of someone hurting my sweet Liv.

"I came to do research for work." She pauses and looks back at me for just a few seconds, leaving me with a sad smile. "Take care, Vinny." And then she's gone

CHAPTER 7

Liv

My morning started out almost as hellish as the night before ended. I tossed and turned half the night feeling emotions I hadn't felt in years come flooding back. Seeing Vinny again messed with my head. When I finally fell asleep at four this morning, I was so exhausted that I completely missed my alarm going off at six thirty.

Running late, I forgo washing my thick hair and settle for a fast and easy slicked back ponytail. A quick coat of mascara does little to hide the dark circles under my eyes, but I'm hopeful coffee will at least help me wake up. In my haste, I quickly pour almost half the pot into my travel mug, not realizing I didn't screw the top on correctly. I attempt to take a sip and the entire contents spills all over my favorite cream skirt and chocolate silk blouse. Hot coffee soaks me through and through. I'll even need to change my bra and panties.

Surprisingly only twenty minutes late to the office after oversleeping and having to change my outfit, I'm relieved that no one seems to notice. There's not a lot of time left to make a good impression and I'd never forgive myself if I lost the job of my dreams because I was late to work a few times.

I pull out the Stone research file, the one I should have pulled out *before* walking into the gym to get the surprise of my life, and begin sifting through mounds of photos and clippings. There are dozens of pictures of Vince "The Invincible" Stone in the ring. The ones where his arm is being raised in victory catch my eye each time. He looks so proud and confident. No matter our past, I can't stop myself from smiling, feeling happy at his victory. He's waited a long time for his moment, started fighting before I'd even met him in high school.

Then I come to the candid shots and my smile quickly fades. In photo after photo, there's a different girl under Vinny's arm. Walking on the street, outside of a bar, in front of the gym. It seems things haven't changed much over the years. I actually take my time to look at the women because I'm curious to see if any of them are repeats. Apparently, Vinny loses his interest after one night.

There's no denying the women are attractive. There are brunettes, blondes, redheads, short, tall…it appears Mr. Stone doesn't have a specific type. Unless you call provocatively dressed a type, that is. The bevy of women clinging to Vinny in the photos begins to get on my nerves, so my careful study of each shot soon turns into a quick flip. Until I get to the last couple of photos. One is of a handsome man who appears to be about Vinny's age. He looks familiar, only I can't place why. Startling pale blue eyes and a masculine, cleanly shaved jaw captivate my attention and I find myself staring. Lack of sleep does that to me, makes my gaze linger longer than usual. Flipping the print over to read the back, which normally contains data on the photo, I'm surprised to find it blank. Perhaps it's an opponent of Vinny's?

The last photo in the file is of an older man. There's a resemblance to the younger man in the previous photo and I hold them up, studying them side by side, thinking they may be father and son. The older man is nice looking, distinguished, even more familiar than the younger man in the photo before. Perhaps he's an actor, someone I've seen on television? He's wearing simple slacks and a sweater, but you can tell by the way he holds himself that he's confident. Definitely an actor. Maybe the last few were just misfiled.

Closing the photo file, I attempt to forget the gorgeous fighter in the pictures. The one with the rugged jaw that always seems to have the perfect amount of five o'clock shadow. It's not an easy task. I type up my notes, although there's not much to write since I didn't actually get to interview the subject. Three quarters of a page of basics is all I can come up with, most of that from memory.

I hate myself for stealing one last look before I turn back in the research photo file to Sleezeball. But I just can't keep my eyes off him… which is why I need to keep far, far away from Vince Stone.

CHAPTER 8

Vince

It's been two days and I still can't stop thinking about Liv. She's stuck in my head. I see her every time I close my eyes. And it's not just the thought of her incredible body that keeps my mind locked in place, although that perfect ass is definitely seared into my brain. Liv's different, always was. Smart, funny, sees life in a way that's pure. Gave me prospective. Opened my eyes to see good when bad was all I'd ever known. It took everything I had not to pounce on her back in the day. The way she looked at me with those big round hazel eyes, she made the boy I was feel like a man.

I remember purposely failing a few tests, even when I could have passed, just so I could have an excuse to be with her. Hang out with her...in the god damn library even. She was so young and sweet...and innocent. So unlike anything I had in my life.

Liv was different back then. *Is* different. I know it from just being around her again the other day. She's the type of girl you bring home to your mother. If your mother wasn't a fucking crackhead, that is.

I'm just finishing up my workout when I catch the front desk guy, Sal, pointing a woman in my direction. Not just any woman, a hot piece of ass. Now this is what I need to get my mind over little miss big eyes.

"Mr. Stone?"

I'm done with my workout, but I start one handed pushups as she approaches anyway. Might as well give her the full show. I stand and take off my sweaty shirt, using it to wipe my face. Her eyes go right to my abs. It's like taking candy from a baby.

"Who wants to know?" I smile at her while I ask.

Her eyes come up to mine, and she flips her hair back a bit before she extends her hand to me.

"My name is Summer Langley. I'm with the *Daily Sun Times*. I was wondering if I could talk to you for a little while. We'd like to run a story on you and your upcoming title fight."

"Sure." I hold the handshake longer than necessary as I speak to make my point. "As long as you don't mind me getting you all sweaty." I wait until I get a reaction from her face, and then point my eyes at our sweaty joined hands for her eyes to follow.

"Not at all." She grins back at me and I know we're on the same page.

"Come on, we can take this conversation somewhere more private." I lead her to the small kitchen in the back of the gym and put out my hand, offering her to go first through the doorway. It gives me a good shot of her ass in that tight little skirt of hers. It's nice, but too skinny. Nothing like Liv's heart shaped, perfect ass. Fuck, I gotta stop this shit with thinking about Liv. Especially when I have a hot number standing right in front of me, smiling at me like it's already a done deal.

"So, you're a writer?" *Liv's a writer too.*

"Yep, I'm actually an intern right now. I'm competing for a full writer position. It's down to two of us, so I'm hoping I get something juicy from you to help put me over the top." She emphasizes the word juicy and almost purrs at me. Oh, I'll give you something juicy alright. At least I won't have to work too hard for this one. I think she's almost as ready as I am. Maybe more so. But that's okay, even though I usually like to hunt for my dinner, sometimes it's nice to just call in for delivery too.

We sit and skinny Summer takes her pad out of some expensive designer bag that probably cost more than my last car. She smiles at me with perfectly straight white teeth that I'm sure cost her old man a fortune.

"So, Mr. Stone. Tell me about yourself. Were you born and raised in Chicago?"

"Yep, been here all my life. Went to South Shore Elementary and High School."

She jots down some notes on her pad. "Oh, that's where the other reporter is from. I'm surprised you two didn't know each other."

"What other reporter?"

"Olivia Michaels. The reporter who had this story originally."

Fuck. Me. Liv did say she was at the gym doing research. Guess she failed to mention that her research was me. "What happened to the other reporter?"

"I'm not really sure, but she gave up the assignment." Summer smiles at me like she's ready to eat me. "But I'm glad she gave it up. I can't wait to get to the juicy part."

I should be thanking the gods for what they delivered to me. Yet instead, I'm fucking pissed. Really pissed.

CHAPTER 9

Liv

Sleezeball calls us both into his office. I say good morning to Summer and she doesn't even look my way. She's in a worse mood than usual. Daddy must have cut her allowance.

"So ladies." Sleezeball comes around and sits on the corner of his desk, his arms folded over his chest. "Looks like we have a problem."

Summer folds her arms across her chest and raises her chin. Looks like the problem must belong to the princess. I try not to smile as I speak. "What's the problem and how can we help, James?" I'm such a brown noser, but I don't even care. Six more weeks. I can finally see a light at the end of the tunnel and I'm not above a little ass-kissing to make sure I'm the one that makes it there first.

"Well it seems Mr. Stone has refused an interview with Summer." I look to Summer for an explanation, but she snubs me. My face turns back to Sleezeball, waiting for more information.

"He'll only give his story to you, Olivia." Sleezeball shrugs his shoulders. "So you're back on the story, Liv." He sighs loudly. "I'm not even sure why this guy's story is so important, but my boss wants it. And since Mr. Stone has decided he wants you, that's what he'll get. You."

My mouth is still hanging open when he dismisses us. I almost make it out before Sleezeball speaks again. "Olivia, stay for a minute.

Summer, close the door on the way out." Really, could my day get any worse?

"Listen, I know you asked to be let off this story for personal reasons. However, it seems we don't have a choice here anymore. So, take this assignment as a learning experience. Whatever you and Mr. Stone have going on, exploit it and get me a good story."

Total sleezeball.

Summer is still stamping around our shared workstation when I get back to my desk. I'm guessing being rejected is new to the little princess. Although I'm pissed as hell at Vinny for interfering with my work, I have to admit, seeing her knocked off her high horse does have its perks.

"I don't know what game you're playing Olivia, but making me look bad in front of James is going to cost you." Her face distorted in anger, she doesn't look quite so attractive. "I'm not just going to win this job, I'm going to wipe the floor with that ratty little head of yours."

I can't help but laugh at her threat. Who knew the princess had it in her? Game on.

I leave the office and head straight to the gym I know Vinny works out at. I have no idea if he'll be there this time, but he's getting a piece of my mind if he is. Instead of a few hours calming my initial anger, it's made it worse. Worse to the point that I've gone from a light simmer to a full-blown boil and the top is about to come flying off the pot...and hit someone in the head.

How dare Vinny screw with my work? Who does he think he is? I've worked too damn hard to get where I am to let some old crush interfere with where I need to be. He wants to play games, he's going to find out I'm not the same little girl he thinks I am. I've grown up since he broke my heart in high school. A lot.

I enter the gym and look around. It's filled with bulky guys with tattoos and I'm surprised when a pretty, albeit very pregnant, woman walks up to me. She looks out of place dressed in a stylish red suit, her hand mindlessly rubbing the basketball she looks to be carrying around in her stomach.

"You look lost." She smiles at me warmly. "Are you looking for someone?"

"Ummm...yes, I'm looking for Vinny Stonetti." Hesitantly I respond.

"You must know Vinny for a long time?" The pretty pregnant woman tilts her head assessing me. Oddly, her inquiry and stance feel motherly, almost protective, although she certainly isn't old enough to have a child as old as Vinny.

"Actually I do. We went to high school together." I furrow my brow in confusion. "But how did you know that I'd known him for a while?"

The woman smiles warmly, "Because he made the change from Vinny Stonetti to Vince Stone a few years back. No one calls him Vinny around here anymore. Well, except me and my husband, Nico. I've known him since he was a teen, so he's still Vinny to me. My husband still calls him Vinny too, but that's to piss him off more than anything."

I smile at the woman, I can tell in the tone of her voice she has a soft spot for Vinny. It doesn't surprise me. Most women do. Until he screws them over and leaves them devastated. Like he did me. "Is Vinny...eh...Vince around?"

"He's not here yet. But he usually comes in about now. He trains with my husband."

"Oh. Okay, I'll come back later. Or maybe I'll just call and set up an appointment."

"You're welcome to wait. I was just going to have a cup of tea in the back. Why don't you join me? We can exchange embarrassing stories about Vinny."

I don't have to think about it long. I'm already here and maybe I can get some material for my story from her too. "Sure, sounds good. By the way, I'm Olivia." I extend my hand.

"I'm Elle." Smiling, she shakes my hand and then it returns to her belly. "And this here is Nicholas Jr. I think he's already practicing his kicks. He's just like his daddy, strong and full of energy."

We walk through the gym and into a small kitchen on the far side of the room. Elle puts on an electric kettle and pulls down two mugs. "I only have decaf. My husband read way too many baby books and threw out anything with caffeine within an hour of us finding out I was pregnant." She smiles and rubs her belly protectively as she continues. "We waited a long time to have this little guy. My husband finally retired from fighting last year. He's a little on the protective side when it comes to us."

Smiling at her frankness, I respond, "Decaf is fine. I'm still wired from the three cups I had at the office."

Elle and I chat for a while, the conversation comes easily, almost as if she's an old friend I'm catching up with rather than someone I barely know. Oddly, it feels as though I could sit around for hours in my pajamas watching old movies and eating ice cream straight from the container with her after one of us has had a bad breakup. She just seems like that kind of girlfriend. I don't know how much time passes but it's easy to forget I just met this woman. There's just such an instant friendship that we find ourselves giggling most of the time. As we finish our tea, Elle looks into her now empty cup with remiss. She sighs. "I miss coffee. Tell me what your three cups tasted like today. I'm that desperate. My health nut of a husband doesn't even drink coffee. Some weeks I go without even the smell of it."

Smiling, I'm more than happy to play along. Aside from being acutely addicted to coffee, I love to tell a good story. "Well, today I started with straight up Kona coffee. Fresh brewed, with a little bit of Bailey's flavored Irish Cream in it. It tasted like nutty cream freshly harvested from the mountains of Kuai."

Elle arches her eyebrows at my description and giggles. "You're killing me. But go on." She closes her eyes and smiles and waits.

"Then, in the afternoon, I needed a little pick-me-up, so I went over to Barto's for an espresso." I lean in close and lower my voice to a playful whisper. "A double."

"Mmmmm…Barto's. What did that one taste like?"

"Dark, thick, confident. Arabica beans." I pause for effect and Elle licks her lips, a dreamy smile still on her face. "The first sip tempts the tongue and brings the urge to roll the steamy liquid goodness around to make it last. Yet you can't slow it down, can't stop yourself…because you know what comes next. The unmistakable taste of dark chocolate. It coats the hint of sour and brings you deep into rich flavor. Flavor that makes you close your eyes and picture the Tuscan hills, grasses off in the distance swaying in the breeze."

Elle's eyes are still closed as she speaks, a huge grin on her face. "Mmmm…I think I can actually taste it a little. Tell me more. Tell me about the third one." She sounds like a little girl waiting anxiously for her mom to continue her bedtime story and I can't help but giggle.

I'm just about to dive into my description of my Caramel Frappuccino when a deep voice interrupts my thoughts. "Yeah, tell us more. Tell us how much you like the steamy liquid goodness, Liv." Vinny. His voice snaps me back to reality and I turn, finding him leaning casually in the doorway, one eyebrow cocked and a dirty grin on his ridiculously perfect face.

"Vinny, where have you been hiding this one? I think she might be my new best friend." Standing, Elle smiles at me and waits for Vinny to respond.

"I don't know where she's been. But I'm hoping to make up for lost time." Vinny looks at me, his playful smile gone, replaced by what could almost pass for sincerity on his face.

Elle hugs me before leaving. "Here's my number. Call me in three weeks." She rubs her stomach. "This little guy is due to make an appearance in two. We, my new friend, are going for coffee." She smiles and heads toward the door, stopping before she exits. "I'm thinking we may need to go on a binge…hit up at least three or four shops."

Vinny laughs and makes his way to the table I'm still sitting at. "I see you met Elle."

"She's great."

"Yeah, she is. I would've been out a long time ago if it wasn't for her. She gets in the middle of me and my trainer…her husband, Nico. He's a pain in the ass, but he's the best trainer out there now that Preach retired."

"She seems like a fan of yours, too." My words and smile are genuine. There was no mistaking that Elle seems to adore Vinny.

Vinny smiles and pulls a chair over to where I'm sitting. He turns it backwards to sit, his forearms leaning on the top of the back of the chair as he straddles it. I'm instantly brought back to the library, oh so many years ago.

"So what brings you back here, Liv?" A lopsided, knowing, cocky smile on his face. He knows exactly why I'm here.

"It seems you had a little problem with Summer?" Arching my eyebrows, I wait for his explanation.

"I didn't want Daddy's Little Princess writing a story about me. Thought someone I know would do a better job. Someone that has been writing since she could hold a pencil."

I can't help but smile at Vinny's assessment of Summer. Daddy's little princess, so spot on. "She wasn't a happy princess."

"I bet she wasn't. Looked like it might have been the first time she was ever rejected."

Vinny looks at me and the smirk on his face fades away as our eyes meet. There's an unmistakable intensity in his beautiful pale blue eyes, like looking into a calm ocean with a storm lurking dangerously under dark grey clouds in the distance. I break our gaze intentionally. The need to pull myself away is great, although the task is not easy.

"Why, Vinny?" He looks at me, confused for a moment. "Why did you insist on me writing your article?"

"Because I wanted to see you again." His statement is spoken very matter a factly, without a hint of shame for interfering in my life.

"You could have just called me."

"Would you have agreed to see me again?"

Okay, so he has a point. I open my mouth to respond, but close it quickly and say nothing.

A smug smile on his face, "I thought so."

Changing the subject, I pull out my notebook and a pen. "How about we get started then?"

"No."

"No?"

"You can interview me over dinner. Tomorrow night."

"I don't think so, Vinny."

He stands, righting the chair back to its position and calmly folds his arms over his chest. "Well, it was nice seeing you again then, Liv."

I narrow my eyes at him. "You're screwing with my chance at the job of my dreams, Vinny." Perhaps maybe a little guilt will soften him up. But I'm not surprised he doesn't budge an inch.

I stand, not sure of my next move, but I can tell I need to bend a little. "Lunch."

"Dinner."

"Meet me half way, Vinny. Lunch."

His gaze narrow and face unreadable, I realize the strong boy has become a determined man. One who still plays by his own rules. Unsure if he would call my bluff, I hold my breath waiting for his response.

"Fine, lunch tomorrow."

"I can't tomorrow, I have plans for lunch already."

"With who?"

"I don't think that's really any of your business."

"Cancel your plans."

I look into his eyes, hoping to find some indication that he's joking. But he's not. He's dead serious. "Fine."

"I'll pick you up at your office."

"I'll meet you at the restaurant."

Vinny closes his eyes and bows his head slightly, shaking it back and forth before taking a deep breath. He takes two steps forward so that we're standing toe to toe. Close enough to feel the heat resonate from his body, but not quite touching. "Tomorrow. Twelve. Lombardi's."

I nod, unable to form a cohesive sentence with him so close. Finally, after a long minute, I force my brain to resume control from my traitorous body and I smile hesitantly and head to the door. "See you tomorrow."

"Can't wait, Liv."

Relieved to be home after what seemed like the longest day of my life, I head straight for the fridge and pull out a corked bottle of wine.

"You haven't even put your purse down. Bad day at the office, Honey?" Ally, my roommate, calls out teasingly from the living room.

"You want one?" I yell back.

"Of course, it would be rude to let you drink alone." I can't see Ally from where I'm standing but I can hear the smile in her voice.

I pour two full glasses of wine into sparkly crystal glasses, emptying the bottle, and head into the living room. Plopping myself onto the couch, I kick off my heels, exhale a deep breath, and slump into the cushy seat before downing a big gulp from my glass.

"Spill it. You look frazzled." Folding her legs Indian style onto the couch, Ally turns to face me, clicking off the television with the remote.

"I saw Vinny again today."

"Get. Out. I thought you had his story reassigned."

"I thought so too."

"What happened?"

"Vinny happened, that's what." I take another gulp of my wine. "He refused to do the interview with Summer, said he would only give me his story."

I look up at my best friend and she's smiling at me excitedly.

"What the heck are you smiling at?"

"I think it's kinda hot that he demanded you." Ally laughs. "Always was fearless. Is he still gorgeous?"

Grudgingly, my mind wanders to Vinny Stonetti. Vince Stone. The years have only made him sexier. While he was always gorgeous on the outside, something about his confidence and strength made him even more so. A force of nature, something I'm not quite sure I'm ready to reckon with. "Yes, he's still gorgeous. But that's not the point. He screwed me once, I'm not going to let him do it again."

"He can screw me instead." Ally wiggles her eyebrows. We've been best friends since grade school. Although we seem to have the same taste in men in looks, I keep away from the bad boys. Ally, on the other hand, keeps away from the good boys.

"So how did the interview go?"

"I didn't interview him yet. I'm meeting him tomorrow for lunch."

"A date. Nice." Ally smiles and sips her wine.

"It's not a date."

"Are you meeting him at a restaurant and eating together?"

"Yes, but that's not the point. It's a business meal."

"Couldn't you have interviewed him when you saw him today?"

"I tried, he said no. Wanted me to interview him over dinner."

"So you negotiated dinner down to a lunch date?"

"Yes. Wait, no. It's not a date."

"Whatever. As long as I get all the details afterwards, you can call it a communication session with ingestion for all I care."

CHAPTER 10

Vince

"Who was the girl here earlier?" Nico's damn nosey. The fucker thinks training me means he gets to control every inch of my life. Been this way since I was thirteen.

"An old friend." I hit the bag with a roundhouse kick and one of Nico's feet drops back to keep his position. I've been trying for more than ten years to take him down. Figured after he retired he'd lose a little strength, slow down on his workouts. But no, a year after he retired and the fucker is still in pristine shape. Once. I was able to take him to the ground once in ten years. And I paid dearly for it. Came in to train high and Nico called me on it. We got into it and half the place had to pull us apart. Got me thrown out of the gym and lost my trainer for six months until I could prove my sobriety with random piss tests.

"Elle went on about her for two hours last night. Says she's great. Nice girl, would be good for you. She rambled on something about needing coffee and then got pissed off at me because I *could* drink coffee. Even though I don't drink the crap. Pregnancy has made her crazy."

Nice girl. Yep, that's what Liv is. A nice girl. One I'd like to bend over and fuck. Hard. Damn it, I should know better. Me and nice girls don't go together. I tried that route once. Even managed to have a somewhat normal relationship, went at it missionary style for almost a full month. But it's not who I am. Eventually I gave her a taste of the real me and she went running scared. Wasn't even the hard core stuff. Just a little spanking and hair pulling and I'd freaked her out. Probably went and found someone named Biffy to marry. Biffy, who would give it to her missionary style and keep his deviance for the whore he keeps on the side. "Yeah, she's a nice girl. But it's business. She's writing a story on my next fight."

"Elle was business when I met her."

I was twelve or thirteen when Elle and Nico met. At first I thought it was a strange coupling. Elle, an attorney, always dressed in her girly business suits, helped Nico get out of a contract. She was just so different from the semi clothed women that I normally saw prance through the gym once. Twice if they were lucky. But all that shit stopped the day he laid eyes on Elle...and went after her with his usual relentless pursuit of getting what he wants. I may not have understood the pairing at first, but it didn't take long to figure out there was no one else for Nico Hunter.

"Whatever, I'm not you."

It's late when I finish up at the gym and all I want to do is head home and crash. But my pain in the ass mother looked bad yesterday, so I stop in and check on her. I can't stand the sight of the woman, yet I feel compelled to take care of her. She's been a drug addict as long as I can remember. Hasn't held a steady job in all her life. When she was younger, she danced at night. Left me alone from the time I was five to work nights at some seedy place for a guy she wanted me to call Uncle Wally. Uncle Wally my ass. All his girls were high, he kept them that way. Made them more dependent on him.

She sobered up once. Even left *Wally's Den*. I was about seven. Lasted almost three months. I remember the months clearly. The house was clean and we had food regularly. And no losers sleeping all over the house. Even took me to the zoo once.

It didn't last long. Uncle Wally got her to come back. Two weeks back working at the *Den*, the house was a mess and the losers returned. Been that way ever since. Some days are better than others. Yesterday was a bad one. She looked like shit. Split lip and a lot of shakes. Swore she fell and split her own lip, but I don't trust Jason, the new loser she's hanging out with.

I knock once, but there's no answer. So I use my key. The TV is blaring so loud, I'm surprised the neighbors haven't called the cops. I find my mother sitting on the couch. She's crying. She tries to hide it when she catches sight of me, but it's too late, I've seen it. "What's going on, Mom?"

"Nothing, Baby. Everything is fine. You can go home. I told you, you don't have to check on me every day." Her eyes dart to the bathroom and back to me. She has one hand on her cheek. I'd thought she was wiping her tears when I walked in, but she's hiding something from me. I walk to her and take the hand from her face. There's a hand mark and it's bright red. Fresh, like it's just been made, and the color hasn't had a chance to change from stinging red to welted pink yet.

I look at the closed bathroom door and back to my mother. "Is he in there?"

"Don't, Vinny. Jason's a good man. Helps me out financially too."

Yeah, helps her out by paying for her drugs. Then raises his hand to her. What a great fucking man he is. No fucking way. I can't help it. I see red when his dirty, skinny face walks through the door.

He's so fucking high, he can't even protect himself when I beat him to within an inch of his life. What's fair is fair. Mom was the same way when he raised his hand to her. Fucking useless piece of shit.

Mom didn't even argue after the first punch. She knows how I get. There's no stopping me once I get going. Especially when it comes to protecting my mother. I can't keep her from pumping that shit into her own veins, but I can damn well keep her from being smacked around. It's not the first time I've taken care of a loser who thought raising his hand to my mother would make him feel like more of a man. Started when I was fifteen. Lost count of the assholes over the years.

Leaving the piece of shit on the floor, I carry my mom to her bedroom and tuck her in. She couldn't walk if she tried. Too high and frail. Needs to eat more. I kiss her goodbye on the forehead and walk back to pick up the loser and toss him outside to the curb. I can't stand my mother, yet I can't let her be.

CHAPTER 11

Liv

I get to the restaurant and find Vinny at the bar. Ignoring all her other customers, the bartender stands and talks to him, leaning suggestively over the bar so he has a clear view of her ridiculously large, obviously fake breasts. Her stance clearly intentional. Unexpectedly, I feel a pang of jealousy, but I push it down and force myself to ignore my innate reaction.

"Hey." I walk over to the bar and greet Vinny. He stands and kisses me on the cheek, one hand on my hip, quickly forgetting the conversation he was in the midst of. His strong grip on me sends goosebumps racing and a tingle washes over my skin. I almost jump back at the power with which it hits me. Damn, I need to keep some physical distance from this man. I smile politely at the waiting bartender, but she shoots me a nasty look when Vinny leads us away without so much as a glance back at her.

We're seated in a booth off to the back of the restaurant. It's quiet, perfect for an interview. Although not an easy task, I force my thoughts back to business. But instead of sitting on the other side of the booth, Vinny settles in beside me, his arm casually draped around the back of the wide seat.

I've sometimes seen couples sitting beside each other in a booth and thought it looked odd. It just seems more natural to have a conversation sitting across from someone. Only now do I see what the appeal is. It's intimate, allowing low spoken conversations and innocent brushes from the close proximity. But sitting this close to Vinny makes me flustered. I'm also seated on the inside, against the wall. It makes me feel cornered somehow, and it pisses me off that my body seems to like it, regardless of what my brain is telling me.

"Wouldn't you be more comfortable over there?" I point to the other side of the table.

"No. I like it here. Does it bother you?" he says, a knowing smirk on his face.

"Not at all, it's fine," I lie.

Vinny twists at the waist and pulls one knee up on the seat so he's facing me. He's dressed in low hanging jeans and a black V-neck sweater, making him look casual and understated. With the way the clothes hang on his body, he looks more like a model than a fighter. A model who doesn't really care about his appearance, yet he looks perfect without effort.

I take a deep breath and try to delve into my work. "So tell me, are you nervous about the upcoming fight?"

"No."

"Your opponent has slung some mud at you, claiming you're a drug addict. Do you want to respond to his accusations?"

"No."

"Are all of your answers going to be this short? Because it's going to be difficult to make an article out of the word no."

"Ask better questions then."

Offended, I take a defensive attitude. "There's nothing wrong with my questions."

"How about we take turns. I'll give you longer answers, but we go question for question." He scooches an inch closer to me.

"I'm not the one being interviewed."

"Apparently, then neither am I." Leisurely grabbing a breadstick from the table, Vinny casually bites off a piece. A twinkle in his eye tells me he's quite enjoying himself.

"You're really going to make this difficult, aren't you?"

"It doesn't have to be that way," he says.

I get the urge to smack the smug smile off his face. He knows I need this interview and he's arrogant enough to hold it over me to have his fun.

"Fine. But I go first."

"Always." The flirtatious smile is back.

"Do you have a drug problem?"

Vinny shoots me a hard glance. "No. But I did. I started doing some stupid stuff after I broke my arm last year and couldn't fight. In the beginning, I told myself it was to stop the pain. But it got out of control. Quickly. I've been clean for six months. Nico, my trainer, wouldn't train me unless I was. He does random testing to make sure I stay on track."

His honesty makes me feel less guarded. Studying his face while he speaks, I can't help but take in every masculine feature. The way his mouth moves, the five o'clock shadow that brushes onto his chin and frames the squareness of his jaw. I find it difficult to stop staring.

Vinny's gaze slides over mine and a wry half grin graces his sinfully beautiful face as he speaks. "My turn."

I smile hesitantly. The playfulness in his voice, coupled with the dimples peeking out of his smile, makes me think he is enjoying himself, even though he just revealed something difficult.

"Are you seeing anyone?"

A pretty waitress comes to take our order and Vinny orders for both of us without asking. Lasagna. For lunch. It's not something I would ever order at this time of the day, but I find it sweet he remembers what I'd always ordered for dinner when we studied late back in high school.

Returning his attention to me, he turns back and makes an expectant face. "So, what is it, yes or no?"

"No."

"Now you're giving me a one word answer. I thought we agreed those aren't gonna cut it. Unless you want to start over with my answers all being no…"

"Fine." I try my best to act annoyed. Rolling my eyes, I continue with my response. "I don't have a boyfriend, currently. Two long-term relationships while I was away at college, the last one ended when school did. A date every once in awhile, but I'm pretty busy with my work most of the time."

Vinny nods, pleased with my answer. My turn. "You turned down a fight with Ravek last year, saying you weren't ready for a title fight. What makes you think you're ready now?"

His eyebrows arch in surprise at my question. "You've done your homework." I smile at the compliment and await his response. "I was considering joining the military last year. I may have been ready physically, but my head wasn't in the game for that level of a fight."

I remember back to when we were in high school. He'd always worn dog tags around his neck that belonged to his father. "Your dad was in the military, right?"

He reaches in under his sweater and pulls out the same tags I remember dangling so many years ago. "Haven't taken them off except to fight since I was a kid. He died in the line of duty when I was a baby." His face looks sad at the memory, but he quickly recovers. "That's two you owe me now."

"Did you go to the prom with Evan Marco?" Vinny asks.

The name brings back sad memories. "No."

"Why not?"

"He was too injured to go. Wonder how that happened?" I respond with sarcasm. I'm actually surprised that he would even bring up Evan, no less push me to talk about what happened back then. I was only in tenth grade, so I was shocked when Evan had asked me to the prom. He was two years older and captain of the football team. Every girl wanted him to ask her. Yet he asked me. I hadn't even realized he knew my name. I was just a wallflower, one of the smart girls who took advanced classes. But he did, and I was excited to go...even though deep down I secretly would've rather gone with Vinny. Then Evan got into a fight with Vinny a few weeks before prom and Evan canceled on me. I'd bought my dress and everything. I was devastated, but Vinny got it worse. He was already on probation for fighting and Evan's father was on the school board. No one was surprised when Vinny was expelled.

My turn. "Why did you beat up Evan?"

Vinny's eyebrows arch in surprise. "Olivia Michaels, are you asking me a personal question, not for your article?"

I blush, hating myself for asking. But I'd always wondered. Vinny got into fights often in high school, but it wasn't usually with the jocks. He'd even been friendly with Evan before that. "I guess I am."

He smiles halfheartedly, tension creeping back into his face. "He said something I didn't like."

"He said something you didn't like?" I mock his answer in disbelief that he'd gotten himself expelled over something so trivial.

"That's gonna count as another question if I have to repeat myself." Vinny warns with a grin.

Almost two more hours go by and Vinny's answered every question I've thrown at him. And I can tell he's done so truthfully. In between our question and answer sessions, we reminisce about the time we spent together in high school. I'm surprised how much he remembers about me. My favorite foods, the music I listened to, how I rewrote my own endings to the classics, my dream of becoming a writer. It's sweet and unexpected.

Vinny pays the check even though I tell him the paper would pay the bill. "Can I get one more question, Liv?"

I roll my eyes playfully, but somewhere along the line in the last few hours I let my guard down...he knows I'm kidding. "Go ahead."

He leans in closer and whispers to me, "Can I kiss you?"

I don't respond right away, mostly because he doesn't give me time to. Instead he kisses me. At first it's hesitant, controlled, gentle...almost unsure. He tastes sweet, like the tiramisu we just shared. Incredibly delicious. After a minute he pulls back, our lips still touching after his gentle kiss, and a low moan escapes my lips before I can stop it. And then gentle goes out the window and he's on me, kissing me hard, his tongue pilfering my mouth and demanding I allow him to take the lead. The tension gripping my body for the last few days since I saw him again begs for release. I find myself grabbing at his shirt, clenching, pulling him even tighter against me than his already strong hold has us pressed against each other. He sucks on my tongue desperately and bites down on my lip when I move to pull away for air.

Panting breathlessly, eventually we come up for no other reason than we need to breathe. Shocked at the intensity of my reaction, embarrassment starts to seep in. I begin to pull away, but Vinny follows, not allowing our contact to break. He nuzzles the side of my face, and I listen to his hard breathing so close to my ear. It's insanely erotic and I need to put space between us to stop myself from doing something stupid. "I need to see you again, Liv." His voice is low and rough.

I do my best to pull my thoughts together, but my head is spinning, my mind a tangled web of mixed emotions, some old, some new. "What about Krissy, or Missy, or whatever her name is?"

"Over." His response is quick, tone clipped.

"Since when, I just saw you together last week?"

"Since right now."

Shit. I wish I didn't love his response, but I do. It's defiant and socially improper, but it's also raw and honest. And everything that attracted me to him so many years ago. He is who he is, and makes no apology if it's not what you expect. In a strange way, I was always a little envious of him. The ability to live your own life, truly for yourself, is such an easy thing to say, but such a difficult thing to do.

CHAPTER 12

Liv

Saturday morning I go to yoga. I really don't want to drag my lazy ass out of bed, but I need it. More for my mental well-being than my physical. My brain feels jumbled the entire drive there, my usual morning clarity evading me. Being with Vinny yesterday confused me. I'd been hurt by him once, and it took a long time to get over it. Longer than I care to admit. It wouldn't be wise to go for a second chance. Missy may have turned into Krissy, and fighting in the hall turned into fighting in a cage, but he's still the same. The same boy that takes what he wants and doesn't look back. Except now he's a man. God, he's all man.

But that kiss. It was unlike anything I've ever felt in my life. Filled with passion and desire, it made me forget where I was. *Who* I was. Being near him is dangerous. I could easily fall for him again, which is why I know I can't see him anymore. I'd told him I'd think about it, but my decision wasn't difficult to make. Once I put distance between us, I was able to think clearly.

I'm more relaxed and focused after yoga, but still not nearly my organized self. I stop downtown to grab some groceries, and I struggle to find my ringing phone in my bag while carrying my packages to the parking lot. I don't immediately recognize the number.

"Hello?"

"Liv?" A woman's voice. It's familiar, but I can't match the face immediately.

"Yes."

"It's Elle."

"Oh, hi Elle. How are you feeling?"

"Like I swallowed a ten pound watermelon," she sighs. "Listen, I'm dying for some coffee. Are you busy? I'll have decaf, you can have the good stuff and describe it to me as you drink it."

I smile thinking of our first and only meeting. We'd become fast friends and I liked her. I'd described the taste of my coffee that she was so desperate to consume. "Sure, I'd love to. I'm downtown, how about Barto's?"

"Perfect, I'll meet you in half an hour."

Elle and I sit and chat for a while. She tells me how she met Nico while doing some contract work for him. I tell her about the job I'm desperately trying to land and my backup position with the *Post* in New York. An hour into our chat, she quiets for a minute before looking up at me sheepishly, I can see she wants to say something.

"I have a confession to make."

"Okaaay." I drag the word out, unsure of what will come next.

"Vinny asked me to contact you. See if I could convince you to go out with him. Don't get me wrong, I think you're awesome. I wanted to get together anyway. But I feel dishonest now, sitting here without full disclosure."

My initial reaction is to feel betrayed, but I can see Elle feels badly, so I put her mind at ease. I really do like her, feel like we could be good friends. "Thank you for telling me. I appreciate you being honest."

"Sorry. For some reason, I just can't say no to that boy. I've always had a soft spot for him. I met him when he was only twelve or thirteen.

We've been through a lot together over the years. Especially with his mom and all."

I'd always suspected that Vinny's mom had problems. Every time he got in trouble at school, he'd stood for his punishment alone, his mother nowhere to be found. I feel bad for goading Elle into telling me more. Clearly she isn't aware that his home life is unknown to me, but I want to find out more for some reason. "How is his mother?"

Elle makes a growling sound in response. "Still high. Still dragging Vinny into her mess on a regular basis. Still a total loser." She sips her decaf coffee and wrinkles up her nose. "Why can't they make decaf that tastes more like the real thing? We send men to the moon, images through cell phones to the other side of the world, but decaf still tastes like sour water."

When two o'clock rolls around, my cell phone alarm goes off reminding me I need to pick up Ally from school. She'd decided to go back to school and start her graduate work and I volunteered to play taxi for her weekend classes since she doesn't have a car anymore. Elle and I have spent more than two hours at the coffee shop, yet it only seems like ten minutes. "I hate to run, but I have to give my roommate a ride."

We both stand and hug, laughing at her belly getting in the way between us. "So what do I report back to Vinny?" Elle raises her eyebrows and bites her bottom lip. There's hope in her eyes. Clearly, she adores him. I find comfort in knowing that Vinny has a woman like Elle looking after him. Especially after what I just learned about his mother.

"I don't know, Elle. I know you care about him…and, oddly, I find that I still do too. But I just don't think he's right for me."

Elle looks disappointed, but smiles anyway. "I hope we can still be friends?"

"I'd really like that."

CHAPTER 13

Vince

I've been on a tear since Elle came back and gave me the news that Liv wasn't planning on seeing me again. I put in nine hours at the gym today. It's too much, I know I'll pay for it tomorrow, but right now I don't give a shit. Nico locked the place up an hour ago, but didn't tell me to leave. He knows I need to work something through. Understands how my brain works, leaving me restless, unable to stay still until I work myself to the point of exhaustion. He gets me because he's the same way. Plus, he knows how I would have handled feeling like this six months ago, so he's happy to keep me busy in the gym, rather than out partying.

"You wanna talk about it?" Nico lives upstairs in the loft above the gym with Elle, but he comes down to check on me. He gets behind the bag that's swinging from my kicks and steadies it, giving me a firmer target to attack.

"No." I throw a few punches at the bag and Nico's forced two steps back from the sheer force of my hits. Whatever I'm feeling now has me hitting harder than usual. Too bad you can't bottle this shit and pull it out when you really need it.

"Elle says it's the girl." Nico pushes, he always does.

"I don't wanna fucking talk about it."

"Watch your mouth."

I stop swinging and still myself. He can't be serious. "Are you kidding me? I'm not god damn thirteen anymore."

"Yeah, I realize that. But you're down here acting like you are. And you're also yelling and my very pregnant wife is worried about your sorry ass for some stupid reason and her hearing your foul mouth upstairs is showing her disrespect."

Give me a god damn break. "You know what, I'm outta here." I push the bag at him as hard as I can before I storm off. The bag wasn't doing it anyway. I need to find another way to blow off steam tonight.

Less than an hour later, I'm showered and back on my bike heading to the nearest bar. It's late and the place will be packed with GIMPS. It won't take long to find one ready for me.

Downtown's busy for a Saturday night. I feel like I've caught every damn light since I hit the street. I stop as yet another one turns red in front of me, bringing my feet to the ground as I balance and wait. I look around, taking in the high rise buildings surrounding me. It's a path I often take, but I've never noticed the sign on the building I'm sitting in front of until now. *Daily Sun Times.* Fucking figures. A week ago, I hadn't seen her in years, now she's everywhere I damn turn.

It takes less than ten minutes from the time I walk into Flannigan's for Krissy to find me. She cuddles up to my side, pushing her groin into my leg. I know I can have her now, no extra effort on my part necessary. And she likes it rough. Normally I'd be all over the easy lay, but tonight it's just pissing me off. I ditch her at the bar, leaving through the back door, not bothering to tell her I'm not coming back after the bathroom.

Back on my bike after less than a half an hour at the bar, I'm pissed that I'm alone, but I have no interest in being with a woman tonight. Except one. One woman who has no interest in being with me. Fucking great.

CHAPTER 14

Liv

I work till six on Monday, rushing out the door to try to make a seven thirty yoga class. There's a mass exodus to the front door, with people lined up waiting to exit through the only two turnstile glass doors. I attempt to dig my ringing phone out of my bag as I push my way around the turnstile, taking the necessary baby steps to keep from banging into the glass. I almost miss the opening to get out as I fumble to bring the phone to my ear while righting the two shoulder straps back onto my shoulder.

"Hello."

"Liv?"

His voice stops me in my tracks. Literally. The person behind me bangs into me when I halt unexpectedly. "Vinny?"

"Yeah."

"How did you get my number?"

"I stole it from Elle's phone."

I smile to myself at his honesty. "Is everything okay?"

"I want to see you."

I take a deep breath. Just hearing his voice makes my conviction waver. Distance is definitely necessary to keep from falling under his spell. Perhaps even keeping away from the phone might be a good idea. The sound of his voice just melts me. "I can't, Vinny."

"I don't think you have a choice, Liv."

"Why is that?"

"Because you're about to walk right into me."

I practically drop the phone when I look up and find him leaning casually against a Harley, a cocky smile firmly in place.

I stop. "What are you doing here?" Like an idiot, I'm still talking to him through my phone, even though he's only about fifteen feet away from me.

Vinny smiles and holds up his phone to me, shrugging his shoulders. He looks amused, but lifts his phone back to his mouth to respond anyway. "I wanted to see you."

"So you come to my job and wait for me?"

"If that's what it takes." I watch as Vinny pushes off his bike and stands, tucking his phone into his pocket. He walks to me slowly, almost as if he's not sure if I'll run. I don't move.

I'm still talking into my phone when he closes the distance between us, standing directly in front of me, close enough to touch if I lean forward even slightly. He's so near I can smell him. God, he smells incredible, it makes me heady and dazed. "But why? Why do you want to see me?"

Slowly, Vinny lifts one hand and tucks a lock of hair the wind has forced across my face back behind my ear. His hand lingers on my cheek and then he gently glides it under my chin and lifts my head, forcing me to meet his gaze. His voice is low and tender when he speaks. "I can't stop thinking about you."

Swallowing hard, I try to push down the lump that's formed in my throat so I can respond. "Vinny, I can't."

His arms snake around my waist, locking me in. "You can." His tone changes from soft to firm, almost commanding. It does something to me, stirs something inside of me and I feel the surge of arousal from his forcefulness. Everything on the street ceases to exist, and my body becomes completely in tune with him. It unnerves me how I can be so completely turned on by something that should make me run the other way.

He buries his head in my neck and breathes deep. "You feel it. I know you do."

He's not wrong. I feel it too. All the way down to the tips of my toes. I want him. Badly. But I've gone down that road before with him. And I know I'd be starting something that he would finish. Sooner than I was ready to. Again.

His arms, loosely wrapped around my waist, tighten, pulling me to him until our bodies are touching. I can feel the heat radiate from his hard body, and the hunger in his stare. "Kiss me, then tell me I'm wrong." His voice is hoarse and strained.

Unconsciously, I lick my lips that have gone dry. He groans, the erotic sound setting fire to my body instantly and my breath catches as he looks down at me intensely before sealing his mouth over mine possessively. His kiss is aggressive, but well skilled, leaving me no choice but to follow his commanding lead.

I don't even notice my bags dropping to the ground, but it frees my arms. My hands reach up and dive into his unruly hair. Entwining my fingers, I pull hard, deepening the kiss. Vinny growls and squeezes me hard as he lifts me off my feet, bringing me closer against him. I can feel his throbbing erection against my stomach and it makes me lose my mind. My body aches for him and I kiss him back with such force it takes even me by surprise.

Too soon, he gently settles me back onto my feet. My knees are so weak from his kiss that I'm thankful his grip is still tight around me, for fear I might fall.

"I want you, Liv. I can't stop myself. Tell me you don't feel what's between us and I'll go."

I don't look up at him, my mind is still racing as fast as my heartbeat and I'm afraid what looking into those beautiful, pale blue eyes will do to me in my already weakened state.

"Look at me."

Something about his tone makes it so I have no choice but to obey. My judgment becomes clouded at the sound of the strength of his will and demand. It takes over me, bringing me into my own little universe where only the two of us exist and I feel the inexplicable need to please him.

My eyes open slowly and I look up at him. His focus so intently keen on me, I find it difficult to breathe. "Tell me you don't want me."

I want to tell him I don't want him, but I can't. Because I do. I've never wanted anything more in my life. The feelings he conjures up in me are just so overpowering and consuming. "It's not that I don't want you," my voice comes out as a mere whisper.

"Then what is it?"

"It's you." I shake my head, not fully understanding myself. "It's just you. It's all too much, too fast, and too intense, and it scares me. Scares the hell out of me."

The corners of Vinny's mouth curl up, and I watch as his face visibly relaxes before my eyes. "I want to promise you I'll slow down, take things slower, but I don't want to start things off on a lie. I'm not sure I can do slow around you, Liv." His voice is back to gentle and sweet. "But I'll promise you I'll try. If that's what it takes, I will...I'll try." Vinny pulls back his head to look directly into my eyes. "Trust me about one thing, Liv...whatever is going on between us, it's going to happen. You can make it as difficult as you want, but we, Liv, are *going* to happen. Neither one of us can stop it."

Somehow, down deep, I just know he's right.

Vinny doesn't give me the chance to back out or reconsider agreeing to see where things might take us. He senses that time and distance between us will make me change my mind, and he's probably right. Most definitely right. I've only been away from him for an hour and I'm already having second thoughts as I pull up to the gym I've agreed to meet him at. He's talked me out of yoga and into trying a kick boxing class he teaches just outside the city.

He's already at the front of the room when I walk in. The few women surrounding him look like they're going to an athletic wear photo shoot, rather than to really exercise. He catches my eye as I walk in and crooks one finger at me, beckoning me to the front of the room. The ladies surrounding him trace his line of sight, curious what has taken his attention away from them when they've obviously worked so hard to keep it. They scowl at me as I approach.

"Ladies, we're going to get started in a minute, why don't you go take your places." He's talking to them, but his eyes have never left mine. I point to myself, smirking, questioning if he is directing his words at me, but he grins and shakes his head no.

"Front row. Right in front of me, Liv." He gives me a crooked smile and reaches down, grabbing the hem of his shirt and pulls it off in one swift motion.

I roll my eyes in his direction, but take my position in the front nonetheless. The view is just too good to not be front and center anyway.

"Warm ups ladies. Or are you ladies already ready for me?" He smiles at the full class of hopeful women and I watch their reactions in the reflection of the mirror in front of me. I think I might even take in the scent of female pheromones wafting their way to the front of the room, determined to attract their intended target.

Vinny's eyes find mine and he grins at me knowingly. I roll my eyes playfully in response. He walks the class through a series of stretches and I catch glimpses of him in the mirror as he weaves his way through the class giving instructions. He stops when he gets to me and puts his hand firmly on my lower back as I bend over stretching to touch the floor with my hands.

"A little deeper." He applies pressure as his hand slowly strokes up and down my spine. Leaning down next to me, he whispers into my ear so that only I can hear him. "Jesus Christ, you have an amazing ass, Liv." I feel his words slide over me and I'm grateful we're in a room full of people, instead of alone.

The forty-five minute class is harder than I expected, but Vinny makes it fun. He's playful and attentive to the class. I can see how they all look at him, but he keeps a certain distance from them as a few try hard to entice him as he works with them individually. I find myself wondering if he's always this professional with his students, or if his act is merely for my benefit.

I'm a sweaty mess after the class, even worse than I would've been in yoga. "That was fun, I can't believe how fast the time went by." I wipe the sweat from my forehead as I speak.

"I'm glad you liked it. You're good, a natural at swinging those legs."

"Thanks."

"You ready to get something to eat?"

"I really need to shower."

"I could use a shower too." Vinny arches his eyebrows suggestively.

"That wasn't an invitation."

Vinny finishes packing up his stuff. There's a few women still hanging around talking, but most have already left. Standing in front of me, he reaches around my waist with his one free hand and pulls me closer to him, uncaring if people are still in the room. "That's a shame, I was looking forward to you washing my back."

"I think you're going to be taking care of yourself today." I arch one eyebrow playfully, the double meaning in my statement intentional.

Vinny laughs, shaking his head as he throws his arm around my shoulder, holding me close as he leads us to the door. "I'll shower alone, but it won't be as much fun. But I'm taking you to dinner. Give me your address, I'll pick you up in forty-five minutes. I'm not taking any chances by giving you more time than that."

We drive to a part of town I haven't been to in years, not far from our old high school. I'm surprised when Vinny parks behind the library and comes around to open my door without explanation.

"Why are we at the library?" Vinny takes my hand and helps me out of his truck, grabbing a bag from the back seat.

"Come on, I'll show you."

We walk for a few minutes and I finally catch on to where he must be taking me. The tree. For years after Vinny left school, I couldn't look in the direction of that damn tree. It was our spot. A few months after I started tutoring him in the library, the weather had finally warmed up enough and Vinny had insisted we needed to study outdoors. So we found a quiet place under a big tree and spent almost every afternoon after school under it. To me, it was our tree, a special place where I fell in love for the very first time.

Vinny opens the duffle bag, pulls out a blanket and spreads it over the grass, motioning with an exaggerated hand gesture and bow for me to sit.

"Our dinner." He reaches in and pulls out another bag, handing it to me before he sits close on the blanket.

I know what's in the bag, but I check anyway. I can't believe he's remembered so much. Most afternoons we'd share a hero. Roast beef and provolone, mayo only on his half.

"I can't believe you remembered all of this."

"Of course I remembered."

I try to force a smile at Vinny, but he sees on my face that something's bothering me.

"What's the matter?"

"Nothing. I guess I'm just surprised that you remembered all this."

"Remember? Liv, those months with you…I'd never forget."

When we spent time together all those years ago, I never doubted that there was something between us. I was young and inexperienced, but my heart told me he cared about me too. Then it just ended. And I spent the next year of my life feeling stupid for thinking he felt something for me too. To say I was devastated would be an understatement. It crushed my faith in so many things...young love, trusting my judgment on boys, giving my heart to someone else. "Then why, Vinny? Why did we stop spending time together after you left school?"

Vinny sighs, raking his fingers through his dark blond locks. It makes his unruly hair even more wild and only that much sexier. "My life was just so screwed up. My mom had problems, I'd just got kicked out of school, and I didn't understand things about myself." He reaches for my hand. "You were young, Liv. You weren't ready for what I needed from you."

Softly, the words escape my lips before I can catch them. "I didn't care about any of that. I just needed you."

I watch Vinny's throat work as he swallows. For a second, I catch a flash of the boy I once knew in the man, only this time, he's forlorn instead of angry. But the flash quickly passes, shuttering over the sadness. "You needed someone better. I would've dragged you down." His words are spoken resolutely. It's clear by his clipped tone he intends the conversation to be over. We're both quiet for a long time, neither of us wanting to speak first.

I don't even realize I'm staring at our joined hands, avoiding eye contact, until Vinny finally puts his hand under my chin, forcing my head up to meet his gaze. "Do you understand?"

"Sort of. I guess." My tone wavers. Because, the truth is, I really don't understand.

"I cared about you, Liv. A lot."

I can tell he's sincere and it makes me feel better. A little at least. I smile half-heartedly at him as he runs his knuckles gently along my cheek. "You better eat. When I look at you sitting here, it reminds me of all the things I never got to do with you." His sweet smile is replaced by a dirty grin. "To you. I have a whole list of things I wanted to do *to* you."

Eating breaks the tension that was building between us and we spend the next hour laughing and catching up, filling in all the missing pieces from our years apart.

"So what made Nico take you back to train?"

"My dad." Vinny rubs his chest as he speaks, unconsciously reaching for the dog tags beneath his shirt. I doubt if he even knows he's doing it.

"Your dad?"

"Yeah. The local chapter of The Angels MC do a bike run to raise money for the Children's Hospital every year on Veteran's Day. Most of them are vets like my dad was. So I started riding with them in his honor when I turned seventeen and got my first bike. Last year they needed to raise more money. The hospital's working on funding a new wing for families of kids with cancer to stay while the kids get their treatment. So I asked Nico to ride, get some of the guys from his gym to join too."

"And he said yes and then started training you again?"

Vinny laughs. "Nothing with Nico Hunter is that easy. He asked me if my dad would be proud of what I was doing. I was out of control, doing too much partying. I got a four hour lecture, but in the end he agreed to ride for the fundraiser. After it was over, he told me to be at his gym the next morning at 6AM. I thought he was going to train me. Instead he made me take a drug test. I passed. Then he made me come back at random times for a month. One day I showed up and he told me to get in the ring, instead of handing me a cup."

"Sounds like you had to earn back his trust."

"Yeah, I'm still working on that part. I haven't touched anything except booze in six months, but I still get randomly tested."

"Does it bother you?"

"What?"

"That it's taking you so long to earn back his trust?"

Vinny doesn't respond right away. Instead, he looks into my eyes and holds my gaze for a minute before speaking. "I don't mind working for something important to me." His eyes drop to my mouth and back. Slowly, he leans in and kisses me. It's gentle and sweet, full of meaning, and I feel yet another crack in the wall I've built around my heart to protect myself from this man.

It's almost 3AM before Vinny finally drives me home. I've been with him for close to ten hours, yet it feels like the night's ending too soon. Vinny parks and jogs around to open my door, giving me his hand to help me get out. He doesn't release me once I'm standing. Instead he pulls me flush against him, his grip tight as he holds me close without saying a word for a full minute.

"I want to come up, but I'm not going to ask." He speaks into the top of my head, his cheek still buried in my hair.

I pull back my face, enough to look up at him while I speak. I'm just about to respond, tell him that it's too fast and I can't invite him up yet, when he takes my mouth in a kiss. His large hand wraps around the back of my head, holding me in place while he gently traces the outline of my mouth with his tongue before sucking my lip into his mouth and biting down roughly. My innate reaction is to pull back from the pain, but it's no use, Vinny has my head in his grip and doesn't give me the chance to respond. Instead his tongue infiltrates my mouth and he kisses me with so much passion that I can't help but feel it throughout my body. My skin heats, every nerve courses at warp speed with electricity pumping through my veins, and I kiss him back as hard as he gives it.

"Soon, Liv," he mutters between impatient kisses when we come up for air. "I want you in my bed. Underneath me, on top of me, bent over...fuck, we're going to invent new ways for me to have you."

A small moan escapes my mouth and his grip tightens even more around me. "You better run now, Liv. If I hear that sound one more time, I'm going to be breaking my promise to take it slow and I'm not going to stop until you can't walk for a few days."

Begrudgingly, Vinny loosens his grip around me and slowly releases me. It's clear he's struggling and I open my mouth to speak, but Vinny puts his hand over my mouth silencing my attempt at words. His words a stern warning, "Go. Now."

The sun is starting to come up by the time I finally relax enough to fall asleep. But when I finally do, I find the boy that I once knew, rather than the man I've just left, take over my dreams.

I'm sitting up against the tree, my knees drawn up to my chest, arms locked around them tightly. I look down at him, lying so casually and relaxed, his toned body sprawled out on the dark green grass. Hands folded behind his head, he smiles up at me and his pale blue eyes sparkle, contrasting beautifully against his tanned skin in the afternoon sunlight.

"Kiss me, Liv."

I freeze at his words. I've kissed a boy before, but not one like Vinny. It's pretty much all I could think about doing for the last four months. Yet here I sit like a deer in the headlights when the opportunity finally falls right into my lap.

"Liv." Vinny's voice breaks me out of my daze. For a minute, I think I must have imagined that he just told me to kiss him. I even feel a little relief that it was all in my head. But the relief is short lived. His beautiful eyes lock onto mine and this time there's no mistaking that I haven't imagined his words. "Come here, Liv. Kiss me."

Still lying with his hands casually linked behind his head, he makes no attempt to move toward me. He sees the confusion on my face. "Lean down, Liv. Bring your mouth down to me and kiss me."

"Why?" Finally, I find my wits and speak.

"Don't you want to?" he says, a knowing smile on his face as he speaks.

My face reddens before I even speak, giving away my embarrassment before my answer. "Yes."

"So kiss me then."

"But..."

"Liv."

"What?"

"Just do it. Stop thinking for once."

So I do. I lean down and, hesitantly, I touch my lips to his and kiss him. Gently, with closed mouth.

I sit back up and open my eyes and find Vinny smiling up at me. I smile back at him, feeling relief. "Now really kiss me, Liv."

My smile quickly disappears, replaced by worry and nervousness. Unconsciously, I bite my lower lip. Vinny arches his eyebrows, waiting patiently.

Slowly, I lean back down to him and cover his lips with mine. At first, I'm hesitant to open my mouth, but then I do. I force myself to push all my fears away and I slip my tongue into his mouth. And that's all it takes. Vinny growls and hooks his hand around my neck, pulling me closer as his tongue takes over the lead. We kiss for what seems like forever, coming up only for a few seconds each time, both of us panting wildly, gasping only for enough air to allow us to continue.

Eventually Vinny breaks the kiss, ending the passionate embrace with a series of sweet, gentle, closed mouth kisses. Loosening his grip on the back of my neck enough to allow me to pull my head back to look at him, I find him smiling at me.

"Why?" I ask.

"Why what?" Vinny's thumb strokes along the back of my neck gently as he speaks.

"Why didn't you kiss me? Why did you make me kiss you first?"

"I was giving you time to say no." He smiles at me with a cocky smile. "Even though I knew you wanted to. I didn't know if you were ready for me."

CHAPTER 15

Vince

"You're dragging your ass. Do I need to ask what you were up to last night, or do we go straight back to random testing?" Nico's in the ring with me. He's right, I'm wiped this morning, but it has nothing to do with partying for a change.

"I was with Liv late last night. Got home and couldn't sleep."

Nico laughs. "Been there, done that."

"Yeah, took me three hours to fall asleep after leaving her."

"And you didn't stop at Flannigan's on the way home to pick up someone to help you work it out of your system?"

"Didn't even think about it." The thought never crossed my mind to pick up a GIMP, help work through the frustration I'd taken with me when I made Liv walk away last night.

"My little boy might be growing up after all." Nico climbs into the ring and raises the cushioned protection pads for me to begin my strikes.

"Funny."

Nico laughs. "I think so."

Swinging my right leg in a roundhouse kick, I connect with the pad and Nico takes a step back from the momentum of the impact. "Looks like hard up works for you. Again. Other leg. Knock me on my ass or you're doing six miles on the treadmill when we're done here."

Fucking Nico. Always using that god damn treadmill against me. Ever since I was a little kid. I rear back and strike hard with the other leg. Nico takes two steps back, but remains standing. "Looks like you have a good run after practice today." Nico laughs and I spend the next forty minutes trying to knock him on his ass, purely for my own personal satisfaction. I'm unsuccessful and the six mile run actually helps me cool off after another few hours of feeling frustrated.

I swing by Mom's on the way home from the gym. The front door is open and I feel the frustration I just ran off knot its way back through my body. She's careless when she's wasted, totally disregards her own personal safety. And since she's wasted most days, she's pretty much always putting herself out there at risk.

I'm surprised to find my mother sitting up on the couch when I enter. Most days she's passed out and junkies are lying around haphazardly, like trash before the cleanup after a rough night of partying. There's two men sitting opposite my mother. Unlike the usual ones I find, these appear clean, their clothes aren't torn and dirty, and it's likely they've shaved in the last day or two.

"Mom?" All eyes turn to me, they hadn't noticed I entered the apartment with the heated discussion going on.

"Hi, Baby." My mother looks to me, and then back to the two men staring at me, and I can see she's nervous. Whoever they are, they're bad news. They may look better than the usual losers I find, but the vibe coming from my mother tells me that they're just as much trouble.

"Who are you?" I tilt my chin to the closer of the two men and wait for a response.

"We're friends of your mother's." The man stands and folds his arms over his chest. He's trying to intimidate me with his size, only the fucker has no idea who he's dealing with. I don't give a shit if he does have a few inches on me.

"Yeah? What do you want from my mother, *friend*."

The guy still sitting slaps his hand on his knee. "Holy shit. You're Vince Stone, the fighter, aren't you?" He seems pleased with himself for the discovery.

I completely ignore his question. He still hasn't answered mine and I feel my adrenaline start pumping up, readying me for a fight. "I've asked nicely twice, now I'm starting to lose my patience. Who the fuck are you and what do you want from my mother?"

"We're looking for a friend of your mother's...who has something that belongs to us."

I look to my right and then to my left with dramatic emphasis. "I don't see anyone else here...so get the fuck out."

The guy still sitting chuckles and stands. I watch as he lifts his hand to his waist and pats what's tucked into the band, silently letting me know that my fists are no match for his fire power. He motions to the other guy with his head toward the door and the two make their way to the exit. The one carrying stops before he walks out and turns back to me. "Listen, I've seen you fight. Got a lot of respect for you, man. Love to see a local kid make it big time. It's a shame it's gonna go down like this. But your mother there," his chin points back in her direction, "she's got two weeks to come up with our cash or our stash," he pauses, "or find that dirtbag Jason she vouched for. Otherwise we're coming back. And all the muscle in the world you got ain't gonna help her."

CHAPTER 16

Liv

"I was just about to check if you were still breathing in there. How much longer do you really think I can hold out for details?" Ally doesn't even wait until both my feet are through my bedroom door before starting in on me.

"Coffee," I grunt in response. There will be absolutely no talking before I get at least a loading dose of caffeine in my body. Ally isn't deterred by my grumpy response. Instead she plants herself up on the kitchen counter, directly across from the coffee pot where I lethargically prepare the antidote to my slumber.

"I waited up till two and you still weren't home, so I'm guessing your date with the sexy beast went well?"

"Sexy beast? I thought he was just the beast?"

"That was in high school, when he broke your achy breaky heart. I forgive him now. I mean who wouldn't? That man is a sexy beast."

"You forgive him? You haven't spoken to him since high school. Exactly what has he done to earn your forgiveness?"

"He took off his shirt for that picture in the paper this morning." Ally wiggles her eyebrows suggestively and motions to the newspaper lying on the kitchen table. It's open to an advertisement for Vinny's, actually, Vince "The Invincible" Stone's, upcoming fight. Except for the date and time, there's little writing, yet I can't seem to stop staring at the picture.

"You can take it back to your room and use it for inspiration later," Ally teases, a wide grin on her face. "I want details first." My best friend folds her arms over her chest. Clearly she isn't going to go away quietly.

Walking past her with the paper still clenched in my hand, I grab my coffee and make my way into the living room. Ally follows closely behind.

"I don't know, Ally." I let out an exasperated sigh. It's not for effect while telling my story, I truly feel conflicted. "When I'm around him, it's so easy to feel like I can fall for him again. Like we could pick up right where we left off, almost as if he didn't walk away one day and forget I ever existed. It scares me how easy it was for him to leave."

"Maybe it wasn't as easy as you've thought all these years, Liv. Did you ask him?"

"I did. I didn't want to, but I couldn't help myself…I needed to know how it was so easy for him, when it was so, so hard for me."

"And what did he say?"

"He told me what I wanted to hear."

"Which is what? Different from the truth?"

"I don't know, Ally. I'm afraid to believe it's the truth. That I can trust him. That maybe we could pick up where we left off. Or better yet, start over. As adults."

"Guess you have to decide. Is he worth the chance? The chance that maybe if you let him in, he'll stay this time?"

I'm in a fog as I run through all of my weekend errands. My mind keeps finding its way back to Vinny at every turn. At the gym for my spin class, I think about the smooth lines of his muscular, carved abdomen stretching as he led the class through a series of kicks yesterday. At the dry cleaner, a nice looking man in an expensive suit smiles at me and attempts to strike up a conversation. But my mind only thinks about how much better Vinny would look in the three thousand dollar Armani the handsome man is sporting. All roads just seem to lead my mind back to one place.

I stop by the bookstore after my last errand. There's nothing better to clear my mind than spending a few hours perusing the aisles and sipping a caramel latte from the in-store coffee bar. I pick up a few novels I've been meaning to check out. Flipping a few pages into the first chapter of one, I begin to read, attempting to decide which book I'll be spending the evening with.

His thick, throbbing erection slips past my opening, landing on my aching clit. A low moan escapes me in a deep throaty breath and it fuels my lover's desire. With a growl, he rears back and thrusts into me, filling me deeply in one heavenly plunge. Oh my, and I'm only on page six. I'm thinking I may have found my newest purchase, my date for tonight, when my phone rings, bringing me back from a place I was just beginning to enjoy.

"Hey." Just hearing Vinny's deep voice makes me smile

"Hi."

"Are you home?" he asks.

"No, I'm at the bookstore."

"Looking for something for work?"

"Actually no. I was just trying to decide on a good book to snuggle up with tonight."

"What kind of book?"

"Ummm…romance."

"Snuggle up with me instead tonight."

I laugh because he's teasing, but something in his tone tells me it's also a real invitation. "But I was so looking forward to reading my smut tonight."

"Smut? Bring it, you can read it to me. We can act out the scenes."

Suddenly, my throat goes dry. Visions of Vinny acting out the short scene I was just reading makes my head spin and my hormones get the best of me.

"Liv."

It takes me a minute to snap out of my daze and respond. "Yeah, I'm here."

"Buy the book that's in your hand right now."

"How do you know there's a book in my hand right now?"

Vinny chuckles. "What's it called?"

"Ummm." Shit, couldn't I pick up something with a less telling title. *His Thick Heat.* "I don't have a book in my hand," I lie.

"Buy the book, Liv."

"You're insane, you know that?"

"So I've been told. Buy the book, Liv. I'll pick you up at seven."

"But..."

"No buts. Seven, Liv...with the book."

And then he's gone.

CHAPTER 17

Vinny – 7 years earlier

The last few weeks we've spent more time fooling around than working on English. Only in this subject, I'm the tutor and Liv's the student. The hottest little student I've ever seen. And a damn fast learner too. It's been hell taking it slow. All I want to do is be inside her, and she wants it too, I can see it in the way her eyes glaze over when I slide my fingers into her. She's so tight and hot, and her body responds perfectly to my every touch. And she makes this little sound that drives me crazy. I doubt she even realizes she's doing it. A sound that's a cross between a moan and a purr, and I'm afraid I might explode if I ever hear it with my dick inside her.

It's almost nine and the park is empty, just the two of us rolling around on the blanket under our tree. Ever since that night when I made her kiss me, things just keep going further, moving faster each night. More just isn't enough. Tonight it's hot and heavy, both of us grinding against each other desperately through our clothes. Dry humping Liv feels better than the real thing has with any of the slutty girls I've been with. I reach down between us, finding her magic spot through her shorts and rub small circles, the way I know makes her feel good. She's not a talker, but her body tells me everything I need to know.

As she's about to come, I cover her mouth with mine. She tries to pull her tongue away as it takes her over, but I force her to keep kissing me. The sound of her moan being stifled by me makes me fucking insane. It's the hottest thing I've ever heard in my life. If she were anyone else, I'd have taken her four different ways and been done with her by now. Only she's not just anyone. She's sweet little Liv, and every once in a while I let myself pretend I'm the good guy she thinks I am.

As she comes down from her orgasm, she reaches for me and somehow her hand is down my pants and squeezing me at the base before I can stop her. The feel of her soft little hand wrapping around my thick throbbing cock makes my control slip. Then I feel the heat of her mouth at my ear and I fucking lose it when I hear her say, "Please Vinny, I want you."

Screw it. I'm done being good. Less than two minutes later, both our clothes are off and I'm just about to get what I've been waiting so patiently for. My cock lined up perfectly at her opening, she looks up at me and our eyes meet. Her big hazel eyes are wide and filled with emotion, but that's not what I see that scares the living shit out of me. I see trust. She's giving me all of hers and I don't fucking deserve it. Not for a minute. God knows what it will do to her when I screw things up. And it won't take long either. Nothing good ever lasts.

So I close my eyes, I fucking want her so badly that my body aches, but I can't look into those big eyes when I rob her of what she's about to give me freely. Only closing them doesn't help…I still see her, even though my eyes are pressed shut. A picture so vivid stares at me that it takes a second to be sure I'm not actually looking at her anymore. So I try to stop thinking, squeezing my eyes shut so hard that I'm sure my face looks like I'm in pain. But it doesn't work to erase the god damn picture of her sweet, innocent, trusting face in my head. Not at fucking all. A few more seconds pass, my body beginning to shake as I keep myself steady, so ready to enter her, but unable to move.

"Fuuuuuckk!" I jump up as I growl, my roar so loud it echoes in the quiet, hands frantically wrenching at my hair, mind racing, trying to figure out what the fuck I am doing. Shit. Shit. Shit. I can't fucking do it to her.

"What's wrong?" Liv's voice is hesitant. I must be a scary sight, yet she reaches for me without fear.

Jerking my arm away from her reach, I can tell that I've scared her, but I can't let her touch me. Need to get the fuck away from her before I change my mind. "Get dressed." My voice is cold and distant.

"What?" She's confused.

"Get dressed, Liv. I'm taking you home."

Neither of us says a word the whole drive back to her house. I pretend I don't see her tears as she tries to hide wiping them away.

For the next two weeks, I avoid looking in Liv's direction when I catch sight of her in the cafeteria. Today as I walk in, I see Missy to the left and Liv to the right, so I decide to find a new table to sit at. I take a seat next to Evan Marco and some of his football team buddies. He's full of himself, but not a bad guy. A bit too Biffy for my taste. Daddy's got deep pockets, makes him think he's got value. Nothing life won't eventually smack him in the face with and teach him a lesson. They're in a heated debate about the point system to some game it sounds like they've been playing together for a while.

"The only way Evan or Kyle have a shot at winning this thing is to bag a virgin at prom. Ryan's got five points on both of you from his two on one with the two blondes from the bonfire the other night." Caleb Andrews has a little notebook with pages upon pages of markings and notes he's studying as he speaks to his friends.

"Speaking of which, did anyone verify the Ryan twofer?" Evan throws out to his friends.

"Yeah, man. I fucking saw it with my own eyes. He had one giving him head and was making out with the other with his hand up her skirt. Wanted to burn my eyes out when I got a good look at his little pin dick," Caleb laughs as he speaks.

"You guys keeping tabs on getting laid?" I smile, why wasn't I in on this action. This sounds like one organized sport I would have actually joined at this crap school.

"Don't even think about it Stonetti. We wouldn't let you in giving a hundred point handicap, pretty boy. Chicks love the whole trouble thing you got going on." Caleb is only half joking when he speaks.

"So who's winning?"

"Well as of now, Ryan. But he's got no more chances to earn. Banging a virgin at prom is a premium, but he's taking Laurelyn, so that's definitely out," he laughs.

"So Evan and Kyle are taking virgins and can pull off an upset?"

"Yep. This is gonna go down to the last night of the damn contest."

"What's the winner get?" I'm thinking a long term game like this has gotta have big stakes.

Evan smiles. "A dollar."

"A dollar? Are you fucking kidding me?"

"We're in it for the game bro, not the cash."

"Whatever you say man, but both would be nicer in my book." The bell rings and we all stand. I find Liv and watch as she walks out the door before I even attempt to move in her direction. "Who's your prom date, Evan?"

"Olivia Michaels."

CHAPTER 18

Liv

I've taken the book in and out of my bag at least ten times by the time the buzzer rings right at seven. It's currently hidden in the bottom of my bag, but if he takes more than thirty seconds to get up to my floor, I'm pretty sure it won't be in there by the time he knocks.

I hear Ally open the door, but I stay in my room a few more minutes to compose myself. Eventually, I hold my breath and force myself out of hiding and make my way into the living room.

Ally is standing in the kitchen pouring a glass of wine while Vinny sits on a stool at the breakfast nook. He turns and stands as I walk into the room, leaving Ally talking to the back of his head.

"Hey." He stands and watches me walk toward him, a slight smirk on his handsome face. I stop in front of him, suddenly feeling awkward about how I should greet him, but the feeling doesn't last for long. Vinny hooks his hand around my neck and leans down to kiss me gently on the lips.

Looking up, I find a smile on Ally's face and her eyebrows arched in question at the greeting I've just received. Her glass of wine in hand, halfway up to her mouth, she looks at my face and changes her mind, extending her hand with the glass out to me.

Desperate to calm my nerves, I take the glass and silently thank my best friend with a smile.

"You want a glass of wine, Vince?" Ally reaches into the cabinet where we keep the glasses.

"No, thanks. But don't let it stop the two of you." His words and smile said in jest, as I'm already gulping from my glass and Ally is busy pouring another for herself.

Ally and Vinny catch up, lots of talk about his upcoming fight. Most of what he shares, I already knew from interviewing him for my article. I'm surprised when he extends an invite to Ally. "You should come with Liv. I'll give her a few extra tickets."

I wonder if Vinny's aware he just bought my best friend's unwavering support of my new found relationship with him. She's a die-hard sports fan, not to mention that she would never turn down an opportunity to ogle men with eight packs wearing only boxers, surrounded by a few thousand manly men hyped up on extra testosterone in anticipation of watching said men beat the crap out of each other.

I finish my glass of wine in record time and interrupt the little love fest the two seem to be sharing. "Who said I was going to your fight?" Arching one eyebrow in question, I turn to address Vinny.

"You don't want to come?"

"I didn't say that."

"So what's the problem then?"

"You seem to be making a lot of decisions for me without consulting me first," I fold my hands over my chest as I respond.

"And you don't like the decisions?"

"I didn't say that...but..."

"But what, Liv?" Vinny shrugs his shoulders. Clearly he's clueless as to the point I am trying to make here.

"You're supposed to ask people what they want before you decide things for them."

Vinny folds his arms over his chest, mimicking my stance. "Seems like a waste of time when you already know what the other person wants."

My mouth actually drops open. The arrogance of the man is just so unbelievable. "And what if you're wrong as to what the other person wants?"

Vinny shakes his head and closes the distance between us, wrapping both his arms around my waist. "I have no doubt you'll let me know if I'm wrong." The cocky smile on his face disappears only for a second while he plants a chaste kiss on my lips.

I've never been to the restaurant Vinny takes me to. It's small and intimate and would normally be something I'd appreciate, but the staff all seems to know him and I find myself annoyed that it's clearly a place he frequents with his conquests. I don't know why it bothers me, it just does. We're both adults, even I've had my fair share of dates and overnight partners. Yet something deep inside me is bothered by knowing he's been here and done this before…with someone else.

The waitress comes to greet us, and I feel my pulse accelerate when she also greets Vinny, no Vince, by name. She's cute, although too thin. So much so that I find myself wondering if she has an eating disorder, or perhaps a drug problem, while her and Vinny take a minute to catch up. Careful inspection finds dark circles under her eyes, even though a thick layer of makeup attempts to conceal it.

"So, what can I get you tonight? Beer for you and…" The waif like waitress smiles at me and waits for my response.

"I'll take a Merlot. Thank you." I bury my nose in the menu, unable to conceal that I'm bothered by his familiarity with the restaurant, the waitress…the entire dating scene. What girl wants it smacking her in the face as she goes out to dinner with a man she is trying to learn to trust?

"Do you like tilapia?"

"Yes." I answer, but don't look up from the menu.

"I'll order for us then." Vinny folds his menu and tosses it on the table, as if the discussion we just began already ended.

"I can order for myself." I'm not successful at hiding that I'm annoyed, even though I really do try.

"I didn't say you couldn't. I just figured since I've tried most of the things on the menu—"

"Looks like a few that aren't on it too." The words come out under my breath, dripping with so much bitterness that even I find the statement catty.

Vinny doesn't respond immediately. Curious as to his response to my immature statement, I lift my head and find him glaring at me. Neither of us says anything for a minute as we stare into each other's eyes, playing visual chicken, both too stubborn to look away.

"I come here with Elle and Nico all the time. I know Lily from outpatient rehab, never touched the woman. I've never taken a date here."

I can see in his face he's telling the truth. Heat seeps up to my face, I'm embarrassed for jumping to conclusions, but even more embarrassed at how I reacted to the conclusion I drew. Like a jealous girlfriend, unsure of herself.

"I'm sorry."

"Don't be." There's a slight uptick in the corner of his mouth. "I'm glad you're territorial, because I feel the same way."

"I'm not—"

Vinny interrupts me before I could deny what he's accused me of. "You are."

Exasperated, I let out a sigh and wave my hand. "Whatever." It earns me a full-fledged, panty dropping, dimple bearing smile.

The tension from earlier in the evening long forgotten, we spend hours catching up.

"So you were valedictorian?"

Surprised he knew I'd received any accolades, I correct him. "Salutatorian. You kept tabs on me?"

"Isn't that like, number two? And yes." He arches his eyebrow. Clearly he remembers how competitive I could be.

"Scott Julian beat me by .002." It's been years, but the agony of defeat still grates on my nerves. "I got a B+ in gym." Rolling my eyes at my own admission.

My response earns a chuckle. "You lost number one because of gym."

"Yep." I lift my wine to my mouth and drain the glass. It pisses me off, but I can find the humor in it too. Finally. Well, maybe a little anyway.

"That was the only class I ever got an A in."

"What about English? You did well when I tutored you."

"Got a B." He finishes his beer. "Tutor was hot." He shrugs, a grin on his face. "Distracted me."

"So it's my fault you didn't get an A in a real subject?"

His brows narrow. "Gym *is* a real subject."

"Pfsst." I pooh-pooh his answer. "Gym is *not* a real subject."

Eyebrows popping, he finds amusement in my answer. "Bet you Scott Julian agrees with me."

"Whatever." I squint, my hand waving away our argument as no big deal, even though it's one I could clearly argue for hours. One that still sits uneasily with me. "You just like to get a rise out of me," I accuse.

One lip turned devilishly upward, an eyebrow arched suggestively, he doesn't even need to speak his retort. We both know what it would be.

Through dessert, I tell him stories about Ally and I going away to college together, bringing him up to date on her four changes in career choices since we graduated high school. He tells me stories about Elle and Nico. There's a lot of history there. They seem to have become his family. I notice he doesn't often mention his mother.

After he pays the check, Vinny stands and offers me his hand to help me up. Though he doesn't release it when I'm fully upright. Instead, he gathers me close and lowers his mouth to mine. I feel the heat of his breath and a brush so soft on my lips, I can't even be sure if we've touched. "Did you bring your book?" he says softly, but with a huskiness to his voice that warms my body all over.

"Yes." My breaths coming quicker and shallower from the close proximity, the word drops from my lips in almost a pant. This man can take me from zero to sixty in only a few seconds.

"Good girl." He slightly pulls his head back to take in my face. The mischief I find makes my heart skip a beat. "You know I always loved it when you read to me. I had to sit on my hands to stop them from finding their way up that little black skirt you used to wear. I'm guessing this book is gonna be a lot more fun than the stuff we read in high school. And I'm definitely not sitting on my hands." A damn sexy grin mixed with his deep raspy voice melts any conviction I'd had left. "Let's get out of here."

He doesn't tell me where we're going, and I don't ask either. We're both quiet as he zips his truck through the downtown streets, his attention clearly focused on getting to our next destination. My mind races and I struggle to separate it from my body that seems to have ideas of its own. At this point Vinny could probably tell me that he's a serial killer, but if his hard, warm body is pushed up against me, I know my brain would lose the battle to the relentless pursuit of my body to fill its own needs.

He leads me into his apartment, both of us still quiet. I'm nervous and anxious and he senses it. Knows I'm teetering on the verge of changing my mind...not that I've been given an opportunity to make up my mind anyway. One large arm wraps around my waist pulling me close to him. I lean my head into his chest, still feeling conflicted, although the close proximity tips the scale slightly on the side of seeing this beautiful man naked.

After a minute, Vinny runs a hand slowly down my cheek, stopping at my chin, using his finger to gently lift my head so my eyes meet his gaze. "I want you, Liv. I wanted you seven years ago. Want you even more now. So much that I can't think about anything else. Need you." He exhales deeply and leans his forehead into mine, composing himself before he continues. "All you gotta do is say no, Liv. But, I'm giving you fair warning...if you don't tell me no, I'm going to take you." His serious face changes and I watch as his pupil's dilate, heat pouring from his body as he continues, his grip on the back of my neck tightening. "And then you're mine to do with as I please."

My breath hitches at his words, and I'm a goner. His long, thick fingers ravel tightly in my hair and he yanks my head back further to take my mouth. The roughness of his actions startles me, but at the same time sends a bolt of electricity mixed with fiery anticipation throughout my body making every little hair stand at attention.

My body presses into his as I kiss him back with a desperation I've never known. Slowly, he licks the rim of my mouth before diving in to suck on my tongue and my nipples harden with anticipation. Nibbling on my bottom lip, I can't help but get the feeling that it's more than a kiss. He's showing me what he wants to do to me with his hot, wet mouth. My eyes roll into the back of my head at just the mere thought of his licking and sucking other places on my body.

His arm that isn't tangled in my hair pulls me possessively closer to his body, so close I can feel his erection pressing up against my belly. The hard length of him digs into me and a low moan escapes my lips.

One minute I'm standing in the living room being kissed senseless and the next thing I know I'm being lifted effortlessly and carried into his bedroom. He gently sets me back down on my feet. I feel the bed against the back of my knees, but together we remain standing.

"Take off your shirt," he says, his voice sinfully gruff and low. The commanding tone makes my body tingle all over.

Vinny takes one step back and waits. His hooded eyes are filled with desire, it makes me feel wanted. Worshiped. Adored. Slowly, I lift my shirt over my head, revealing my black, lacy bra contrasting starkly with my pale, alabaster skin. Vinny's eyes rake me over approvingly and I stand still for a long minute letting him drink me in.

"Your turn." My eyes find his and lock, expecting him to comply with my request as easily as I did.

Vinny smirks, a knowing grin on his face and shakes his head back and forth. "Doesn't work that way." He reaches forward and runs a finger across one nipple, barely concealed behind the black, lacy fabric. My already engorged nipple swells to his touch. Satisfied with the response from my body, Vinny moves to the other breast and my body again responds easily to his demands.

"Turn around."

My eyes that were glued to watching his hand explore my body, jump to meet his. He says nothing else, but patiently waits for me to do as I'm told. Wrapping his long arms around my waist, he pulls me close to him, my back pressed firmly against his front. Burying his face in my neck, he trails a line of wet kisses from the nape of my neck up to my ear. His hands cup my breasts and his fingers pinch my nipples, eliciting a moan from my throat I didn't even feel rise to the surface.

Pulling me even closer to him, his hardness grinds and throbs against my ass. "Feel that, Liv?"

Unable to speak, I swallow hard and nod my response.

"I'm going to bury myself so deep inside of you it'll leave you feeling hollow when I'm not with you."

Jesus. My body begins to pulsate on its own. I can feel the blood coursing through my veins, my heart beating wildly with anticipation.

Vinny pinches my nipples again, this time harder, more forcefully. Pain shoots through my body, but it only ratchets up my need. "Is that what you want, Liv."

"Yes." My hips push back, pressing his thickness even further into me. I moan as I begin to rock my hips. I've wanted this for what seems like forever.

"Tell me. Tell me what you want, Liv." He pushes harder against my ass.

"You."

"Say it. Tell me what you want me to do to you."

"Take me. I want you to take me."

"Turn around."

I turn, not wanting to lose the connection, the contact...but the look in his eyes is even more intimate than his touch. It tells me he wants me, that he feels the same way I do. Yet even though I see wild in his eyes, he still manages to maintain his control.

"Take off your jeans."

With him fully dressed, I feel exposed as I wiggle out of my jeans and stand before him in nothing but matching lacy demi cup bra and black thong lace panties.

Unhurriedly, Vinny slowly gazes up and down my body taking in every inch with heat in his eyes. I see lust and adoration, and it fuels me as I stand there so completely bared before him. When his eyes finally meet mine, I see what he's thinking before he says the words. "You're so beautiful, Liv."

I smile back at him. But it doesn't take long for his sweet smile to turn devilish. It's a barely discernible change, something in the way his eyes squint and a gleam shines from his pupils. Yet it's there and I notice it.

"Lie on the bed."

Slowly, I sit, then lay back on the bed, looking up at the man looming over me.

Vinny leans in and takes both sides of my panties, slowly pulling them down my legs until they're off. Gently, he unhooks and slides my lacy bra off, allowing his callous fingers to leisurely graze over my pert nipples. Leaning over me, he brings his head to mine and gently kisses my lips before speaking. His voice is low and throaty. "Reach up. Grab the headboard with both hands. If you keep them there, I won't bind you to it."

My eyes go wide as saucers at his threat. A devilish grin on his face, he continues, "this time."

He waits and watches me intently, saying nothing more until I finally comply, reaching both arms above my head and taking hold of the headboard.

He lowers himself down my body, stopping at my breasts to suck in each sensitive nipple. Each suck ending in a nip that shoots a burst of pain down my body, but turns into desire before it reaches its final destination. His hand reaches between my legs and his wide thumb strokes my clit as he inserts one long finger into me expertly. Reacting to his touch, my body coats his finger until its slick, easily allowing him to slip in and out of me.

A moan I don't even attempt to stop escapes as he glides a second finger into me, leaving my body feeling replete. Instinctually, my hips grind up to meet the rhythm of the thrust of his fingers and my hand reaches down to entwine in his hair.

Abruptly, Vinny stills, leaving me dangling from bliss. "Headboard, Liv. Last warning."

I hadn't even realized that I'd released the grip I had on the cool metal frame. A minute ago my knuckles were white as I held on for dear life, then suddenly they were grabbing for him with a mind of their own. Returning my hands to the headboard, I take a deep breath and do as I'm told, grasping the headboard with white knuckle strength. It seems to satisfy Vinny because his fingers are back moving inside of me again. He sucks in my nipple and my hips begin to circle of their own accord.

Another moan escapes me and I hear Vinny growl before his fingers begin to pump furiously into me. The slow circle of my hips grows larger as I push up to meet his slick pumps. Just as I begin to feel my body contract on its own, his fingers are gone, only to be quickly replaced by the heat of his mouth on me.

He circles my clit with his tongue, at first gently, teasingly swirling round and round. But the pressure quickly increases to a full suck as he reinserts his two fingers into me and draws harshly down on my clit. Every nerve in my body ignites and I cry out as I climax, my body shaking and pulsating uncontrollably with the sudden intensity of my orgasm.

I'm still reeling from the power of my body giving itself over to Vinny, vaguely aware that he's taking his clothes off, and I hear the crackle of a wrapper before I feel the weight of his body covering mine.

"You can let go of the headboard if you want."

I hadn't even realized I was still holding it. I begin to release my death grip, then reconsider my actions. After the most intense orgasm of my life, I want to see what comes next. I grin up at Vinny and firm up my grip on the headboard with a wicked smile.

"Fucking perfect." With a groan, Vinny surges inside of me and fills me deeply. His mouth covers mine and tasting myself on his tongue has me on the brink of another orgasm before he can even begin to move. Once he's fully seated inside of me, I brace myself, expecting a rough and thoroughly heated performance. Instead, he takes me by surprise, slowing our kisses down from wild to sensual as he begins to slowly rock in and out of me.

I want to reach out and touch him so badly, feel the hard corded muscle on his back as it strains and contracts with the rhythm of his body. But I don't. He's giving slow and sensual to me, a trade for the control I've allowed him to take.

Unlike my first orgasm that hit me hard, head on, dizzying me into euphoria, the second one builds slowly, with Vinny stroking it from me one amazing thrust at a time. And when it finally begins to take over me, I watch as Vinny's own orgasm hits him simultaneously and, together, we fall over the cliff with our moans stifled between our kiss.

I don't even remember falling asleep last night, but I wake up completely wrapped in Vinny. My head on his chest and our legs firmly entwined, I have no desire to move, but I see the sun beginning to peek in through the blinds and I remember I need to turn off my phone alarm before it blares and wakes him. Slowly, I do my best to extract myself from our mess of tangled limbs. I'm careful not to wake him. Stretching to reach my phone, my body responds with a mass of aches and soreness. I hit the button to turn off the alarm that is due to sound in just under five minutes, and a warm hand wraps around my naked belly and pulls me back in place.

"Mornin." Vinny's early morning voice is gravelly and deep. Sexy as all hell.

"Morning." I smile at the sound of his voice, but he can't see it with my back pressed firmly against his front.

"You trying to escape?"

"Just turning off my alarm so it won't wake you."

He nuzzles his head into the back of my hair and gently kisses the back of my neck before speaking. His warm breath warms my whole body. "Got a class to teach at Nico's gym this morning. I have to run."

I'm disappointed, but I try to feign otherwise. "Oh. Okay."

Vinny kisses me on my shoulder and rises from the bed. A chill runs through me as the warmth from his hard body disappears, cool air in its place. I wait until I hear the bathroom door close before getting up in search of my carelessly strewn clothes.

By the time Vinny returns, I've gathered most of my clothes, but I'm still wrapped in a sheet, searching for my panties.

"Where you going?"

Did he forget the conversation we just had? The one where he tells me he needs to leave? "Ummm…home."

"I thought you weren't trying to make an escape?"

"I wasn't. But you're leaving."

Vinny slips on a pair of running shorts and reaches down to the floor, pulling up the panties I'm still searching for. "You looking for these?" He twirls my sad excuse for underwear around on his one finger with a devilish grin.

"Yes." I reach out to grab them, but Vinny's too quick. He folds them into one hand and hooks his arm around my waist, pulling me to him with the other.

"Stay. I'll be back in less than two hours."

"You want me to stay?"

Leaning down, his mouth close to my ear, he responds, "I want you in my bed waiting for me when I get back."

His words are kind, and I appreciate him offering them to me, but it's not necessary. I'm a big girl, he doesn't need to coddle me after a night of passion. "It's okay. It's sweet of you to offer, but I have errands to run anyway."

Vinny turns me to face him, tilting my face up to look into his eyes. "I don't do sweet, Liv. I want you to stay because I'm selfish. I want back inside of you. I'm hard just thinking about the sound you make when you come for me. So fuck your errands and get back in bed and try to get some rest. Because you're gonna need it."

My lord. Maybe I should be offended at the harshness of his words, but I'm not. Instead they make me feel drunk with desire and I find myself staring back at him at a loss for words. Vinny grins, he must know he's gotten to me.

"Okay?" He kisses me chastely on the lips.

"Okay," I finally respond with a smile that lets him know he's changed my mind.

Grabbing his keys off the dresser, Vinny opens the palm of his hand revealing black lace. I'd forgotten that he even still had my panties in his hand. "I'm keeping these." With a devilish grin he shoves them into his pocket as he walks out.

CHAPTER 19

Vince

I'm full of energy as I run the women in the self-defense class through a series of techniques. I normally pick my assistant to demonstrate moves on based on the shape of their ass or size of their rack. But today I took the closest person to me, a plump woman, probably in her fifties. Oddly, it's the most fun I've had demonstrating in months, aside from the day with Liv. She's ticklish and sensitive to touch, and each time I grab her to show a position, she giggles and laughs with a snort. Usually I'd find an overly happy person annoying at this time of the morning, but today her laugh seems to be contagious.

After class is over, the woman gives me a hug, thanking me for making her day. Totally out of character for me, I kiss her on the cheek and tell her it's me that should be thanking her for making my day. Packing up the last of my things into my duffle bag, I'm not surprised to hear Nico's voice. I haven't earned his trust back yet and he still feels the need to check up on me every time I'm scheduled to teach.

"You're in a good mood today."

"Guess I am." Giving nothing away, I pull the strap for my bag diagonally across my chest, anxious to get my ass back home. The thought of what's waiting for me makes me salivate.

"You have the key to the back door? Elle took off with both sets of keys and I want to lock up the garage before I head out for a few hours."

"Sure." I reach into my pocket to pull out my keys and don't even notice that something tumbles to the floor.

Nico's eyes point downward, directing me to the scrap of lace material lying on the floor. "Think you dropped something."

I quickly scoop up the lace at my feet and feel a tightening in my chest. It pisses me off that Nico's seen anything that belongs to Liv. "Fuck off."

Nico's taken aback. "Since when are you protective of some GIMPs belongings?"

"It's not some GIMPs." Anger resonates from my every word as they're spoken through my clenched teeth.

Nico looks confused for a minute, and then seems to come to some sort of understanding, even though I haven't offered him an explanation. He slaps me on the back and walks with me to the door. "Glad to hear it. Now get out of here and go enjoy Liv."

How does he know?

I stop on the way home and pick up lunch and the paper. It's been years since I bought a freakin newspaper. The only time I even glance over at one is when I see a picture of myself, an ad for an upcoming fight. And then I read from the back page forward, stopping before I get to any real news. But it's Liv's paper, the one she works at, and I figure she probably reads it every day.

It's quiet when I walk in. For a minute I think she might have left. Then I walk into my bedroom and catch sight of her. She's lying in the middle of the bed wearing the shirt I had on last night. Her face is so peaceful as she sleeps, I almost pull the door closed and let her rest. Almost. But then she shifts in her sleep, one leg already bent at the knee lifts higher, taking the hem of my shirt with it revealing her porcelain, naked ass. And I just can't resist.

I strip out of my clothes, my eyes never leaving the curve of her half naked ass. The way it rounds as it meets her thigh, toned muscle shaping the sides into a heart that leaves me salivating. There's nothing I want to do more than turn that silky white skin a hot shade of red with my hand. It's hard to resist as it peeks out at me, taunting me to slap it. Hard. So that she feels the sting on her ass as she sits down. So that she remembers me inside the hollow of her empty pussy when I'm gone. Remembers who put it there. Who taught her to enjoy the pleasures of a little pain…

I'm two seconds away from waking her with the sting of my hand, followed by ramming myself into her for another round of hard, deep penetration, when her eyes flutter open and she looks up at me with a smile. It's sweet and innocent, and an expression I'm not used to. One that I can't remember seeing from another woman directed at me. Not ever. Not by any woman. I watch as her eyes come into focus and drift down to realize I'm naked. And hard. Her eyes look at my body with appreciation, but then our eyes meet again and she smiles even wider. Women usually don't find my face again after their eyes drop below the neck. That works for me. Usually.

Pulling the sheet to the side, Liv rolls onto her back and reaches up her hand without words. So I take it, forgetting the pain I was so ready to inflict and following her lead instead. There's always later…

CHAPTER 20

Liv

I split the paper in two offering Vinny the sports section as I delve into the business section. Sitting with my back against the arm of the couch, my legs lying over Vinny's lap, he begins to rub my feet.

"Oh my god, that feels so good." My voice drops, doing little to disguise the pleasure of his touch. My body instantly remembers the feel of his hands on other parts of my body. I close my eyes, releasing the paper I was intent on reading, completely forgetting the topic of the piece within seconds.

"I'm here to service."

Vinny presses his thumb into the arch of my foot with one hand as the other kneads the ball of my foot, the part that carries my weight most days as I wear high heels to the office. "Mmmmmm." The sound escapes me as my eyes roll into the back of my head. My shoulders slump, tension easing, even though his touch is at the other end of my body.

"Jesus, Liv. I can't be responsible when you make that sound and you look like that."

"Sorry, can't help it. You have really good hands."

"So I've been told."

Like being plucked from a blissful dream as you sit on fluffy white clouds, my body tenses and I rip my feet from his grip. My voice hardens as I respond, "It really doesn't interest me to hear about the opinions of your Krissys and Missys."

Eyebrows drawn, Vinny has the audacity to look annoyed at my response, when it was his words that were a slap in the face. "I'm a fighter, Liv. Remember? I've been told I have good hands by *trainers and opponents*." He drags a hand through his hair. "Nice to know you think so little of me that I'd brag to you about other women."

"I, I...I'm sorry...I thought you meant..."

"Yeah, I know what you thought I meant." Abruptly, he stands and it looks like he's going to walk away, but then he stops and turns back to speak again. "How did it make you feel to think I was talking about being with other women?"

"I...I don't understand, the question."

Vinny leans down, his hands pressing into the couch on either side of my face, caging me in. "Simple question. Simple answer. You're the smart one."

Not wanting to admit the truth, I go for vague and deflection. "I thought it was rude. How would you feel if you thought I was talking about another man while I was touching you?"

I watch as the dark pupils in the middle of the pale blue grows wider and wider in his eyes, leaving only a thin shadow of color as the darkness takes over. Jaw clenching, the anger resonates from his body. "Like I want to rip someone's head off. Answer the damn question, Liv." His eyes narrow with anger.

"Jealous. Okay? Are you happy?" I yell my response.

"Good."

"Good?" You've got to be kidding me. "You *want* me to be jealous?"

"I want you to stop finding reasons to run away from me every few hours. Jealous at least means you give a shit."

I open my mouth twice to respond. But each time I realize I have nothing to throw back at him. Vinny's eyes watch me and wait. They say so much. Dear Lord, they say everything as they blaze into me with so much intensity it takes my breath away. "You scare me, Vinny."

I pause. *"We* scare me," I whisper, feeling embarrassed at what I feel. But I'm honest. Finally.

Vinny's eyes close for a minute and I watch as his throat works as he swallows. When he opens his eyes, they're different, less angry, yet still full of emotion. Lifting one of his hands from the side of my head as he still looms over me, he gently cups my jaw. "You scare me too, Liv."

I turn, leaning into his touch and kiss the inside of his hand. Returning my sight to his face, a thought dawns on me that makes me grin. "I scare Vince 'The Invincible' Stone?"

Vinny returns my smile. "You're really asking for it today, aren't you?"

One eyebrow arched, I can't help myself...he's left himself so perfectly open. "And what if I am, does that mean you're going to give it to me?"

He groans, and before I can even protest, I'm lifted out of my seat and flung over his shoulder as he stalks into the bedroom. The next few hours we alternate between reading my new book and Vinny giving me what I asked for.

It's almost midnight when Vinny drops me back at my place. There's no parking near my building, so I tell him to drop me off, but he insists on walking me to the door. We don't even notice Ally sitting in the living room while we spend ten minutes making out like teenagers in the doorway before I actually have to push him out of my apartment. Shoving him through the door was for his own good, as much as mine. We both have to work tomorrow. At least mine is mostly sitting. His is physically demanding.

I close the door and lean my head against it. "Looks like you had a good time." Ally's voice startles me.

"Do you sit there in the dark waiting for me to come home just to scare the shit out of me?"

"Maybe."

"You need help."

"I need one of those." She motions to the door that I've just closed behind Vinny.

Laughing, I walk into the kitchen. "I was going to go to bed. You want to have a glass of wine first?"

"Does Vince Stone make women drool?"

Shaking my head, I pull two crystal glasses out of the cabinet. There are plenty of nights that we do takeout, sometimes eating our delivery straight from the carton. Yet our wine is always in crystal. "I'll take that as a yes."

"Damn straight."

I can't help but smile at Ally's excitement as we sit on the couch facing each other. "That man is *so* into you."

"He certainly was a few hours ago."

Eyes widening, Ally smiles and claps her hands together. "Now that's the stuff I want to hear!"

I sip my wine and lean back into the couch with a dramatic sigh. "Jeez, Ally, he's just so...so...intense. It's like he can see right through me. There's nowhere to hide."

"Well why do you want to hide anyway?"

"I don't know. I just feel like I need to go slow. Keep some of what I'm feeling to myself. But he's hard to refuse. I can't explain it."

"He hurt you once, Liv. You're being cautious," Ally winks and smirks. "Just enjoy the sex and see where it takes you."

Finishing my wine, I feel the effects go straight to my head. I'm a lightweight normally, but even more so when I'm sleep deprived. "Oh, I'm definitely enjoying the sex."

"Hate you." My best friend smiles.

"Hate you too." I smile back and lean in to kiss her cheek before standing to turn in for the night. "Sweet dreams, Al."

"Just tell me one thing," Ally yells as I reach my doorway. "Is he a take control kind of partner in bed?"

Smiling, I don't turn around when I respond. "You have no idea."

CHAPTER 21

Liv

Sitting at my desk staring blankly at my computer screen, I shift in my seat to find a comfortable position. My body still aches from the long weekend of sexual escapades with Vinny, and I find myself replaying his words over and over again. *I'm going to bury myself so deep inside of you it'll leave you feeling hollow when I'm not with you.* Fidgeting in my chair, I realize he's done it. It's only been three days since I've last seen him, yet I feel empty this morning without him.

As if on cue, my phone rings and I smile lifting it to my ear. "I was just thinking about you."

"Oh yeah, what were you thinking?" Sex exudes from Vinny's deep raspy voice.

"I…" Remembering where I am, I look up and find Summer's eyes glued to me, waiting for my response. "Ummm…I'll have to tell you later."

"Oh no you don't. You started it, you're going to finish it. None of this leave me hanging crap, Liv."

Lowering my voice, "It was just something you said."

"Who's sitting so close to you that you have to whisper?"

"A co-worker."

"The princess?"

Laughing, I respond, "Yes."

"That's even more reason to tell me. Come on, Liv. Let me hear it," he says, his voice low and enticing. "You know you want to."

Lord, this man is impossible to keep things from. I really need to start watching what comes out of my mouth in the future. "It was about feeling hollow." I whisper and look up at Summer, finding her wide-eyed. Guess I didn't whisper low enough.

Vinny groans. "You feel hollow without me buried inside of you, Liv?"

I hesitate, feeling my face flush. "Yes."

"Say it."

"Are you crazy? I can't. I'm at work."

"I'll pick you up at twelve for lunch."

"Vinny," I warn.

"See you in a bit, Liv." He hangs up before I can respond again.

Looking up, I find Summer still staring at me. If eyes could shoot daggers, I'd look like Swiss cheese about now. "Sorry," I shrug my shoulders and offer, my voice as thick and sweet as maple syrup, matched perfectly with my over the top fake smile. It's clear that neither is sincere.

I struggle through the next few hours, my eyes constantly checking my phone for the time. By the time twelve rolls around, I'm anxious and equally excited. After our weekend together, being apart for a few days feels like a lifetime. But my work schedule took me out of town for two days and then Vinny was busy doing promotional stuff for his upcoming fight.

The minute I push through the revolving glass door, I catch sight of him. He's leaning casually against a half concrete wall to the right, his legs casually crossed at the ankle. He stands as I make my way to him, but makes no attempt to come to me. Instead, he watches my every move with a devilish grin on his face.

As I stand before him, neither of us says a word. Vinny hooks one arm gruffly around my waist and pulls my body to him as his head lowers and he takes my mouth in a kiss. It's so powerful, I literally lose track of where I am for a minute as we both come up breathless.

"Hey." He leans his forehead against mine.

"Hi."

His eyes dart over my shoulder and then quickly return. "I think we have an audience."

Turning around, I find Summer gaping. She's stopped in her tracks, her mouth actually hanging open. Embarrassed, I turn back to Vinny to hide my face. God forbid he follow my lead and try for low key.

"Hey, Summer." The hand not around my waist raises in a casual wave and I want to kill him for making it worse.

"Ummmm...hi." She scurries off, completely frazzled.

We spend the next hour catching up. Vinny tells me about his promotional photo shoot and pokes fun at the photographer, a man who made no secret of his crush on Vinny and spent four hours calling him "Mr. Sweet Muscles."

I'm ten minutes late by the time he walks me back to my office, so there's no time for games when Vinny locks me in his grip and demand I tell him what I was thinking about earlier.

"Do you really need your ego stroked that much?" I tease.

"If you're not stroking something else, I do."

Rolling my eyes, I try for serious. "I'm late coming back from lunch."

"Then you should hurry."

"But you're holding me."

"You know what you need to do to get released."

"You're such an arrogant ass." Playfully I smack at his chest and try to pull out of his grip.

"You knew that seven years ago."

Smiling, I can't help but laugh. He's so right. He's always been confident, the pendulum leaning towards the side of arrogant on the full of himself scale. "Seriously, I need to get back."

"Say it."

Lord, this man is not going to give in. "Really?"

A huge grin on his face, he nods his head. "Really."

Rolling my eyes, I give in. "I was still a little sore this morning from, you know, from our weekend. And I was thinking about something you said."

"Go on," he says, his smile wide and eyes sparkling.

"Fine. You told me you were going to bury yourself so deep inside of me that I'd feel hollow when you weren't inside of me."

"And do you?" Vinny beams, clearly delighted at being quoted.

"What?"

"Feel hollow?" he says, a cheeky dimpled grin on his face. He clearly already knows the answer.

"Yes, Vinny. I feel hollow without you inside of me. There. I said it. Do you feel better now?"

"I'd feel better buried inside of you."

"You're impossible. You know that?"

"Whatever, hollow woman."

"Mr. Sweet Muscles."

"I kinda like it coming from you."

Laughing, he almost makes me forget how late I am. Almost. "Seriously, I'm so late. I have to go."

He kisses me chastely on the lips, not yet releasing me. His voice low and sexy, "I got tested a week ago during my pre-fight physical. I'm clean." Leaning his forehead against mine, he offers and waits, searching my eyes cautiously for a response.

Barely able to swallow, my mouth dries up as I try to form the words to respond. "I'm on the pill. No partners since my last physical."

A mischievous grin spreads across his face. "You aren't gonna be hollow for long then."

The heat from my blush spreads from the tips of my toes to the top of my head. Vinny chuckles, clearly enjoying my embarrassment. "Tomorrow night?"

"Tomorrow night." I walk away feeling his eyes keen on the sway of my ass.

Back at my desk, I'm greeted with a scowl from Summer. Jealousy doesn't befit her. It makes her normally pretty face contorted and mean, ugliness crawling out and making its way to the surface.

"Guess I know why Vince requested you. He wanted someone easy." Looking down at her manicured nails, she tries to act like it doesn't bother her, but I know better.

Before I can respond, Sleezeball comes out from his office and beckons us both to his lair with a leering smile that makes my skin crawl.

I smile at Summer, determined not to sink to her level. Grabbing a pencil and pad, I head to Sleezeball's office. Normally, I try to avoid alone time with him, but today I'm thinking even his company is better than the princess's.

Sleezeball comes around from behind his desk, and inserts himself in the little space between us and the front of his desk. As if sitting with my eyes almost perfectly aligned at eye level with his crotch isn't bad enough, he reaches down with his right hand and adjusts himself before he speaks. Gross, just totally gross. "So ladies, we need to do a little juggling of assignments. Summer, I'm going to need you to take over covering the publishing merger story."

"But…," I attempt to protest. I've been working on that story for three weeks and it's going to be a big story. One that could help me land the job in the end.

Summer smiles. I'm sure she doesn't even know anything about the merger, or what's going to make it a big story. But she sees how upset I am and that's enough to satisfy her. "No problem, James. I'd be happy to fix up whatever Olivia has started."

Fix up? She's got to be kidding me. I see the chance of finally landing my dream job dramatically decreasing and I can't let it slip away without a fight. "James, I'm almost done with the story…I really only need another few days and I can piece it all together. I wouldn't want Summer to have to go through all the work to get caught up on all the research I've done."

Waving away my plea without even considering it, Sleezeball walks back around to the other side of the desk. "Summer should be able to handle it just fine. In fact, Summer, why don't you go grab Olivia's file on the story and start going over it. Give Olivia and I a few minutes."

Gloating, Summer smiles at Sleezeball and smirks at me. I can see in her step as she leaves the office she thinks victory is within her reach. And I'm afraid she might be right. There's no way I'm giving in this easy. "James, I…"

Interrupting me, as if I wasn't in the middle of speaking, Sleezeball talks right over my short lived attempt to protest. "Olivia, you're being given a special assignment. One that can make or break your career."

Now he has my full attention.

"We have it from a very reliable source that Senator Preston Knight has an illegitimate child."

Without question, *that* is a life-size story. One that drives newspaper sales to daily highs and is read, and noticed, by people around the globe. I'm excited, but surprised, that they would let me, a nobody, take a shot at such a story.

"Wow. I can't believe it. The implications are huge." Preston Knight is running for his fourth term. His re-election campaign is squarely centered around his Christian values. But even bigger than the effect such a news story could have on the man himself, if he loses his seat in the Senate the majority will shift, allowing the other party to regain control.

"It sure is. And we're trusting this to you. Do you know how big this is?" Sleezeball leans back in his chair and clasps his hands together, a failed attempt at looking dignified.

"Absolutely..." My mind races. "I don't want to sound ungrateful in any way...but I'm surprised you chose me."

"I didn't. The editor-in-chief did." Sleezeball leans in and motions for me to move closer, as if he's going to tell me a big secret. Even though the door is closed and we're the only two in the room. Whispering for added drama, he continues, "And I've been authorized to tell you, Olivia, if you land this story, the job is yours." He winks.

It's the opportunity of a lifetime, and yet I sit here feeling jittery for some reason. "That's amazing. I can't wait to start."

"Good, good, I'm sure you'll do great, Olivia." Reaching into his drawer, he pulls out a file in an inconspicuous manila folder. "One more thing."

I don't know why, but my heart drops. Something just told me there was more. More that meant something big.

Opening the folder, I'm confused as he begins to turn pages and pages of blown up photographs. All of them, the same subject...Vinny. In the gym, on his motorcycle, coming out of the vitamin store...he turns and turns until he comes to one that makes my heart stop...me and Vinny kissing in front of the building. Not more than two hours ago.

"I don't understand."

"Our source believes your new friend, Vince Stone, is Senator Knight's illegitimate son."

The familiar picture in Vinny's file, it wasn't an actor, it was the Senator. Blood thunders so rapidly through my veins it feels like an out of control train that will eventually jump its track and meet its final destiny with a brick wall. My breathing becomes labored and for a second, I think I might throw up all over the pictures. Clutching at my chest, I feel the color drain from my face so fast that even Sleezeball picks up on it and gets nervous.

"Olivia. Are you okay?"

No response.

"Olivia." Standing. Louder now.

No response.

"Olivia!" Yelling. He comes around and touches my shoulder, startling me and I almost jump out of my chair.

"Are you okay?"

"Yes....um....yes, I'm fine," I lie.

"Are you going to be able to handle this assignment?"

My response is delayed, but I finally give him the answer he's looking for. "Yes."

"Good, why don't you take some time to go through the research. Let me know if you have any questions."

I stand, a bit unsteady on my feet, but I make my way toward the door without falling.

"Olivia?"

I look back, not really seeing anything at all when I turn. Though at least the response appears normal.

"Get the story. Get the job. It's that easy."

Yeah, sure. Easy.

CHAPTER 22

Vince

I blow through three sparring partners in less than an hour. I'm so pumped full of adrenaline, I feel like I could take Nico at this point. Jumping up and down on the balls of my feet wearing nothing but my headgear and a pair of shorts, I impatiently wait for Nico to fasten the next victim's headgear. I've seen the guy around the gym. He sucks. Normally I could take him with a few jabs and two heavy leg strikes, but I'm not feeling normal today. I'm wired. Without any extracurricular help to get this way.

"Come on, it's taking you longer to get his headgear on than he's going to last in the ring."

"Don't get too full of yourself, kid." Nico responds, but I can tell he's enjoying himself, taking pride in how good I look today. He doesn't really mind my arrogance. Mostly because he's full of himself, too.

My fourth sparring partner finally gets in the ring and shit was I wrong. I must have overthought it. Underestimated myself. It only took me one strike and one jab and he's splayed out on the floor. So much for light sparring.

Nico laughs and shakes his head. Extending his arm to the poor guy on the floor. "What am I going to do with you today?"

Still bouncing, I respond hastily. "Get me a real partner."

Nico looks around, there are a few guys working out, none of them even close to a contender. Raising both arms from at his sides, he responds in question, "Who?"

"You."

He laughs. "I don't think so, kid." He begins to climb out of the sparring ring.

"You afraid?" I yell loud enough to get the attention of everyone in the gym. It's gonna take some assistance to get him to do this.

Nico turns and raises an eyebrow. "Don't ask for things you can't handle, Vinny."

"Not sure who's the one that can't handle it anymore, old man."

The guys that were working out stop what they're doing and respond with a series of oohs and aahs, a couple of "you gonna take that Nico" thrown in for good measure.

"Give me your headgear." Nico turns to my last sparring partner then back to me. "Don't say I didn't try to walk away."

Smiling, I bounce around the full perimeter of the ring, putting on a big show for the muscle heads that have stopped to watch us.

Headgear on, Nico lifts his hands and faces me, a smirk on his face, "You've had this coming for a long time. This is gonna be fun." And then he strikes. Unexpected, hard and fast…he connects with my ribs. I stumble back two steps but somehow manage to stay on my feet.

So I respond, winding up for a roundhouse kick that lands on Nico's shoulder. The sheer momentum from the windup catches Nico off guard and he stumbles, forced back three steps, his back hitting the rope as he struggles to stay on his feet. I expect him to lunge at me, but then he stops cold. I trace his line of sight and find Elle, one hand on the bottom of her belly, her face showing signs of distress.

"Nico…I think it's time."

"Shit." Hopping over the ropes in one swoop, he tosses me the keys as he lands next to Elle. "Pull the car around, Vinny."

Once inside, Elle doesn't want Nico to let go of her, so I drive them to the hospital, both of them in the backseat, chauffeur style. It's a quick ride, even quicker when you drive twenty-five over the speed limit. We arrive at St. Joseph's and Nico and I both run around to help Elle out of the car. None of us even notice the engine's still running and three doors are left open. Nico speaks to the admitting desk and they tell us to take a seat, it's going to be a few minutes before the doctor can take Elle in.

Contractions subsiding, Elle sits in a chair and looks up between me and Nico, flanked on either side of her, standing. Looming. A big goofy smile on her face quickly turns to laughter. "Do you two realize what you two look like?"

I look between myself and Nico for the first time, realizing we're both wearing nothing but shorts. No shoes, no shirts. Just two jacked fighters, a sixteen pack between us, hovering over a very pregnant Elle. Looking around the room, I find all eyes on us. Nico and I join Elle in her fit of laughter.

Three hours later, we're all back at the gym. Braxton Hicks contractions or some shit like that, otherwise known as false labor. I grab my bag and say goodnight to Elle with a kiss on the cheek. "I know you threw that labor. Saw us fighting and didn't want your washed up, has-been of a husband getting embarrassed in his own gym." I smile and Elle smiles back, shaking her head.

CHAPTER 23

Liv

Sitting on my bed, hundreds of documents and photos strewn all over the place, I feel sick…like a big hand has reached into my chest and squeezed my heart so tight it struggles to pump blood through my veins. There are pictures, birth records, interviews, incomplete genealogy studies, and hours and hours of countless research on both Senator Knight and Vinny.

I've learned so much about the last ten years of Vinny's life, so many pieces to the puzzle that all seem to fit together, making him the man he is today. But they're things that he should have been the one to tell me. Things I should have learned a little at a time, as we got to know each other again.

Staring down at the photo I haven't been able to take my eyes off for the last four hours, I find Vinny's captivating baby blues looking back at me. Staring. Only the photo is of Senator Knight. There's no denying the resemblance. The broad shoulders, the squareness of the jaw, even the way they both hold themselves while they stand. Confident, firm, with authority that instantly makes you feel like they're in charge.

Testimony dates back almost twenty-five years, before Senator Knight was even elected. In his mid-twenties, Preston Knight was a rising star at one of Chicago's most prestigious law firms. Married to his college sweetheart, he was the living, breathing picture of perfection. He seemed to have it all when he became the youngest partner at Kleinman and Dell at only twenty-eight.

Sources place the first meeting between Vinny's mother and Senator Knight at a celebration held at a place called *Wally's Den*, the night he was voted in as partner. A gentlemen's club, known back then as the place for influential and powerful men to let loose in private, Vinny's mom had been a cocktail waitress. One that apparently caught the attention of Senator Knight, and he pursued her relentlessly for a month before finally getting what he wanted.

Stories confirm Senator Knight was extremely unhappy when he learned of Vinny's mother's pregnancy only two months after they began their affair. Senator Knight's wife was already expecting their first child, a son born only a few weeks before Vinny.

The trail of their affair goes cold after an incident that left Vinny's mother in the hospital. Apparently she was attacked one night coming out of *Wally's Den.* She was beaten so badly the doctors were amazed that she didn't lose the baby. Especially since the beating seemed to focus on her stomach. The police never caught the attacker, as Vinny's mother was vague on the description. Although internal investigation reports seemed to suggest that Vinny's mother was hiding something, possibly even knew and was protecting her attacker's identity.

My phone rings, startling me from the daze I've been in since I started sifting through the mounds of documents.

"Hey." Hearing Vinny's voice melts my heart.

"Hi."

"Did I wake you?"

"No, I was just doing some work."

"Anything interesting?"

"No." My response is so quick, I wonder if my guilt travels through the phone, smacking Vinny in the face on the other end of the line.

"Well I had an interesting day."

I freeze, convinced he knows what I'm doing, maybe even able to see the pictures that lay on the bed in front of me. I know it makes no sense, but that doesn't stop my paranoia from kicking in.

"Liv?" There's concern in his voice from my lack of response.

"Sorry. I dropped the phone for a second," I lie.

"Oh."

"What made your afternoon interesting?" Hesitantly, I ask the question and hold my breath waiting for his response.

"Elle went into labor."

"Oh." Exhale. "Wow."

Paranoia and guilt mix for a potent cocktail, leaving me feeling hungover, even though I've just been given a reprieve.

"Yeah," he laughs. "I'm not sure who was more nervous. Me, Nico, or Elle."

"Did she have the baby yet?"

"No. Turned out to be false labor."

"Oh. They must be disappointed."

"Think Nico looked more relieved than anything." I can tell he's smiling, enjoying his trainer showing fear. "Big guy was looking pretty scared."

"Maybe he's nervous about seeing his wife in labor. Watching her in pain."

"More like he's afraid of what comes after the labor."

"You like the thought of him being afraid of a little baby, don't you?"

"Yep."

I can't help but laugh at his honesty. We talk for another half an hour. He tells me stories about Elle and her little brother Max. Clearly, he adores them, the excitement about the baby coming through in his voice.

After I hang up, I lie back in my bed, my head spinning from the day. The feeling of being on a runaway train with no means to lessen the impact of the crash that would inevitably come overwhelms me. The job I've dreamed of since I was a little girl is dangling from a fragile thread right in front of my face. So easy to reach out and grab it. But if I don't, if I let the chance of a lifetime slip through my fingers, there'd be no bracing for the impact of the fall. The job would be Summer's.

My phone ringing again, not ten minutes after I hung up with Vinny, makes me debate ignoring the call. But I don't, I answer it, although without the enthusiasm I usually greet people with.

"I'm still thinking about you. The look on your face after I kissed you outside your building today. I'm lying in bed with a hard-on remembering the way your body reacts to me." Vinny's voice trails off. "Even in public. It's uncontrollable and so god damn sexy, I just needed to hear the sound of your voice again."

Swallowing hard, my voice is throaty when I respond, "It was a good kiss…"

"Tomorrow night. I'm going to do things to you that'll make you scream my name over and over."

Ummm…how do you respond to that? Other than having your nipples harden and feeling the flesh between your legs swell in anticipation. "Okay," I say softly.

"Night, Liv."

"Night, Vinny."

I hang up, tossing my phone into a pile of papers, and eventually drift off to sleep with visions of Vinny making me scream, rather than thoughts of the story I had to come to terms with writing.

CHAPTER 24

Liv

I woke today with a new outlook on life. I've decided the story just isn't true. God just couldn't be that cruel to bring this man back to me and then make me crush his only honorable family memory. One that he utterly cherishes. Lots of people have pale blue eyes and rugged square jaws. Hell, there's a whole community of beautiful people out there that could pass for a relative of Senator Knight or Vinny.

Arriving at my office bright and early, I'm ready to dive in head first. I just need to clarify a few things with Sleezeball before I get on my merry way.

"Good morning, James. Do you have a minute for me?"

"I've got whatever you need. Come on in." His dirty smile tells me his choice of words is not coincidence. I feel the need to shower at his gross double entendre. Yet I smile all the same as I take my place in the seat he motions for me to sit in.

"I spent a lot of time thinking about the Senator Knight story last night."

"I figured you would." Sleezeball leans back in his chair, touching his fingertips together in a praying like pose.

"What happens if I work the story for the next few weeks and, in the end, it turns out that Senator Knight is not Vince's father? Where does that leave me with the job?"

"We're confident we're right with this one." He sits up in his chair. "But no one has been able to prove it one way or the other. Bring us the proof and the job is yours. They've had some heavy hitters working this one for a while now, but Senator Knight has it tied up tighter than a virgin's ass. The fighter's our only way in...and seeing those pictures of you outside, I'm thinking pillow talking that man will be like taking candy from a baby."

Ignoring his crude remark, I go for professional and to the point. "I'm going to need travel and expense funding."

"Done."

"I'll also need a cover story, something to get me time with Senator Knight. I was thinking we suggest a multi-page expose on him and his family. Tell him we want to recreate the Kennedy feel in our family values article. That will get me access to his wife and son."

"You got it." He sneers. "I like the way you're thinking now."

That comment alone should scare the shit out of me.

CHAPTER 25

Liv

Friday night I have no desire to go out and celebrate. It's been such a long week, I'd much rather crawl into bed in the fetal position and sleep for twelve hours straight than spend the night barhopping with Ally. But it's her birthday and I promised her we'd have fun. I know I need to put the week of dead end research behind me and let it go for a while, but it's easier said than done. I feel guilty for keeping my assignment from Vinny, but I don't want to hurt him by making him question his father for no reason. A soldier he never knew, a man he always cherished.

I'm still surprised that Ally invited Vinny to join us the other night when he came to pick me up. Normally birthday celebrations are strictly girls night out. But apparently one mention of bringing a few of the guys from the gym was all it took. The birthday girl is easily swayed at the mention of hard bodied fighters with tattoos.

"What do you think?" Ally emerges from her bedroom wearing a skimpy skirt and heels so high she must be close to six feet, even though she's normally just five foot six.

"Is that a shirt or a skirt?" I tease.

"Some of us don't have a sexy beast ya know."

"I'm guessing you'll attract a beast with that outfit." I take a sip from the glass of wine I just poured, hoping it will relax me a bit.

"Ya think?" Not catching the sarcasm in my voice, Ally takes my comment as a compliment, looking down at her outfit. Satisfied with what she sees, she continues, "Go get dressed...we need to find this birthday girl a gift to unwrap later." She wiggles her eyebrows.

It was never a question in my head what I was going to wear. Every girl has that one outfit she loves, the one that gets more compliments than she receives in total for the rest of the year. Mine is emerald green. The simple dress is fitted on the bottom, hugging my curves and coming a little above my knee. The top blouses out after it reaches my waist, and lies draping artfully from my shoulders. From the front it's simple, the color and fit being the most impressive part of the dress. The emerald green color contrasts with my pale skin and auburn hair, setting off a beautiful palette that people definitely seem to notice.

Although it's the back of the dress that's the showstopper and I know it. The same draping that shows just a hint of demure cleavage on the front, hangs on the back, only the draping extends lower on the back. Far lower. Revealing a scant hint of pale white skin from the top of my neck, down to just above the top of my ass. Like a treasure map, it leads the eyes down my back to where the emerald color gathers tightly across my ass. Something tells me Vinny is going to love the dress. I've noticed he seems to have taken a liking to my backside. I may pretend I don't notice where his eyes frequently drift to as we go about mundane things, but I do. And tonight I'm dressing for him.

Pouting playfully as she sees me come through my bedroom door dressed, Ally confirms I've picked the right outfit. "It's my birthday. How is anyone going to notice me when you wear *that*?"

The second bar we stop in, the one we are supposed to meet Vinny and his friends at, is packed. Squeezing our way up to order our drinks, Ally wastes no time in letting the bartender know it's her birthday.

"Two Long Island Iced Teas." She yells over the deafening music playing from speakers that have way too much bass blaring. The thud is so loud I feel the vibration on my hands as they sit on the top of the bar, my heart jumping to join in on the rhythm.

"Make that one and a water," I yell, and the bartender smiles and nods.

"It's my birthday! You have to celebrate with me!"

"Someone has to take care of you. One Long Island Iced Tea and you're going to need to be carried."

"I'll sip it." She smiles.

"Heard that before."

Half a drink later, Ally giggles through her words as we both eye a couple sitting quietly to themselves on the other side of the bar. They look uncomfortable as the woman stirs her drink and the man checks his watch.

"Last night they went out. It had been nineteen months since she got laid. *Nine-teen months.*" She drags out the last words for emphasis before continuing. "They met on Match.com. Wait, no, Churchdate. com. You know, the place where the god-fearing go to meet other people that get up way too early on Sundays to spend an hour listening to an old man preach." Ally takes a breath, long enough to gulp down another inch from her glass before she continues her rant. "Chatted online for a month before he got the nerve to ask her out. They met at a coffee shop last night, seeing each other for the first time in person. Both were highly disappointed."

Raising an eyebrow at her story, I point to Ally's glass, "I'm afraid to hear what happens after you slam down the rest of that thing," I tease.

Not deterred in the slightest by my comment, Ally continues with her story. "So Elgin, that's the guy's name," her grin widens, "suggests they go for a drink. You know, beer goggles and all, everyone looks more appetizing after a few." Another sip from the innocent looking, yet highly potent, liquid she's drinking like it's lemonade. "They both drink four vodka tonics. Elgin's a big guy, but he's a lightweight, just like Penny."

"Penny?" I question, smiling. Ally always picks the best names. Personally, I've never known a Penny, but the woman sitting on the other side of the room fits the name perfectly. I wouldn't be surprised if Penny was actually her real name.

"Yeah, that's his date's name. Quit interrupting, you're making me lose my train of thought." Sure, it's my question and not the drink containing five shots of different, highly flammable alcohol she's consumed that's making her fuzzy. "Anyway, Penny and Elgin, they go back to her place. Which, by the way, contains an enormous collection of stuffed Hello Kitty's. I'm talking hundreds of them. That alone should have sent up the warning flags to poor Elgin. But, alas, alcohol and wood in his pants kept him from seeing all the signs." Ally sighs, as if to say she sympathizes with poor Elgin.

"So what happened in Hello Kitty land?" Sadly, I'm anxious to hear the rest of the story.

"They got into it fast. Two horny, sexually starved CPA's going at it. Anyway, turns out, she's a meower." Ally empties the last of the liquid from her tall glass, slamming it down on the bar with a little too much enthusiasm.

"A meower?" Brows knitted, I'm beginning to think I'm already seeing signs of drunk, nonsensical Ally.

"Yeah, a kitty fetish. She likes to pretend she's a kitten while doing the dirty deed."

"What?"

"Yep. Now the secrets out, they're both sober and this," she points to the couple still sitting awkwardly at the table on the other side of the room, "is the day after date they both feel obligated to do after kitty cat clawing, dirty monkey sex."

"Monkey sex?" Vinny's voice takes me by surprise, I'm focused on Ally, doing my best to follow along with the story being told by my crazy best friend.

Forgetting her story entirely, Ally lights up like a Christmas tree, throwing her arms around Vinny's neck, giving him an overzealous greeting. "I'm so glad you came!" Yep, she's definitely drunk. Happy, buzzed, Ally has arrived.

Amused, Vinny grins and raises his eyebrows to me in question. Shrugging, I smile as I watch Vinny handle himself with tipsy Ally. He introduces her to the three friends that he's brought with him, one more ripped and tougher looking than the next. The tallest of the trio has a shaved head and ink sticking out from beneath the collar of his shirt. I'd bet money that he grunts and growls instead of speaking. It's not hard to guess which one will be the subject of Ally's attention tonight.

"Hey." Vinny comes to me, hooking his arm around my neck and kissing me possessively on the mouth. I never would have dreamed that something so cavemanish would do it for me. Before Vinny, public displays of affection weren't for me, especially ones with the intensity that oozes so naturally from him.

"Hi."

"You look beautiful," he says, his voice low and sultry. He gazes slowly up and down my body approvingly, making no attempt to conceal his appetite. Oddly, it's one of the things that I find so attractive about him. He's confident, real, no beating around the bush. Pure, unfiltered honesty.

"Thank you." Taking a compliment in stride has never been something I was comfortable with, but Vinny makes it easy…because I believe he means it.

"So who's having dirty monkey sex?" He grins and I feel my face heat with embarrassment.

"It was just a made up story. A game Ally and I like to play."

Motioning for the bartender, Vinny orders a beer for himself and gestures in the direction of Ally, "And two of whatever she's drinking."

"Ummm…I wasn't drinking." I hold up my water. "Water. I'm being the responsible one tonight. Someone has to carry Ally home."

"I'll carry you both home. Have fun. I'm not taking my eyes off the two of you in here anyway." Surveying the room, he takes the water from my hand and places it on the bar, replacing it with the drink the bartender delivered.

Grinning, I sip the drink, "Okay, but you don't know what you're in for. Ally is crazy when she drinks too much and I'm a lightweight."

Taking a pull from his beer, Vinny redirects the conversation to a place he's not going to let me off easily from. "So. Monkey sex?"

"Not going to let go of that one, are you?"

"Nope." His devilish grin and boyish dimples combine for a face that's simply irresistible.

Sighing dramatically, I gulp a heaping sip of liquid courage from my glass before delving into the game Ally and I have played since we were kids. It all started at a party we were bored at in high school, but our game has morphed into something more creative over the years. "Bar Forensics."

"Bar Forensics?" Apparently, Vinny's not heard of our wonderful game.

"One of us picks a couple and the other has to make up their background…a story about the history between the two."

"Who had monkey sex?"

Sheepishly, I point to the couple sitting on the other side of the room, still looking terribly uncomfortable.

"They didn't have monkey sex, Babe."

"How do you know?"

Raising an eyebrow as if to say "duh…" he takes a swig of beer and turns to canvas the room.

"Tall skinny guy in the black sport coat talking to the brunette wearing…," he falters, looking for a word, "not much." Vinny moves to stand next to me. Our backs to the bar, both of us lean casually with elbows supporting our weight. I guzzle from my glass and waste no time in developing my story.

"Brendon." I turn my head to look directly at Vinny, a mask of seriousness readily in place. "That's his name."

Vinny's eyebrows arch and he smirks, amused, waiting for more.

"Is a computer programmer," I continue. "He was with his ex, Julie, for six and a half years. Being a computer programmer, he spends a lot of time on his laptop. Julie was feeling frisky one night…"

Vinny interrupts me, "Frisky?"

"Yes, frisky. There's no interrupting during a forensic recreation, Mr. Stone." I smile, arching one eyebrow, silently daring him to challenge me.

Playfully, Vinny puts his hands up feigning surrender and motions for me to continue.

"So anyway, Julie was feeling *frisky* one night and went looking for Brendon in his home office. Not expecting anyone, the door was cracked open, giving Julie a front row seat to his show. She caught him red-handed, getting himself off as he video chatted with a woman he had been secretly chatting with online for almost a year."

I pause and drain more from my glass. Damn this thing tastes good, it's so easy to forget how potent it really is until you feel your head begin to become weightless.

"And the woman there, is she Julie or the video woman?"

"Neither. Julie left him. Moved out the next day. Turned out the video woman was married herself, so poor Brendon got dumped twice in twenty-four hours."

"So who's the girl then?"

"He met her at Nordstrom's. He went in to buy a sports jacket. Was planning on spending about $300, but met her. She works in the men's department, sold him that overpriced $1,500 jacket. He had to put it on a credit card because Julie took everything from their bank account. Sweat was starting to form on his brow as little miss no clothes rang him up…worried his card would decline."

A real, full laugh tells me Vinny appreciated my story. "You made that whole thing up just now from your head?"

Feigning offense, I retort, "It's not made up, it's their story."

Ally's bubbly voice pulls my attention back from my playful banter with Vinny. She's jumping from side to side, doing what's commonly known as the pee-pee dance. "Come with me."

Kissing Vinny on the cheek, I smile and push off the bar and allow my friend to begin dragging me in the direction of the restrooms. I make it three steps when a strong arm wraps around my waist, stopping me in place.

"What?" I turn to find Vinny's face serious.

"I'm coming."

"To the bathroom?"

"Yeah, I'll wait outside," Vinny growls his response.

"Why, what's wrong?"

"I just saw the back of your dress."

Two hours later, Ally's in rare form and I'm feeling no pain. Two of Vinny's friends disappeared into the crowd, never to return. Me, Ally, Vinny, and Shaved Head hang out at the bar, being entertained by Ally's crazy antics. The last round of Bar Forensics consisted of Ally slurring her words while depicting a tale of mommy issues that the poor couple we picked struggled to overcome.

After Ally drags Shaved Head to the makeshift dance floor, Vinny pulls me close to him, my back to his front, and wraps his arms snuggly around my waist.

"You wanna dance?" I ask, although I'm pretty sure I know the answer before he responds.

"I don't dance."

"Never learned how?" I inquire as he dips his head into my hair and finds a tender spot on my neck to nibble on inconspicuously.

"Didn't say I don't know how, said I didn't dance."

"You can dance?" My voice begins to show my distraction as his nibbling moves to my shoulder. He roughly tugs at my dress to expose more flesh, trailing little nibbles on my sensitive skin.

"Of course, but I prefer to dance with you horizontally."

Oh my. Me too. Keeping me close, he turns me in his arms and locks his arms behind my back, pressing our bodies firmly against each other.

Looking up at him, our eyes locked together, it makes me wonder what he's thinking. Except I've had too much to drink and that wondering is done aloud. "What's our Bar Forensics story?"

Pulling his head back, he looks into my eyes, his quiet confidence captivating me as I wait for his response. "The guy? He wandered around for years looking for something, only he had no idea what it was he was looking for. Just felt like a piece to his puzzle was missing. Then he met a smart, beautiful, funny woman who liked to get lost in her head."

The icy wall I've built around my heart to protect myself from this man melts, leaving me vulnerable. Emotions I'm fighting to contain get the best of me, showing in my strained voice. Barely a whisper, I prompt him to continue as I wait, hoping the story has a happy ending, "What happens after they meet?"

Gathering me even closer in his arms, Vinny places a soft kiss on my lips. His hypnotizing, beautiful eyes warming my thawed heart, he continues, "Slowly, a little bit more each day, she let him into her head and one day he woke up and realized he wasn't wandering around anymore. He wasn't sure when it had happened or why, he just knew. Whatever he had spent the last seven years looking for wasn't missing anymore."

Unable to speak, my breath literally stolen from my lungs, his words wash away all my doubt, leaving the path to my heart free and he takes one step closer to owning it. Again.

Two hours later, I'm tipsy as Vinny opens the car door for me to get in. Throwing my arms around his shoulders instead of climbing in, I catch him off guard and he smiles as I kiss the tip of his nose. I feel badly for ending the party before Ally was ready to go, but the drinks went right to my head. Plus, Shaved Head had already promised to see her home and she looked more than excited at the prospect.

"You're cute when you're drunk."

"I'm not drunk." My words come out with just a hint of a slur, no matter how sober I try to sound.

He kisses me chastely on the lips and surprises me by scooping me off my feet and gently placing me in the passenger seat. He buckles me up, closes the car door, and jogs around to the passenger side.

"Your place or mine?" He starts the engine.

"You're awfully presumptuous." I giggle and turn myself in the front seat to face him.

"Just want to take care of my girl."

Furrowing my brows, Vinny sees the confusion on my face.

"I owe you a dance." His voice turns low and thick.

I swallow, shifting in my seat to calm the throb between my legs as I think of the rhythm I can't wait to feel pounding through my body. "Your place."

Vinny smiles, putting the car into drive.

"Drive fast," I whisper, resting my hand on his thigh.

"Sweetheart, you were going to my house either way. It's closer and I'm not sure I can make it ten more minutes after staring at the back of that dress half the night."

CHAPTER 26

Liv

Vinny doesn't turn on the lights as we enter his apartment. Instead, he keeps a firm grip on my hip and maneuvers me through. Turning left from the hallway in the darkness, I lose my bearings, unsure of where we are, but certain the bedroom is the other way.

Guiding me slowly until I bump gently into something in front of me, he's quiet until we reach where he wants us. "Bend." Moving behind me, he applies pressure at the nape of my neck, pushing me forward until I reach something hard and cold. *The island in the kitchen.*

My face turned, cheek resting flush against the cold island top, he loosens his grip on my neck. I feel the strength in his hands as he slowly trails both down the sides of my spine until reaching my lower back. "Reach up, grab the other side of the counter."

Bent at the waist, cheek pressed to the counter, I lift my hands over my head and grab the other side of the counter as instructed. Vinny takes a step closer, pressing his groin against my ass, and leans over me, his torso against my back so that I'm pinned between the hard granite and his muscular body.

The dark room is so quiet, I hear every breath he takes as his mouth comes to rest near my ear. "This dress is a tease." His teeth sink into my earlobe, causing me to cry out from the mix of shock and pain. His tongue quickly follows his teeth, gently suckling my earlobe where his teeth just marked me.

"Did you wear it for me? To make me crazy as I watched other men run their eyes all over you?"

I want to speak, but my voice is stuck in my throat, the words coming out barely a murmur. "I wore it because I thought you'd like it."

"I do. It's perfect. Your tight little body has been screwing with my head all night." His strong hands caress up and down the sides of my body. His fingers feeling every inch as they slowly move across my curves. It's not a gentle touch, it's impatient and rough and his grip on me makes me feel like he needs to hold me this tight or he'll lose the remnants of his own control.

"Makes me crazy to see another man's eyes on you," Vinny growls, as if just the mere mention of another man ratchets up the intensity of his emotions. Gruffly, he lifts my skirt up to my waist, and tears my panties right from my body. The strength of his action arousing me and I wiggle as my bare ass waits for him.

"Everything about you just makes me…" His voice trails off as he stands, the warmth of his body missed as soon as it's taken from me.

His hand moves to my exposed ass and caresses gently. "Are you ready for me?" His voice is gravelly. Strained. Thick.

"Yes."

Tracing a slow path from my ass to between my legs, his fingers dip into me, making sure my response is true. "You're so wet," he hisses as I hear the sound of his zipper going down reverberate through the room.

I whimper as he pushes into me, my body slick but still struggling to take the width of him fully inside. Firmly seated, he settles for a moment, allowing me time to adjust. His voice is hoarse and strained when he speaks. "I want to come inside of you. Fill up that sweet little pussy that's mine."

Pulling out almost fully, he wraps his arm tightly underneath my bent waist and yanks my hips back to meet every forceful thrust in. Each time rubbing against that sensitive spot inside of me, then pulling away just before it can fully send me over the edge. Dangling so close is torture, yet blissful at the exact same time. The intensity of his stroke increases, bringing us both closer and closer with each rhythmic plunge in and out. A loud moan escapes as I feel my body and mind heading toward the shoreline of the ocean that waits to wash over me. Pulling almost fully out, Vinny growls in response to my moan and, unexpectedly, his hand connects loudly with my ass, swatting me hard once before plunging deeply back inside of me. My body reacts to the forcefulness of his actions before my brain can even catch up. Pulsing wildly on its own, my sex clenches down on him as wave after wave of mind shattering throbbing takes over me in the most violent orgasm to ever claim my body. A string of curses leave Vinny's mouth as he finds his own release. The heat from him spilling inside of me extends my own bliss.

Moments later, when our breathing finally slows and our sweaty bodies are still pressed against each other, Vinny reaches down and leans me back, lifting me into his arms, carrying me to the bedroom. I'm still in a daze as I feel him peel the rest of the clothes from my sweat drenched body. Clothes that we hadn't cared were still on in our heated frenzy. Climbing into the bed behind me, he tucks the covers over me gently and pulls me back to spoon him, gently kissing my cheek from behind before I drift off to sleep.

The next morning I wake to the feeling of being watched. I'm sprawled across the bed on my stomach, the sheet tangled around my waist doing little to hide my naked ass.

I turn my head, expecting to find Vinny next to me, but the bed's empty. Instead, he sits a few feet away in a chair, wearing nothing but sweatpants, drinking coffee that smells divine from an oversized mug.

"Morning." He sips his coffee, looking well settled in his chair.

"How long have you been up?" Sleep coats my voice.

"I don't know. Maybe an hour."

"How long have you been sitting there?"

"I don't know. Maybe an hour." He grins.

"You're just sitting there?"

"I'm enjoying the view." A dirty grin on his face, Vinny's eyes motion to my exposed ass.

"You've been staring at my ass for an hour?"

"It's a fucking great ass." Unapologetically, he sips his coffee and shrugs.

Reaching back, I pull at the sheet that I've somehow wrapped around my body like an angry snake about to crush its victim.

"Don't." Vinny stands and walks to the bed, pulling the small piece of sheet I was able to free from my hands. The bed dips as he sits, one arm reaches across the bed, hauling me closer in one swift motion that seems to have taken no effort from him.

"I love seeing my hand print here." He swats my ass hard. Murmuring, his voice changes from playful to deep – sexy and raspy. His hands gently caress my backside. "Are you sore from last night?"

"No." I feel my face flush just thinking about last night.

"Look at me," he orders, his voice commanding.

"Are you okay with last night?" His eyes find mine and lock me into his gaze.

"Yes." It's difficult to admit for some reason, but it's the truth. I'm more than okay with last night. I never would have thought I'd like sex a bit on the rough side. But I'm finding there are a lot of things about myself I didn't know.

Vinny nods, accepting my answer. "Coffee?"

"Oh my god, yes."

Vinny smiles, it's genuine and I see his face relax. I hadn't even realized there was tension there before. But it's gone now. "I'll get it, but that ass better be right where it is when I get back." He leans down and playfully bites my ass cheek.

After a long, hot, thoroughly enjoyable shower we both dry off in the bathroom together. I clear the fog from the mirror as Vinny stands behind me kissing my shoulder.

"Go away with me next weekend?" His eyes find mine in the mirror

"Where?"

"I have an exhibition just outside of Washington on Saturday. Was planning on flying down on Friday morning, but if you can't get off of work, we can go later."

Outside of Washington, really? "I actually need to go down to Washington this week anyway. I have to do an interview. Could we leave Thursday morning so I can work Friday during the day in D.C.?" Staring into the reflection of his eyes, for a split second, I consider telling him what I need to go do. Just blurt it all out. Every day I find myself falling a little more for this complicated man. But the guilt of keeping such a personal secret clouds it, weighing heavily on my shoulders. I quickly reconsider, I can't hurt him just to lighten my load. Especially when I'm not certain if it's even true.

"Whatever you want. There's always guys at the gym that will cover my classes for some extra cash."

"Okay."

Vinny turns me to face him. "Okay?" A questioning smile on his face, he looks so young and happy. Seeing him so stress free and light, it makes me feel like I'm doing the right thing. I don't remember him even looking this carefree in high school.

"Sure, it sounds like fun. Do I get to see your exhibition?" I tease.

"You get to see me kick someone's ass." He plants a chaste kiss on my mouth before tearing off the towel wrapped around my body and hauling me over his shoulder.

"What are you doing?"

"Taking you back to bed."

"I can walk."

"I can carry you."

"Maybe, but I'll make it quicker to the bed."

CHAPTER 27

Vince

"Don't give Preach a hard time. He's doing me a favor going down with you to D.C. since Elle can't travel."

"I'll be fine."

"That's what you said the night before your first fight and I had to pick you up down at the police station at two in the morning."

"I won't be in a bar at two in the morning this time." I jump from the chin up bar, landing in front of Nico. He stands his ground.

"You better not be."

Picking up the jump rope, I don't look in his direction as I speak. "Liv's coming with me."

"Liv's coming?"

"Is there a damn echo in here?"

Nico laughs and shakes his head. "That's good. She seems like she can keep you out of trouble."

"I can keep myself out of trouble." I whip the jump rope, turning at warp speed, two flicks of the wrist with each single jump. Nico has to back up to keep from getting slapped in the face as the rope begins to play a whirling song with each turn.

"Whatever, I'm glad she's going."

"Yeah, me too."

Thursday I stop by my mom's to check in before heading to Liv's to pick her up and leave for the airport. She's in better shape than most days, even sitting up on the couch and capable of having a lucid conversation.

"You look good, Ma."

She laughs, assuming I'm pacifying her. "Thanks, Baby"

"Did Jason resurface and fix things with the two guys that were here last week?" I've started to ask around, the guy's an even bigger loser than I first thought. And I didn't think much of him to start.

Her eyes trained downward, she wrings her hands as she speaks. I know the answer before the words fall from her lips. "No, I've tried everything I know of to reach him, but he's gone. Vanished."

Shit, I knew that dirtbag was no good. Should've finished his sorry ass off when I had the chance the day I found him raising his hand to my mother.

"Ma, those guys aren't screwing around. I asked around about them. They don't make threats lightly. How much are they holding you up for?"

"Two hundred."

"Please, please tell me that you're kidding! Or that you mean two hundred bucks?" I begin to pace. What the hell has she done? Where am I going to get that kind of money? I figured the loser was passed out somewhere on a binge, but it's been too long...the realization just starting to kick in that he's probably hiding. Leaving my mother holding the bag just for vouching for him. Now I'm starting to get nervous.

"I'm sorry, Vincent." She begins to cry. She drives me crazy, screwed up half of my childhood, and is probably responsible for my fucked up relationships with women, yet I still can't stand to see her cry.

I sit next to her, wrap my arm around her shoulder, and pull her close. "Stop, Ma. It's gonna be okay." I have no idea how, but it has to be. "We'll find him, or come up with something." Sobs rack through her. "I promise."

CHAPTER 28

Liv

Vinny's been quiet the whole flight down to D.C. so far. He said nothing was wrong, but I could tell he wasn't being totally forthcoming. He seems preoccupied, I wonder if maybe the exhibition match he has Saturday bothers him more than he lets on. Or maybe he really doesn't like to fly, although it's been a smooth flight so far.

"So after I turn my hair blue and pierce my eyebrow, I was thinking we could go to Target and buy up all the shaving cream in their stock." Vinny nods and smiles, still not listening to a word I'm saying, so I continue, "You know, we may need a lifetime supply of shaving cream if we get that flood they've been predicting. We won't be able to get to the store for a while. Don't you agree?"

Vinny turns to me, finally realizing I'm waiting for a response. He's looking right at me, but doesn't really hear a word I'm saying. "Ummm, sure."

He's still a million miles away, even though we're sitting so close, so I take out the bigger guns. "Oh, okay, great. I didn't think you'd mind. I mean, I agreed to go out with him before we started seeing each other. It will only be one or two dates, so I probably won't sleep with him more than once anyway."

"Wait, what?" Tension shows in his face as he turns to me, I have no idea what part he heard, but clearly something finally sunk in.

"Well, welcome back."

"Did you just tell me you're going on a date?"

"I told you I was dyeing my hair blue and piercing my eyebrow before that and you didn't seem to care...so I thought I'd see how far away you really were." I smile playfully.

"Very nice. But you know what happens when I even think about another man near you don't you?" Vinny leans forward, a menacing face in place of the one that was millions of miles away just minutes earlier.

Startled, I find myself being lifted out of my tiny plane seat and reseated onto Vinny's lap. My protests go completely unheard as he takes my mouth in a forceful kiss with little warning. Never one for a public display of affection, I'm surprised when my traitorous body gives in to him with little coaxing. Within seconds, I'm kissing him back with all that I have, my brain unable to think with my body achingly aware of being held so tightly by this unpredictable man.

I'm so consumed with the feel of his big hands holding my face in place so he can kiss the daylights out of me, that I don't even hear the flight attendant's first attempt at a polite interruption.

"Sir, she's going to need to take her own seat now. We're getting ready for landing."

My face crimson with embarrassment, I want to crawl under the seat when I realize that the flight attendant is speaking to us. Vinny, on the other hand, finds us being caught acting like two horny teenagers amusing. "Sorry, she just can't help herself sometimes." He shrugs and gives her the dimpled smile. "I'll make her go back into her seat."

"Vinny!" I smack his chest and mock glare at him as he winks at the flight attendant.

Once we're checked into our hotel, Vinny seems more like himself. Without asking, he orders a bottle of the wine that I drink and a platter of fruit from room service. I consider arguing with him again about making decisions for me, but then I realize how the conversation will end. *Do you want wine? Yes, but that's not the point. Are you hungry for a little fruit? Yes, but that doesn't mean you had to order it for me.* So I settle on picking battles where I want a different end result.

"So you never told me about the interview you're doing tomorrow. Is it anyone I'd know?" Vinny asks.

Freezing in place, panic overcomes me. Lying has never been my strong suit, but lying and guilt combined isn't a combination easy for me to mask on my face. I'm grateful that my back is to him when I'm forced to respond.

"Ummm…I doubt it, just some Senator."

"Senator huh?" Vinny comes up to stand behind me as I unpack my toiletries. I stop breathing, half expecting him to tell me he knows what I'm up to. Wrapping his arms around my waist, he nuzzles my neck from behind. "Is he young? Should I be jealous?" He kisses his way up to my ear.

His warm breath and light nibbling cloud my thoughts, I stand unmoving, not quite sure how to respond. Vinny nudges me playfully for an answer. My response comes out a bit too defensive, "Ummm… no, he's old enough to be your—"

Lucky for me, we're interrupted by room service knocking at the door. "Do you mind getting that, I need to wash up," I ask.

"Sure." Vinny swats my ass playfully as I practically run to the bathroom. Looking at myself in the mirror, I douse my face with water, desperate to clear my head. After a few minutes, I regain my composure enough to venture back into the bedroom and I'm surprised when I find room service still here.

"Would you mind signing an autograph for me? I'm a big fan. I've seen all your fights. I'm even going to the exhibition tomorrow." The coquettish young server sways back and forth. She's cute, in a Midwestern cheerleader type of way.

"Sure. What do you want me to sign?" I'm pretty sure he didn't even mean the question suggestively, yet I watch as the girl's cheeks turn pink.

Removing a piece of hotel stationary from the drawer, I walk over, interrupting their conversation. "Here you go." I hand the girl the paper and smile. It's a sugary smile, the type that other woman can instantly read and know the true meaning hidden beneath.

Vinny looks at me curiously before taking the paper and scribbling his name.

The little tart bounces up and down excitedly, taking the autograph from his hand before turning back to me, reading my face, and taking the hint. "I'll see you Saturday, Mr. Stone."

I have a full glass of the already uncorked wine poured, before Vinny even gets back from seeing her out. Popping a strawberry into my mouth, I smile and raise an eyebrow. "She was cute."

"Oh yeah? Not my type. Guess I didn't notice." He takes two grapes from the platter, tossing one into his mouth, and gently slips one between my lips.

Sipping my wine, I decide I probably don't want to know, yet I can't stop myself from asking, "So what is your type, *Mr. Stone?*" I mimic the server in response.

Vinny takes my wine glass from my hand and sets it down on the cart. Wrapping his arms around my waist, he pulls me close to him. "I only have one type."

"And that is?"

"You."

I roll my eyes, but down deep, I love his response. He kisses the tip of my nose and pulls me close to him in an unexpected, tender hug.

"What do you want to do tonight?" I ask, content in just staying right where I am for the next three or four decades.

"Whatever you want."

"Really?" I pull back to look him in the face.

"Sure, as long as whatever you want entails staying in this room and me inside of you."

Yet another decision I choose not to argue about.

CHAPTER 29

Liv

"Morning." Vinny's gravelly voice tells me he hasn't been up for long either. I snuggle closer to him, our legs and arms still tangled, my head resting peacefully on his chest as I listen to his heartbeat. Inhaling deeply, I dread the thought of getting out of bed and getting on the roller coaster of a day I have planned.

Vinny trails his finger up and down my naked back, lightly tracing figure eights. The motion soothes me, makes it even harder for me to get out of bed. He does that to me, makes me want to close the door to the outside world and forget it even exists. Especially today. I want to stay in the little bubble of this room, feeding each other fruit and drinking wine between trysts.

The alarm on my phone goes off too soon and I groan as I reach over, turn it off, and begin to climb out of bed. A strong arm pulls me back down. "Where are you going?"

"I have to get in the shower, my appointment is at ten and I need to meet the photographer a half hour before that."

"Give me that mouth."

"But I haven't brushed my teeth."

"Then give me something else to kiss. I'm laying here looking at you naked, if you don't make it fast, you're definitely going to be late."

Kissing him chastely on the lips, I jump out of bed before he can pull me back, even though I'd much rather stay in bed and have him make me late.

Paul Flanders, one of the dozens of staff photographers from the *Daily Sun Times*, and I arrive at Senator Knight's home. Brick pillars hold two large wrought iron gates in place. A camera mounted on top of one of the tall pillars pivots in our direction as we slow to the waiting intercom.

"Can I help you?" A man's voice booms from the little box, mixed with static.

"I have a ten o'clock appointment with Senator Knight. My name is Olivia Michaels, from the *Daily Sun Times*."

"Hold your ID up to the red x on the box."

Fishing out my license, I do as instructed and watch as the camera moves again. A moment later, the gate opens. "Drive to the top of the hill, park in front of one of the garages."

One of the garages? A long road surrounded by manicured green lawns leads up to a stately home looming at the top of the hill. I park the car and look around at the stunning view. Built on a peak, the spectacular storybook home is perched on the top, offering a bird's eye view of the city of Washington, D.C. off in the distance.

"Not going to be hard to find a place to recreate the Kennedy compound feel at this place," Paul jokes as we stand in front of the intimidating, towering, white double doors, waiting to be greeted.

The doors open and I'm surprised to find Senator Knight standing before me. A home like this, I half expected a butler in a full suit with tails to greet us with a fine British accent.

"You must be Miss Michaels and Mr. Flanders. Please come in." Senator Knight smiles and extends his hand to greet us individually as we enter.

Wearing a navy blue sweater and khakis, he looks casually elegant. I find myself staring as he speaks. I'm barely inside, yet I'm already searching his face for telltale signs of Vinny's lineage.

Luckily, the Senator and Paul spend a few minutes discussing places that Paul can shoot on the grounds. It gives me a chance to take in his face without having to participate in the conversation.

His pale blue eyes are strikingly beautiful, contrasting starkly with his deep tan skin. There's no mistaking that the color is almost an exact match to Vinny's, but there's something vastly different too, although I can't put my finger on exactly what it is.

Standing to his side as he points Paul in a direction outside, I'm able to take in his profile. What I see almost stops my heart. The same rugged, squared jaw line, frames a strong face, one I'm intimately familiar with. It almost makes me uncomfortable to see it on someone else, makes me feel exposed for some reason. The two men exchange words and then Paul heads outside to photograph the house, leaving Senator Knight to turn his attention back to me.

"Miss Michaels, I've met many of your colleagues at the *Daily Sun Times*, but I don't believe we've had the pleasure of meeting before." He smiles, it's a practiced smile, one that reminds me he's shaken hands and kissed babies campaigning for votes a good portion of his life. "I'm actually quite certain we haven't met before, I'd remember meeting such a beautiful young lady."

"Ummm...thank you." I think? "I'm new at the *Daily Sun Times*."

"Well I hope this will be the first of many interviews. I have a long history with some of the reporters at the *Sun*. I feel like I watched a few of them grown up over the years."

Smiling pleasantly, I lie through my teeth, "I'd like that. It's an honor to meet you." My background research taught me he likes to impress women. Young women. The more awe struck I could appear in his presence, the more he would talk.

"Why don't we go into the library?" It's a question, but he isn't waiting for a response. He motions for me to follow and leads me down a series of hallways. The big house is beautiful, architecturally stunning, yet cold, almost sterile. We settle into a beautiful library on two couches positioned facing each other. It's not incredibly large in perimeter, but the room spans two floors. A small staircase leads up to a gangway that traces the outline of the room, allowing visitors to reach books on the second floor.

"You like the library?" Senator Knight smiles, watching me take in the room. I don't have to feign awe in here, the room is beautiful, every journalists dream.

"It's stunning." I look up and down the countless rows upon rows of beautifully bound books, spanning at least twenty feet high, if not higher. "It's absolutely exquisite, such simple classic beauty."

"Yes, yes, it certainly is. Beautiful." I turn back to Senator Knight, finding his eyes roaming my face and, for a second, I'm not sure if he's still talking about the library.

Burying my head in my bag to hide the pink that I feel rise on my face, I take my time to dig out my notepad, paper, and recorder, hoping the heat cools as quickly as it rose. "So, Senator Knight. I was hoping to get some background, set the tone for the story. Show the readers your climb to the top." I smile, clicking on the recorder in front of me.

"Whatever you want. I'm an open book."

Sure you are. "You're originally from Chicago. Did you choose to go to law school locally to be close to your family?"

"Great question. There are a number of reasons why I chose Loyola, but yes, being close to my family was important. Family is at the heart of every success story. There was really never any other choice for me. I attended Loyola undergraduate, and their catholic values just connected with me so strongly. It brought me closer to my faith and family life. So when I was given the opportunity to attend law school there, I jumped at it." He smiles and winks. "Plus, I met my college sweetheart there."

Didn't take long for the good Senator to get his strong family values and religious beliefs in, did it? I get the feeling this man could weave the two into a response to just about any question. Politician oozes from him as soon as the recorder clicks on. Like an actor in front of the camera, he comes to life. Quick, someone hand him a baby to kiss.

"Mrs. Knight earned her degree in early childhood education. Did she teach while you were in Chicago?"

"No, no. She did a lot of volunteer work, but we were married pretty young, and she took on the job of raising our family full time. Not a lot of women are willing to commit to that important job anymore."

Or men. His comment is sexist, and instantly annoys me, yet I plaster a smile on my face as I respond with words that taste stale as they pass through my lips. "I hope I'm lucky enough to be able to stay home with my family someday."

Senator Knight sits back in his seat, fanning an arm over the side of the couch, an approving smile on his smug face.

"You were only twenty-eight when you made partner at Kleinman & Dell, that's impressive, you must have had some celebration."

Turning to look out the nearby window, I watch a change settle in on his face. His jaw clenches and he takes longer to respond. If I wasn't digging for a reaction, I probably wouldn't even notice it, but I do, because I'm watching for even the smallest sign. "Yes, well. I was younger back then." A few seconds later he turns back, mask back firmly in place.

We spend the next hour talking, but the reality is I could've written the story without even coming here. There's nothing new in what he reveals. Desperate to find more, to dig deeper, I decide to push more on his family.

"You only have one son, Jackson, right?"

"Yes."

I could be imagining it, looking for something that's not there, but his answer seemed almost too quick.

"I'd love to ask him a few questions, if he would have time? I know Paul was set to photograph him today, but if he's available for a few questions, I'd really like to get a couple of quotes from him. I'm sure he must be so proud of you and everything you support."

Smiling, he stands, "I'm sure he will make time for you, Miss Michaels." Another wink.

Following Senator Knight outside to the sprawling backyard, we find Mrs. Knight being photographed by Paul while she gardens. She's wearing a sheer white shirt, khaki pants tucked into rubber gardening boots, and her perfectly coifed hair is neatly tied back in a pastel colored scarf. Makeup as perfect as her pose, she's leaning in and digging a small hole to plant a tomato seedling.

I find the whole scene almost comical. Who gardens in an expensive white shirt and makeup? Even funnier, I parked alongside the gardener's truck when we pulled into the driveway. But I look up at Senator Knight with my best attempt at awe as he looks on proudly at the fake scene that represents his life.

"Your wife is beautiful." And plastic.

"Thank you." He stands taller with the compliment, as if he is actually personally responsible for the praise I've just given.

"Come on, let's go find that son of mine so you can have a few minutes with him."

Senator Knight leads the way down a brick path to a smaller house that looks like a guest quarters, or perhaps the residence of a live in member of the staff. "Jackson prefers the guest quarters to his mother's constant doting in the main house. This was their compromise when he decided it was time to move out." He opens the door without knocking and yells in, "Jackson, I have someone that would like to meet you."

The house is quiet. The Senator steps inside and looks around while I wait in the doorway. A voice from behind me startles me, "Can I help you with something?"

I jump at the unexpected sound, losing my balance, almost falling backwards as I trip over a pair of running shoes left just inside the door. A strong arm catches me as I teeter. "I'm sorry. I didn't mean to scare you. Are you okay?" Using both arms, he steadies me on my feet as I look up to find the face attached to the voice.

Looking into Vinny's eyes, I freeze, feeling suddenly lightheaded and dizzy. The Senator's eyes are the same color, yet something was different, gave me hope that maybe the source was really wrong. But the eyes staring back at me instantly shatter almost all the hope I clung to.

My mouth hanging open, I stare at him blankly. I'm unable to tear my eyes away from the familiarity of looking into them, even though he's a total stranger. Unable to speak, I nod my head.

Still holding me steady, I can see concern on his face, "Are you sure you're okay?"

Senator Knight interrupts, "Jackson, there you are." Confused, he turns to me, "Are you okay? You look pale."

Jackson answers for me. "I just scared her and almost knocked her over." He smiles at me, revealing a deep creviced dimple. "And I didn't even get her name yet."

Releasing my arms slowly to make sure I'm steady on my feet, he takes a step back and extends his hand in my direction. "Hi, I'm Jax Knight." His smile seems genuine.

"Olivia Michaels." I finally speak as he takes my hand in his. He shakes my hand, but continues holding it as his father finishes the introductions.

"Miss Michaels is a reporter from the *Daily Sun Times*. She's doing a feature story for the re-election campaign. She'd like to ask you a few questions."

"It's very nice to meet you Miss Michaels." A grin on his face, he finally releases my hand.

"Please, call me Olivia."

He nods, "Only if you call me Jax."

"Not Jackson?"

"Nah, too formal. My father here likes to use Jackson, he thinks it sounds more presidential, but my friends call me Jax."

Senator Knight's phone rings and he walks away for a moment, leaving Jax and I alone.

"So what do your friends call you, Olivia Michaels?" The flirtatious smile is back. It's different than Vinny's, but I'm positive it has the same effect on women. There's just something there. A hint of cockiness mixed with good looks is a lethal combination. Jackson Knight is tall, maybe even an inch or two taller than Vinny, and broad just like his father. He's wearing a plain white t-shirt and low hanging sweat pants, making him appear all the more like Vinny.

"Most new friends call me Olivia, but my closest, oldest friends call me Liv."

"Okay then, Liv." He grins. "I was just going to head out for a run, but I forgot my water so I came back." He pauses. "I'm glad I did. Can I get you something to drink?"

"Your mother wants me in the garden for some photos." Senator Knight turns back to us as he makes his way to the door. "Be on your best behavior with Miss Michaels, Jackson," he scolds his son before walking out.

Ignoring his father, Jax motions for me to follow. "Come on, I'll grab us some waters and we can take a walk outside while we talk, if you want."

"That would be great, thank you."

Surprisingly, our conversation flows freely as we walk. Unlike Senator Knight, every question seems to be answered without rehearsed speech. Our banter is easy, natural, and so many of his responses border on flirting, but he doesn't cross the line.

"So, what made you get into the world of Financial Management?" I know he made a name for himself in managing high net wealth personal portfolios. The Wall Street Journal even took notice of the returns he secured last year for his investors.

"My father," Jax responds with a truthful answer that I don't expect.

"Not your first choice, huh?"

He laughs, "Nope. Don't get me wrong, I've done well, and it's an interesting enough job."

"But…," I encourage him to continue. Obviously there's more to his statement.

"But, what I really would love to do isn't exactly a great long term career move."

"And that is?"

Jax smiles sheepishly, he almost seems embarrassed to admit his childhood dream. "I always wanted to get into pro boxing. I've been doing it since I was a kid."

I stop in my tracks. Jax takes two steps more before realizing I'm not walking next to him anymore.

"Liv. You okay? You're scaring me again." One arm quickly reaches for me, as if he's afraid I'm going to lose my balance again.

The reality of what's been hanging over my head since I was given this assignment finally hits me and I feel sick. Allowing it to sink in for the first time that, no matter how much I want the story not to be true, I can't change the truth. Time freezes, my anything's possible life suddenly flashes before my eyes. Doors that I see open in my future slam shut and I just know nothing will ever be the same from this point on.

"Liv. Do you need to sit down?" There's concern on his face and I realize I didn't even notice him coming to stand in front of me, both his arms holding my shoulders tightly. I've actually lost time, stuck somewhere in my own head.

Shaking my head to physically force myself to snap out of it, I finally regain my senses. "I'm fine. I'm sorry. I should've eaten something this morning. Sometimes my blood sugar gets a little low and I get a little foggy," I lie.

"Come on, let me sugar you up inside."

Once inside, Jax makes me sit and eat some fruit and drink a full bottle of Gatorade before he allows me to stand. Yet another thing he has in common with Vinny, bellowing demands that I seem to follow like a petty officer to a drill sergeant.

"You sure you're okay?"

"I'm fine. I'm sorry, I didn't mean to scare you."

"You know, if you want me to hold you, you could just ask. You don't need to pretend you're going to faint."

"What? I wasn't..." I'm about to set him straight when I look up and see he's joking written on his face. He laughs and it helps me relax a bit.

"You sure you don't have any more questions for me?" Jax smiles in response to my telling him I'm done and should probably go. Standing, I casually grab both our empty drink bottles from the table and head to the garbage. Just as I'm about to toss his in, I change my mind and slip it into my jacket pocket. Hoping he didn't notice, I walk to the sink and set my plate down in the basin.

Turning around, I find Jax standing behind me. Close. Too close. My back to the sink, I have no room to back up to put the requisite personal space between us. He notices my looking around, ready to make my escape, and puts one hand on either side of the sink and cages me in, his body close enough to feel the heat resonating from him, but not actually touching. "Have dinner with me, Liv."

Oh boy. "I, I can't. I have a boyfriend." Who I'm pretty sure at this point also happens to also be your brother.

"I don't see a ring on your finger." He arches one eyebrow and smirks. "One date. Tonight."

"My boyfriend is here with me, I don't think it would sit well if I told him I was going on a date tonight."

Releasing me from where he'd cornered me, he grins. "My loss. You know where to find me if you change your mind."

I help Paul pack up his equipment and the entire Knight family walks us to our car. "Thank you so much for all of your time." I address all three members of the family. "It was very nice meeting you." Senator Knight and Mrs. Knight say their goodbyes and chat with Paul about getting advance copies of the photos to review. Jax walks me to my side of the car. I extend my hand. "It was nice meeting you, Jax."

"You too, Liv." He pulls my hand in his toward him and turns my shake into a hug.

Laughing, because it's done playfully more than harassingly, I whisper in his ear before pulling away. "You should give boxing a shot. Don't ever give up your dreams."

CHAPTER 30

Vince

It's starting to get dark as I begin my run back to the hotel. I have no idea where the time went. The five mile run to Arlington Cemetery couldn't have taken more than a half hour, which would mean I spent four hours wandering around and sitting at my father's graveside. I'd seen pictures of the cemetery on TV, but nothing could have prepared me for the emotions I felt walking in and seeing miles and miles of stark white headstones perfectly lined up, many with American flags waving in the afternoon breeze.

Thoughts of lives lost and other kids growing up without a parent should have been what consumed me, but instead I sat next to his grave and played the *What If* head game I've been playing with myself since I was a kid. What if my father had come home instead of being lost at war? Would my mother have been different? Maybe not strung out for most of my childhood? What if he'd been there every night when I came home from school?

All around D.C., I pass families walking together as I run back to the hotel. They're taking in the sights and having a good time. A young boy and his father pose in front of the Lincoln Memorial while the mom takes the picture, all three smiling at the memories they're creating. It makes me run faster. Anger rises from within me, anger for my father not coming home, but even more anger for my mother not stepping up and being the parent she needed to be.

I don't even remember the last mile of the run, sprinting the entire time so fast that I still haven't caught my breath when I walk back into the hotel room.

"Hey." Liv looks up from where she's sitting on the bed, typing on her laptop. I don't respond. Instead I stalk to her and ravel her hair around my hand and yank her head back, giving me access to her mouth that I so desperately need.

She doesn't complain, even though I'm completely drenched in sweat and just marched in like a complete asshole. She kisses me back. Hard. Almost like she needs it as bad as I do.

"Need you," I mumble into her mouth without letting her come up for air.

"Need you too," she whimpers, her words barely heard, smothered under my kiss.

"How was your interview?" An hour later, I finally ask the question I should have asked walking in the door. But I just fucking needed her. Needed her to erase all the shit going through my head. Help me get rid of the anger. I know it's not fair, she doesn't deserve to be on the receiving end of my shit, but I just couldn't help it. Loathing myself for the way I treat her deep down inside, I try to soothe things over, even though she never complained.

"Okay." She's being tight lipped and I don't blame her. Probably thinks if I was really interested, I'd have asked when I walked in the door…like a normal fucking person.

"What did you do all day?" she asks, her head resting on my chest. I stroke her hair, it brings me peace, the urge to wrap it around my fist and pull gone with my pent up frustration, thanks to Liv.

"I went to Arlington Cemetery."

Lifting her head, she props her chin up on her hand resting just over my heart, and looks up at me. Her voice low and full of concern, she asks, "Is that where your father is buried?"

"Yeah." I stroke the hair back from her face. She's so god damn beautiful.

"Have you ever been there before?" Playing with the dog tags resting on my chest, she runs her finger over the swollen letters embossed on the ID.

I shake my head no.

"I would have gone with you. You shouldn't have had to go alone."

The fucked up thing is it never even dawned on me that she would want to go with me. I'm just so used to taking care of myself, going there anything but alone wasn't even a thought.

"Thanks. It means a lot that you would have gone."

Tilting her head to the side, she holds my gaze for a minute before speaking. "Vinny, it's not that I *would have* gone, I *want* to be there for you." She pauses. "There's a difference you know."

Maybe I'm dense, because I don't see the damn difference. But Liv was always better with words. I shrug my shoulders.

CHAPTER 31

Liv

I've never been to a professional fight before. I know it's just an exhibition, but I'm still excited to see it. See Vinny doing what he lives for.

Because it's not a sanctioned fight, each pair of fighters only spends one minute in each of three rounds, instead of the usual three or five minutes. Since Vinny's got a championship fight coming up, he's the headliner of the exhibition, so he goes last, like the rock star after the opening act.

We enter a small room under the building where the fights take place just above us. An older man greets us. It's clear the two men are fond of each other.

"Preach, I've missed you, you old bastard. The place just isn't the same without you." The two exchange a guy hug, a sort of combination hand shake and one armed half hug chest bump.

"You don't miss me you stupid little shit, you miss Nico having someone else to fight with." Smiling, their teasing says a lot about the strength of their relationship.

Preach catches me out of the corner of his eye. "Who you got with ya…this girl's too pretty to be hanging around with a goof like you." He smacks Vinny in the back of the head as he passes by on his way to me.

Coming to stand before me, Preach ignores Vinny's attempt at answering his question, and Vinny looks on from behind, laughing and shaking his head. "Hiya pretty girl, I'm Preach, and I'm single if you're interested?"

Laughing, I extend my hand, "I'm Olivia, it's nice to meet you, Preach."

Preach takes my hand and shakes, but doesn't let go as he talks to Vinny while still looking at me. "Elle told me all about this one when I talked to her last week. Says she's special and I have to be nice."

"Elle's right there." Vinny walks up to Preach and puts one hand on his shoulder from behind. His response is to Preach, yet he speaks it to me, "She is special." He pauses and I watch as his eyes take their time to travel over me slowly, from head to toe before he continues. "Now how about you let go of my girl's hand and come wrap up my hands, old man?"

The three of us hang out in the small locker room for another hour, the two men catching up on different fighters. Preach was Nico's trainer and retired when Nico did. The three men have a lot of history together, and I get the feeling that they've become Vinny's family in many ways.

Eventually, as it gets closer to the time for Vinny to fight, I take my seat inside the arena. Vinny made sure I was on the end of an aisle, almost directly behind the corner where he will be, just two rows back from the cage. I watch the end of a fight and then the announcer comes on. My heart starts to beat wildly in my chest before he even speaks. *"Ladies and Gentlemen, in the red corner, standing six feet tall, weighing in at one hundred eighty-three pounds, the man you've all been waiting for, the contender for the upcoming middleweight champion of the world title, the ladies love him, the men fear him…I give you Vince 'The Invinnnnnnnciiiiible' Stone!"*

The crowd goes crazy as Vinny makes his way down the aisle, his black robe up, shielding his face as he passes, but it doesn't stop women from screaming like fans at a rock concert. A woman two seats over from me is jumping up and down, tears streaming down her face, as she holds one arm out to him and screams, "Vince, Vince, I love you, Vince!"

Almost on cue, as if he's responding to her, Vinny jumps up into the cage and then slowly turns, finding me in the crowd, and winks, a damn cocky grin on his face. I roll my eyes and he smiles, turning his attention back to the announcer in front of him. He has no idea he's made the day, maybe even the year, of the poor clueless woman sitting two seats over. She's holding her friends arm in a death grip and screaming so loud, I can hear her every word, even though the crowd's still cheering. "Did you see that? Did you see that? He just winked at me!"

The announcer goes on to introduce Vinny's opponent and then rattles on about a bunch of rules I've never heard of, nor understand, and the fight begins. Sitting on the edge of my seat, I watch as Vinny takes control of the fight almost immediately. He strikes hard and fast, hitting his opponent with first a kick to the chest and then immediately follows up with a right-handed strike to the face. Every muscle in his back flexes as his strength and raw power leaves the man wobbling not ten seconds into the fight. But the wobbling doesn't last long. Seemingly out of nowhere, Vinny foot sweeps his opponent, turning his momentum against him and the man is quickly on his back with Vinny on top of him. It all happens so fast, I can't even figure out how he did it, even though I've watched the entire thing happen less than ten feet away. Seconds later, the fight is over when Vinny does something to the man's arm and he screams loudly, right before tapping the mat. The entire fight couldn't have lasted thirty seconds. I'm not even sure if Vinny broke a sweat, and he definitely never got hit.

Undaunted by the brevity of the fight they paid good money to see, the crowd goes crazy, yelling and screaming as the referee holds up Vinny's arm in victory. Preach is laughing as the two pass by on their way back out, Preach carrying Vinny's robe that he doesn't bother to put back on, to the pleasure of the women declaring their love as he passes by, a cocky grin firmly in place. He knows the crowd loves him. It's a surreal experience, one that has my heart racing, and leaves me wondering how many more days until I get to see him do it again.

Even though I have a pass allowing me access to the downstairs area, I still wait on line with the others, many of which don't have passes. I wonder to myself why people would even wait, with the size of the security guard checking for passes, until I catch on to what's actually transpiring in line in front of me. Those with passes are let through quickly, those without are sized up. The nice looking women with short skirts and nice legs are all slipped passes. The ones deemed not worthy are turned away. It makes me wonder how many women have found their way into Vinny's room for post-fight celebrations in the past.

Trying my best to ignore the pang of jealousy I feel deep inside, knowing I can't control either of our pasts, I make my way down to Vinny's room in a fog, not paying attention to where I'm going. Clumsily, I walk directly into someone as I'm engrossed in my own thoughts, just before reaching Vinny's door.

"Liv?"

The voice is familiar, yet I can't place it. I look up, confused. "Jax? What are you doing here?"

He smiles, a genuine smile on his face, he looks surprised, but I can tell he's happy to see me. "I could ask you the same thing." He narrows his eyes playfully and leans in, "Are you following me around trying to get me to bump into you, so I have to hold you again?" He's teasing, I know. Although I don't get the chance to respond, when the door we're standing in front of opens and Vinny steps out.

He takes one look at Jax's hand on my arm and his face changes. "I don't know who you are, but get your hands off of her or you're gonna find the beating the guy just took in the cage was just a warm up for you."

Frozen in place, the sight of the two men standing next to each other makes me unable to respond. The resemblance is so much clearer when they are both within my vision.

"Liv?" Jax looks to Vinny and back to me, a confused question on his face.

"Liv." Vinny's voice is pure growl.

Tension resonates from the two men, and I can sense Vinny's about to explode as he takes one step closer to Jax, the two men coming nose to nose.

Snapping out of it, I move to Vinny's side, taking hold of his arm to gain his attention. "Vinny, he was kidding, I know him. It's fine." My words do little to calm the beast standing before me. Worse, Jax shifts his shoulders back, his fists balled at his sides, readying himself for what might come next.

"Who is this guy, Liv?" His words might be directed at me, but he's still standing toe to toe with Jax, the two men having a staring showdown.

"His name is Jackson, he's the son of the politician that I interviewed yesterday." Attempting to refocus his attention, I tug harder on his arm.

"That doesn't explain why his hands are on you."

"I walked into him...he kept me from falling. Really, it's fine, it was my fault. He wasn't bothering me at all."

I watch his face as he deliberates over the information for a few long seconds, sizing up the man standing in front of him. Relieved when I see his jaw relax slightly, I exhale a long breath I hadn't even realized I was holding.

Vinny takes a step back, and nods to Jax, "Sorry man, I read it wrong. I see a lot of crazy shit down here." Pulling me to his side, he wraps his arm around my shoulder possessively.

Jax nods back, and I think maybe we all might walk away

unscathed, until he opens his mouth. "No problem. Don't blame you for being protective of Liv. You're a lucky guy." Jax smiles a cocky grin at me.

Is he insane? Or perhaps he has a death wish. Vinny's grip on me tightens and I brace for his response...concerned it won't be a verbal one. Luckily, Preach steps out, calling Vinny's attention away for a few seconds, so he misses Jax's wink at me.

Seriously?

"Gotta go talk to some reporters. You ready?" Preach catches sight of me on the other side of Vinny and smiles, "Our boy looked good out there, huh, Liv?"

I can't help but smile at Preach, even though I'm still freaking out inside at the two men standing in front of each other. "That he did." I smile up at Vinny, and I'm rewarded with a proud smile. His arm slung around my shoulder slides to the back of my neck and he squeezes it lightly, turning me toward him, taking my mouth in an unexpected kiss. He doesn't care that two men are standing within feet of us, forced to watch as he kisses me senseless, and eventually, I don't care either.

Releasing my mouth with a low growl, I turn to find Jax still standing there. His cocky grin is gone, replaced by something I can't read. Jealousy perhaps?

"Alright, alright, you two can celebrate in private later. Let's get this show on the road, lovebirds," Preach teases.

Vinny begins to lead us away to follow Preach without so much as a word to Jax. Never one for being rude, I turn my head to say goodbye, "Take care, Jax," and I feel every hair on my body stand on end when I look past Jax and find Senator Knight stopped at the other end of the hall, eyes locked on Vinny.

CHAPTER 32

Vince

The exhibition behind me, I need to focus on my upcoming fight. A shot at the belt. And a real shot at it too. Junior Lamaro. He drops his left, leaving himself open to my power right. He's tough, but wrestling is his strongest discipline. Keeping away from the ground is the key to my winning.

I should be in the gym tonight, practicing my technique, but instead I'm in a fucking bar I haven't visited in almost a year, looking for dirtbags that helped drag me down. Drug addicts. Dealers. Total fucking losers. Guys I used to consider my friends. Friends that were only too happy to keep me as fucked up as them when I was footing the bill.

I can't seem to focus on what I need to with my mom's shit still hanging over her head. Over both our heads. As usual, when her own self-induced pathetic life drags her down, I grab her and try to pull her out. Most of the time it winds up dragging me down with her.

The first three guys I talk to haven't seen Jason in weeks. Guys that aren't tied down to much easily disappear off the grid. But I'm finding this fucker. Probably beat him till he's barely breathing for making me waste my time chasing after his ass when I should be training. The last breath I'll let the two goons keeping tabs on my mother take care of.

A hand reaches around from behind me and grabs my groin. She's lucky I didn't respond with a punch, most of the time my reactions are automatic. It's work for me to stop and redirect against something I've spent years training to respond to. Grabbing the hand reaching for me, I turn to find it's attached to Krissy. Great, just fucking great. Could my night get any worse?

"Where you been, Vince?" She rests her two hands against my chest. I remove them quickly.

"Busy." Turning my back to Krissy, I find her friend close behind me. Like two pack wolves, they box me in. I'm pretty sure the friend gave me head in the bathroom when I was at my low, getting high every day. I don't even remember her name. Not that I care to anyway.

"Hi, Vince," her friend purrs.

"Not interested." Not here, not now, not ever again.

"I can make you interested." She reaches up, makes it close to my mouth with her long red fingernail, but I catch her hand in mine before it touches me. Squeezing her little bony hand too hard, I think how easy it would be to fucking crush it, so I force myself to let go. But she gets my point.

"You know, Vince, the two of us could make you forget whatever is bothering you," Krissy purrs from behind me. It makes me wonder how I ever stomached being with her. "We have enough for the three of us to party."

Finally, something she says gets my attention. "You know Jason Buttles?"

"Maybe." Krissy smiles, rocking back and forth. She's being coy and thinks it's cute, but it's not, I find it god damn annoying. But I know how women like her work. I'll get more from her giving her what she wants.

Turning to give her my full attention, I wrap one hand around the back of her neck and lower my face to hers as if I'm about to kiss her, but I don't. I smile instead, "Can you get in touch with him?"

"Probably." The two hands I removed from my chest are back, but this time I leave them be, even though it disgusts me to have them there.

"Do that for me."

She pouts. "Why should I?"

My other hand snakes around her waist and pulls her close to me. "Because I need to talk to him. And once that's outta the way, I can party with you ladies," I lie.

She leans into me, bringing her mouth even closer to mine, she expects me to kiss her. No fucking way I'm touching that with what I got now. I pull my head back. "Call him."

"He doesn't have a phone."

Who doesn't have a god damn phone? Yesterday I saw the fucking homeless guy that lives on the north side of Nico's gym talking on a cell. "How do you get in touch with him?"

"Beeper."

Beeper? What is it, nineteen eighty-two? "Beep him."

Pulling out her phone, she spends a minute pressing buttons and then smiles back at me. "Done"

Great, now I have to wait with these two.

An hour passes and Jason never calls back. I've kept the two of them strung along enough to keep them close, but far enough away not to have to actually spend time talking to them. Luckily for me, a few guys from the gym come in, helping to pass the time.

But I've had enough waiting around. The loser is probably passed out somewhere or doesn't have a damn quarter to use a payphone and call her back. "Listen, I have to run. If you hear from Jason, call me, okay?"

"What about our party?" Krissy pouts.

"I'm gonna have to take a rain check until I hear from Jason." I'm out the door before either of them can respond.

CHAPTER 33

Liv

After work today, I finally unload my whole story on Ally over a glass, no a bottle, of wine.

"So do you think it was a coincidence that they were at the exhibition match?"

"I don't know...Jax is a fighter, not professionally, but he sounded pretty passionate about it. It wouldn't surprise me if he had tickets. The arena was just outside of D.C., so when I first saw him, I thought it was a coincidence."

"What changed your mind?"

"The look on the Senator's face. He was just staring at Vinny."

"Maybe he's a fan?"

I take another sip of my wine and close my eyes, remembering the look on Senator Knight's face. "It was more than that. Something just tells me he knows."

"So what are you going to do?"

Collapsing back onto the couch, I look at my best friend. "I don't know Al, if I give the water bottle to the paper to test, they'll know the results and it won't matter what I decide. They won't wait for me to write a story."

"So have the results tested yourself. Take something of Vinny's and put the two samples into a lab under a fake name. Find out for sure before you go crazy trying to decide what to do."

"I guess I can do that."

"Do it. You never know…maybe it really is all one big coincidence. The blue eyes, the fighting…everything. Stranger things have happened."

I attempt to smile at my best friend. "Thanks Ally. I feel so guilty keeping it from Vinny. But I don't want to hurt him. He loves the memory of his father. I can't explain it…he just believes that's where the good comes from in him. I can't tarnish that memory if I'm not absolutely sure." And I'm not even sure I can do it if it turns out to be absolutely true.

"Look at it this way. If it is true, at least it's you, and you can protect him from what the paper would do if it was someone else writing the story."

I get little sleep, tossing and turning half the night, guilt wreaking havoc on my brain's ability to power down. Trudging into the office, barely making it on time, even though I've been up for hours, I'm greeted by an overly zealous fake smile from Summer.

"Morning, Olivia." Summer's smile is full of sugar, yet far from sweet.

"Hello, Summer." Taking the high road, I respond professionally, as if she hasn't spent the last three weeks ignoring me and slamming things every time I was near.

"How's Vince?"

What the hell is she up to? "He's great, thank you." I somehow manage to maintain my professional demeanor.

Sitting on the edge of my desk, she folds her arms over her chest and crosses her long skinny legs. "Had dinner with Daddy last night."

"That's nice." I pull out a file and power up my laptop, trying hard not to feed into whatever game she's playing.

Leaning down to me, she whispers through her smile. "Can't wait to see how much he likes your little story."

Feeling the sting of tears behind my eyes, I stand, blinking them back before allowing Summer to see them. The thought of yet another person knowing such a powerful secret about Vinny crushing my spirit, I force anger to replace the sadness I'm truly feeling. "I'll admit, when I first met you, I was a bit jealous. Such a beautiful girl, with all the right connections. But after getting to know you, jealousy has turned to pity. Why don't you stop worrying about my life and get your own, Summer. I'm sure there are plenty of men that are into skinny, self-loathing, and desperate."

I pack the laptop I was just firing up back into my bag, no way I can sit here all day and look at her. Catching sight of Sleezeball out of the corner of my eye, I plaster on a cheery face as I continue quietly. Venom bleeding out from beneath my smiling lips, I warn, "Keep the hell away from Vinny."

Smiling back, looking thoroughly satisfied for ruffling my feathers, she responds through gritted, perfect, white teeth, "I'm a patient woman. Someone's going to need to help him pick up the pieces when you tear him apart. Might as well be me."

I spend the day working back at my apartment, finishing off a story that I owe and researching labs that do DNA testing. Printing off a list, I decide the first few are too close. Maybe putting some miles between my life and the lab will make it feel less risky.

My phone rings and Vinny's voice calms me, even though he's the subject of everything else in my life that brings tension these days. "Hey."

"Hey, Beautiful." His voice warms me after a long day of feeling cold.

Sighing loudly, I give in to what I'm feeling, even if I don't fully understand it. How did I go from running from him to his voice bringing me comfort? "It's good to hear your voice."

"Bad day?" I can tell he's smiling on the other end of the phone, even though I can't see him. Male satisfaction throaty in his voice, he likes the thought of making me smile so easily.

"Yeah."

"Wanna talk about it?" The irony doesn't escape me.

"No, but thank you. How was your day?"

"Spent it in the hospital."

"What happened?" Real concern takes hold of me.

"Elle's having the baby. For real this time."

"Wow, how is she?"

"She's doing good. Though the doctor said it'll be hours still. I'm going to run home and shower, came here in the middle of a workout. Think the nurses are eyeing me because I smell."

As confident as he is, sometimes he's totally clueless. "The nurses aren't eyeing you because you smell. They're eying you because you're easy on the eyes."

He laughs, "Well, I wouldn't notice. I only have eyes for one woman these days."

"Good to know." It's the first genuine smile I've had in two days.

"How about if I pick you up after I shower and we can grab a bite to eat and come back to the hospital. Hopefully the little guy will be around by then."

"I'd love that."

CHAPTER 34

Liv

I've never seen Vinny in such a playful mood. We arrive at the hospital and he takes my hand, together we walk, fingers linked, to the maternity ward. "How many kids you want to have?"

His question takes me by surprise. "Two, maybe three."

He smiles at my response. "How about you?"

"Never really given it any thought." He quiets for a minute, thinking. "Six."

"Six?" I respond horrified. The number shocks me.

Vinny chuckles. "All boys."

"Six boys? You do realize you don't get to pick what you have, right?" I tease, nudging him with my shoulder.

As we arrive through the double doors, Nico comes into sight. He's wearing light blue scrubs from head to toe, a cap covering his head, and matching blue paper booties on his feet. His smile is so big, I can see it even before he removes the blue mask from his face.

The two men hug, clinging to each other, tears in both their eyes. "Ten fingers, ten toes. He's beautiful, just like his mother." Nico sniffles back the start of tears.

"How's Elle?"

"She hates me. Screamed something about my head being too big and that it was all my fault, right before the baby came out." The wide smile never leaves his face.

"She'll get over it." Vinny grins, slapping Nico on the back.

"Yeah, nurses said that. Told me it was normal and she'd forget it as soon as they cleaned him up and she could hold him some more." Noticing me for the first time, Nico greets me with a kiss on the cheek. "Hey, Liv. Thanks for coming."

"Congratulations. I hope Elle doesn't mind I'm here so soon after the baby was born."

"You bring her coffee, she wouldn't care if you were in the delivery room."

Two hours later, we finally get to see Baby Nicholas's mom. Coffee in hand, I greet Elle and congratulate her.

She smiles, quickly sipping the coffee. "I knew you wouldn't let me down."

Surprising me, the nurse wheels in a small clear cradle, where the baby lies wrapped snuggly in a soft blue blanket. Thinking we'd only get to see the baby behind glass, I look down at the perfect pink cheeks, mesmerized by the beauty and perfection of this living, breathing miracle that's only hours old.

"You think you can hold 'em without dropping him?" Nico elbows Vinny.

"I'm not you, old man. My hands are still good." He grins.

"Wash your damn hands." Nico chastises Vinny. The two have an interesting dynamic. It's a cross between a father-son and brother-brother relationship, mixed with a bucket load of authority challenging on both their parts. Yet through it all, the two clearly love and care about each other deeply.

Something happens as I watch Vinny gently take baby Nicholas from Nico. A quiet moment, where all the sexual energy that emanates from the confident and controlling man slips beneath the surface, allowing a beautiful, gentle, incredibly loving man to rise to the top. Just watching him look down at the baby in awe of all his perfectness, a protective lion adoring his baby cub, clutches at my heart. I know exactly what he's feeling as tears well up behind his eyes, love pouring out unbridled for no other reason than his heart decided it loved. I know because I feel it too…staring at Vinny.

Elle catches me staring and smiles at me, the two men oblivious to our attention as we watch from just a short distance. "He's a good man, Liv. He'll make a good father and husband someday." She reaches for my hand and squeezes. "When you're ready."

A feeling of peacefulness replacing the playfulness of earlier, Vinny's mood helps ward off the anxiousness and guilt that always seems to lurk nearby lately. Deciding to stay at his apartment tonight, I change in the bathroom and find Vinny sitting at the foot of the bed, head in hands, contemplating.

"You okay?" I stand between his legs, resting my hands on his shoulders.

Vinny pulls me close, turning his head to nuzzle into my chest through my t-shirt. "I'm great, you?" He whispers with a husky voice, the thickness of it telling me he's in the mood, without the necessity of words.

"I'm good. Tonight was nice. Thank you for taking me with you."

Vinny pulls me down to him, seating me on his lap, his big hand gathering my hair aside as his mouth goes to my neck. I feel his words spoken on my neck. "Want to make love to you, Liv."

My heart thuds loudly in my chest, "I want you too."

"More. I want more, Liv."

"I don't understand." Pulling my head back to look into his eyes, he looks down for a minute, avoiding my eyes, contemplating, before his baby blues find their way to me.

"I've never made love to anyone. Closest I came was with you, a lifetime ago. Scared me back then, scares the crap out of me now. But

I want you, Liv. More. Just damn more. I'm not even sure what that means myself, yet I'm surer of it than anything I've ever been in my entire screwed up life."

There are no words to respond with to what he offers me, so I don't, I give him what he's asking for. Sealing my mouth over his, I kiss him with everything I have. It's different than our usual hot and heavy, it's soulful, and beautiful, and forever life changing.

Gently, Vinny lifts me from his lap, and places me in the center of the bed.

Vinny

I force myself to ignore every impulse in my body, telling me to pin her down and sink deep inside of her. Instead, I hover over her, one hand on the side of her head holding myself steady in place, the other lifts her hand and brings it to my mouth. I kiss each finger gently.

She lifts her arms without words as I slip off her shirt. Looking down the length of her, I admire the beauty of her body. It's god damn perfect. Soft on the curves, toned on all the muscle, and creamy white everywhere.

She watches me intently as I slowly lean down, flicking the tip of my tongue over her nipple. It hardens to my touch and I feel my cock twitch from her body's reaction. Sucking the pink pebble into my mouth, I draw firmly, falling short of biting, even though the urge is great.

Nibbling gently from one firm breast to the other, my mouth takes the other waiting nipple as my fingers gently pinch at the other hardened point. Liv moans, and it's that sound that drives me crazy. A throaty cross between a moan and a purr, it made me crazy back when we were just kids, but could drive a man to do feral things as an adult.

I watch as her face goes soft and she closes her eyes and reopens them hooded a minute later. Lining our bodies up, my head looming over hers, my cock is positioned perfectly at her opening. I can feel the wet heat radiating from her slick pussy and I want nothing more than to dive inside, riding her hard and filling every last inch of her.

But I don't. Closing my eyes, I brace myself, hovering over her. Waiting. Watching. My arms begin to shake and I clamp down on every ounce of control within me and reign in my need. Her big, round, hazel eyes meet mine when I look down at her, and I find them filled with emotion. It takes me back seven years, to a time when I didn't trust myself to not hurt her. Just like so many years ago, I find myself staring at eyes that scare the living shit out of me, eyes that trust me. Only this time, I want it. Need it. Finally man enough to take it.

So I kiss her softly on the lips and smile down at her. Wrapping her arms around my back, she smiles back at me and together we make love for the first time. I enter her slowly, our gaze never breaking, even when I'm seated deeply, the base of me flush against her wet opening.

Pulling back out, almost in unison we both take a deep breath in, and still for a minute before beginning to move again. Together, we find our rhythm, moving in and out slowly, unhurried, each breath and thrust in perfect sync with each other. Our eyes never parting for more than a few seconds, only out of necessity to steal a kiss.

Minutes later, I watch as her face changes, my slow thrusts speeding up, her hands on my back slipping down to grip my ass as she comes closer.

"Show me. Show me, Babe. I want to watch as that tight pussy grips me. Need to see you." Her eyes begin to roll back and drift shut, I know she's close. "Open, Babe. Let me watch you give yourself to me."

Glazed over, she struggles to keep her eyes open as her orgasm begins to pulse through her. Her body spasms beneath mine as I tremble to continue, holding back my own release, thrusting in and out, rocking back and forth, over and over again. I feel every pulse of her orgasm grasp and milk me, until finally, I can't hold back anymore. I smother her moans with a kiss. The sound of her being stifled by me is almost too much to bear. Panting and sliding my cock in as deep as I can, I release into her, my own body spurting uncontrollably as she moans my name through our kiss.

CHAPTER 35

Liv

The next morning when I awake, I roll over and find a cold bed where Vinny should be. A note on the pillow catches my attention. "Went for a run sleepy head. Be back soon. Be naked." I smile, amenable Vinny gone, back to the demanding man this morning, not that I mind. I had no desire to get out of bed anyway.

Half an hour later, a knock at the door wakes me back out of my semiconscious state. Grabbing Vinny's shirt from the night before and wrapping the sheet around me, I pad to the door, the floor cold beneath my bare feet.

Opening the door, I expect to find Vinny, instead a vaguely familiar face greets me on the other side of the doorway. One that's wearing a short skirt and has more cleavage popping out of her scant top than breast underneath.

"Can I help you?" Please tell me you're at the wrong apartment. I try to remain hopeful, but deep down I know she's looking for Vinny.

The bottle blonde sizes me up and down, a look of annoyance on her face as she responds, "Is Vince here?"

"No."

"Who are you?" Attitude and all.

"Considering I'm the person wearing his shirt from last night, I think I should be asking you that question," I give it back as good as she gives.

"I'm Krissy. Tell Vince I have what he needs and to call me."

"I don't think you have anything he needs anymore." I respond curtly, barely holding my temper.

With an irritating smile that I know is about to deliver news I won't like, she says, "That's not what he said the other night."

I deliberate staying and calmly asking for an explanation when he gets back from his run, but then my mind starts to question things. Maybe we've never defined our relationship, but holding himself out as my boyfriend and telling me he wants us to make love sure sounds like exclusivity to me. I go from talking myself into there being a valid explanation to thinking I'm a naïve idiot all within the span of ten minutes.

The need to clear my head wins out and I decide to get dressed and talk to Vinny later. Only I'm not quick enough. Sitting on the bed, I'm in the middle of putting on my shoes when Vinny strides into the bedroom.

"You're supposed to be naked in bed." He flirts as he takes off his sweaty t-shirt. His shorts hang low on his hips, the sight of his defined abs a distraction I don't need.

"I was. Until you had a visitor." Standing, I look around for my bag, I must have left it in the kitchen last night when we came in.

Catching on that something is awry from my icy tone, Vinny stops, arching one eyebrow and has the nerve to look like he has no idea what I'm talking about.

"What visitor?"

"Krissy. She said she has what you wanted the other night." I push past him as he stands in the doorway.

He follows. "It's not what you think, Liv."

"Really?" I turn to finally face him. Not even the sight of his ridiculously sexy sweaty body can cool my anger. "Were you with her the other night?"

His jaw clenches. "Yes, but..."

"Get out of my way, Vinny." He blocks the front door so that I can't leave.

"No." Seemingly calm, he folds his hands over his chest and settles in.

"No?" My voice rises higher.

"Give me a break, Liv. I didn't do anything wrong. Don't you trust me at all?" Really? He's annoyed with me? What's that old saying... fool me once, shame on you, fool me twice...

"How would you feel if it were you opening the door to a man who said he was with me the other night?"

He flinches. His jaw tenses and the answer to my question is clear without words.

"Fine. But hear me out. Nothing happened. I was looking for someone and ran into her and her friend. I asked her to get in touch with me if she saw the guy. I didn't think she would come here."

I try, I really try, to accept what he's telling me, his voice even sounds so sincere. But history and my own self-doubt overshadow his words. Then I suddenly realize why she looked so familiar. She was the girl from the gym. The one that Vinny had waiting in the car for him the day we reconnected. It makes me feel nauseous to even think about.

"Did you sleep with her?"

Remorse on his face, words not necessary. "It was before I met you."

"Let me go, Vinny."

Taking two steps from the door toward me, he stands before me. "I haven't been with anyone since the day I saw you in the gym, Liv. I'm a lot of shitty things, but a liar isn't one of them."

It takes all my willpower to step around him and walk out the door.

CHAPTER 36

Vince

I don't even have a number for Krissy. Guess I should have thought things through before asking her to get in touch with me if she hears from Jason. I'm pissed that she came by my place, but even more pissed that Liv doesn't seem to believe me when I tell her nothing happened.

Two minutes after I walk into the bar, Krissy walks in with her head giving friend. "Hey Vince," she coos in her nasally voice.

"Krissy," I nod my head. She really didn't do anything wrong. It's not her fault that I have no interest. For the first time, I feel badly for the way I've treated her…and maybe a fuck of a lot of other women too.

"Guess you got my message." She grins. Any remorse I felt wanes as I realize she enjoyed upsetting Liv.

"Don't fuck with Liv, Krissy."

"I didn't fuck with her. But you're gonna have trouble with that one, she thinks she owns you."

Like running straight into a Mack truck, I realize for the first time, she fucking does.

Fifteen minutes later, I have an address for Jason. Asshole ran clear across the state, rather than man up for the shit he's got himself into. Tomorrow I'm gonna have to take a whole day from training, a long road trip to find the fucker. Pisses me off, but tonight, I've got more important shit to deal with anyway.

Ally answers the door and is surprised to see me. Guess I'm surprised I'm here too. It's almost eleven o'clock and I didn't bother to call first. What's the point, if she tried to blow me off, I was coming anyway.

"Ummm..." She opens the door, but doesn't invite me in.

"I need to talk to her, Ally."

Hesitantly, she steps to the side, allowing me to pass. I look around, finding the apartment quiet.

"She's in the shower."

I nod.

"And she's pretty drunk."

"Drunk?"

"Yeah." She motions to the empty wine bottle on the counter. "I came home, she was slurring her words and rambling on about you and Missy."

"Krissy," I correct her, not that it matters.

"Nope, it was Missy. Trust me. I spent two years listening to her go on about Missy. That's who she was talking about."

I nod as if it all makes sense to me, but I'm actually pretty lost. What the hell does Missy have to do with any of this?

"I'm going to go over to Andrea's. She lives two buildings over. We're going to drink mojitos, watch a movie with a lot of naked men, curse like sailors, and wind up stalking the internet. I'll be gone at least a few hours, so you'll have privacy." She smiles on her way to the door, but then stops and turns to me, a serious face replacing her smile, "Please, don't hurt her again, Vince."

The gnawing unsettled feeling I've had in my gut all day today getting the best of me, I don't wait till she's done. Opening the bathroom door, my voice intentionally low to not scare her, I speak quietly, "Liv?"

"Vinny?" She pulls back the shower curtain.

"Yeah, Babe."

"Why did you pick Missy over me?" With no curtain to deflect the water, a hard stream of water hits her body and splashes onto the bathroom floor.

"I don't understand?"

"Neither do I. I...I...I loved you." Her words are a bit slurred, but she's very much in control of her mind. "And you picked Missy over me." Tears stream down her face, every inch of her body soaked with water dripping everywhere.

Reaching in, I turn off the spray of water, drenching myself in the process. Wrapping a towel around her body, I hastily dry her off before lifting her and cradling her in my arms. Carrying her to the bed, I gently lay her down and crawl into bed next to her.

Brushing her wet hair from her face, I lift her chin and force her eyes to meet mine. "I didn't choose Missy over you. You were so young and sweet and innocent." I pause, thinking of the right words. Although I'm not sure any words are right, since I don't truly understand my own actions still to this day. "And I was a fucked up loser who'd just got expelled. I didn't want to hurt you, Liv. You trusted me, and all I'd ever done is ruin things. I didn't want to ruin you."

Sadness etched on her face, it breaks my heart to know how badly I must have hurt her. "I didn't touch Krissy either."

"I know." A lone tear slips from her face.

I hold her tight until I eventually hear her breathing slow and I know she's asleep. And then, I just keep holding on.

CHAPTER 37

Liv

I wake to a throb in my head that reminds me of how much I drank the night before. I'm content, a warm body holding me tight, but then I remember the night before. Drunk. Shower. A whole conversation about Missy. And Krissy. Ughh…the thought makes my head pound louder.

A full bottle of wine presses on my bladder and I slip from the bed, still wrapped in the damp towel from the night before. Looking in the mirror, I scare myself, wet bed head and streaks of makeup dried down my face. It's not fixable without a shower.

I wash the makeup off my face and I'm just about to put the conditioner in my hair, when the shower curtain opens, revealing a naked, and very erect, Vinny.

He grins and steps in behind me. "Morning." He kisses my wet shoulder.

"You're blocking all the warm water," I scold. He is, but I'm kidding and he knows it.

"I'll keep you warm." He turns me, wrapping his arms around my waist, takes a small step back and holds me tightly so we're both under the stream of hot water.

We stay that way for a few quiet moments, until Vinny pulls his head back, looks down at me, and asks, "We okay?"

"I think so."

"Think?" Putting his fingers under my chin, he tilts my face up, forcing me to look at him.

"I'm just a little scared."

He exhales. "So am I, Liv."

I nod.

"Turn around." Vinny suds up my back, taking his time at my shoulders, rubbing a full day of stress free from my aching muscles.

I groan. "God that feels so good."

"Turn." I obey, dropping my head as he works his fingers into the top of my shoulders from the front. His thumbs dig into my collarbone while the tips of his strong fingers work their way on either side of my spine at the nape of my neck.

My tense muscles relaxed a few minutes later, his hands caress their way down my sides, coming to rest on my hips. His voice changes, lower and raspier, "Open your legs."

I comply. Reaching up, he repositions the showerhead so that it's spraying only on me. Warm, strong streams of water run over my back, as his hands continue their descent downward. His fingers glide across my clit, two fingers settling in to gently rub small circles. The taut bundle of nerves sends a current through my body, my skin reacting with goosebumps even though warm water blankets it.

Leaning forward, he takes one nipple into his mouth and teasingly tugs at it as he bites down and pulls with his teeth. I moan as the two fingers on my clit reach lower, slipping inside of me, his thumb replacing the pressure on my waiting swell.

My breaths coming faster and more shallow, I quickly find myself heading toward my climax. Sensing my body's reaction, Vinny growls, "Don't come."

As if there was anything I could do to stop it from happening, the feeling of euphoria quickly taking hold of me. "I can't," I pant, so close to the brink, needing to free fall over and wash away all of my thoughts, if only for a short time.

Withdrawing his fingers, for a second I want to kill him, leaving me dangling, perched on the edge.

"Turn around, grab the wall."

Desperate to get back to the place where I just was, I comply quickly, turning so my back faces him, bending at the waist and palms pressed firmly against the tiled wall, he wastes no time. Entering me from behind, with the water and my own slick juices, he easily slips into me. I feel every thick inch of him as he gloriously stretches me, seating himself fully in one agonizingly slow, incredible thrust in.

"Slow or fast?"

Oh god. He's giving me a choice. Just hearing him say the words is almost enough to bring me back to the edge. "Fast."

His big hand tightens on one hip, the other snakes around underneath me and lifts me at the waist, bringing my ass up slightly higher and positioning me for what he's about to deliver. I gasp as the hard-driving thrust of his thick cock begins to pound into me with a fury.

Holding me immobile, pinned to the wall as he powers into me, over and over, I moan his name as my core clenches around him, my orgasm beginning to form again in the distance. "Fuck!" he growls, leaning over me, his wet, hard chest pushing firmly into my back as he sinks his teeth into my shoulder. A sting of pain rushes throughout my body, turning my waning orgasm into a tsunami that washes over me, taking my ability to function with it. My body trembles as it works its way through, leaving me completely vulnerable to his strength, unable to even hold myself up.

Hair still damp and skin pruny from a shower so long the water goes cold, Vinny settles in on a bar stool, watching me make us both breakfast.

"You look like a pro in there," he says as I slide a potholder on. I open the oven door and pull out the biscuits just as the timer rings. I tip the oven door shut with my foot and grab the pan just in time to turn the eggs.

"I like to cook, but I don't get to do it often."

"I like to eat, maybe you should come by and make me dinner every night." He grins.

Laughing, I shake my head and pull down two plates from the cabinet. "My personal chef services are pretty expensive."

"Maybe we can take it out in trade?" Vinny arches one eyebrow with a sinister smile. The man has a one track mind, it's a good thing I like what he's playing.

Plating the eggs, bacon, and biscuits, I set down breakfast in front of him and walk around to the other side of the bar to join him. "That depends on what you have to trade."

Catching me as I'm about to sit, he pulls me onto his lap, teasing me with a piece of bacon at my lips, pulling it away as I open my mouth to bite, "You'll cook, I'll feed you."

Leaning forward, I steal the entire piece of bacon with my mouth, nipping at his finger in the process. His eyebrows arch in surprise, but there is no hiding how his eyes dilate instantly at the feel of my bite on his skin. Grabbing my ass firmly, he growls. "Do that again and I'm gonna be feeding you here on the kitchen counter, and your food's gonna get cold while you're busy taking what I'm gonna put in that sexy damn mouth of yours."

My stomach flip flops and I lean in to cuddle into his neck, needing my goosebump laden skin pressed up against him, wanting to show him the effect his words have on my body.

Blind to what's happening around us, I completely miss the clickety-clack of Ally's sandals on the wooden floor, not noticing her entering the room until she's in the refrigerator. "Don't you two have jobs or something?" she asks as she smiles and pours herself a heaping glass of orange juice, guzzling the tall glass in one long gulp.

"Thirsty?" Vinny teases.

I attempt to hop off his lap, but his grip on me tightens, keeping me locked into place.

"Very. And hungry too. Wanna share that egg sandwich, Liv?" She helps herself to a bite that consumes almost half of my breakfast, before I even have a chance to respond.

"Help yourself." Shaking my head, my response a moot point, I smile anyway.

"Can you drop me at school on your way to work? I have to work on a project *with a group*." Her happy face falters as she groans the last three words of her sentence.

"Not a good group I take it?"

"Five girls. I was hoping the big guy with the goatee would be in my group." She wiggles her eyebrows for effect.

Chuckling, Vinny shifts me on his lap to grab his breakfast. "I'll drop you. I'm heading to the gym. It's on my way." Two bites and the entire plate is gone. Perhaps I need to rethink the quantity of food I prepare. I'm definitely not used to cooking for a man that burns more calories in the gym than I consume in a month.

"Do you have your truck or motorcycle?" Ally clasps her hands together excitedly, her posture reminding me of a little girl waiting to find out if her mom bought her a new pony she'd been begging for.

"Bike." Vinny stands, setting me on my feet, and turning me to face him. Pushing a lock of hair behind my ear, his voice low so only I can hear him, "That good with you?"

Nodding my head, finding it sweet that he cares enough to clear my best friend riding on the back of his bike, I ignore the tiny bit of jealousy I can't help but feel at the thought of another woman with their arms wrapped around Vinny. Even if she is my best friend.

"Nico's back today, I'll be at the gym all day, then I have to take a road trip tonight."

"Road trip?" My brows furrow.

"Something I have to take care of for my mom." Sadness darkens Vinny's eyes, his voice reaching for casual, but his clenched jaw and forlorn eyes offering a window into his heart.

"Can I help?"

A genuine smile warms my heart. His hand slides down my cheek, and gently glides to the back of my neck, "Just offering helps." He squeezes the back of my neck and lowers his mouth to mine, kissing me softly, sweetly, on the lips. "Have a good day, Beautiful."

CHAPTER 38

Vinny

"How's the little bambino?" I ask, hitting the speedball.

"He's perfect, but full of energy, just like his mother." Nico smiles. "Elle's a good sport, my niece is upstairs 'helping' her babysit."

"The seven-year-old that wears the pink tutu and cowboy boots?"

"The one and only. I ducked out the door when Elle was changing him and I heard her ask what was inside his *pesticles*." Nico laughs.

Finishing up with the speedball, we move to the ring. "We'll spar for a while, then I have Kojo coming in to work you out on the mat."

"That guy freaks me out. I'm not sure how he even hears out of those cauliflower things he's got growing on the side of his head." I throw a warm up kick as Nico brings up the deflecting pads.

"Yeah, well cauliflower or not, he's got a gold medal in wrestling, and you don't. You want a real shot at Lamaro, you gotta focus, pick up as much as he can teach you in the next two weeks."

Swinging my leg high in the air, I follow the pads, striking each time with a kick almost dead on center of where I aim. Kickboxing is my strongest discipline.

"What's going on with Delilah?" My kick knocks Nico back three steps. Just the mention of my mother's name brings back years of pent up anger. Maybe I should drag her ass to the championship, sit her cage side with a pipe in her hands to keep me pissed while I take it out on Lamaro.

"Trouble, what else is new," I grumble a response, switching to alternating between leg strikes and punches.

"What did she do now?" Raising the pad higher, Nico motions for me to hit him with a series of jabs. We've been together so long, we can basically train like mutes, words unnecessary for most of our communication. Yet he always talks anyway, sticks his nose into my business. Been that way since I was a kid.

"Making bad decisions. Hanging out with losers that pull her down into their crap." I hit Nico with a series of jabs and a strong right, the momentum forcing him back into the ropes.

"Don't let her take you down with her this time. This is your chance Vinny. Chances like this don't come around too often. You're distracted, Lamaro's gonna pick up on it, deliver you a beating. You're focused, things gonna go a whole different way than the bookies are expecting." Nico takes the pads off and stills, wanting all of my attention. "You can take this guy, Vinny. Your right hook and brushing up on your technique with Kojo. You're ready. Just stay fucking focused."

Hours later, I'm standing in a puddle of my own sweat, maybe even a few of my own tears, after the torture Kojo ran me through for three straight hours. I down a liter of water and peel my still soaked shirt from the floor.

On my way up from the floor, I catch a glimpse of long shapely legs sticking out from beneath a chocolate colored skirt that makes my mouth salivate even though I'm pretty sure I'm dehydrated from my water loss. Liv. I'm surprised to see her, but it's a good surprise. I watch as Sal points her in my direction and she looks up smiling, her eyes taking in every rigid muscle of my chest, and she licks her lips unconsciously as she makes her way to me. I don't move, instead waiting for her to come to me.

"Hey." I wrap the towel around my neck.

"Ready for our road trip?" She lifts a bag I hadn't even noticed she was carrying, distracted by the sight of those legs, my mind visualizing them wrapping around my back.

Titling my head, for a half second I think perhaps I've forgotten a conversation we had, but then she smiles. It's mischievous and sweet, and makes me want to grab her and never let go. I squint, not letting her see I made up my mind she was coming the minute she smiled, pretending I'm deliberating her coming along for the ride. She stands her ground, hitching her shoulders back and readying for an argument. Her boldness turns me on. A lot.

Closing the two steps to stand in her personal space, I lean in, towering over her, my face still unreadable. Never wavering, she looks up at me through her long, thick eyelashes, the hazel color of her eyes turning deep green with conviction. Her eyes never straying from mine, I lean my sweaty forehead against hers and wrap my hand around the back of her neck, pulling her close to me. "Ten minutes, let me shower." Kissing her chastely on the lips, she smiles up at me in silent victory.

CHAPTER 39

Liv

It's a four hour drive clear across the state from Chicago to Macomb, even at the speed that Vinny drives. The early evening sky is drenched in the last of the sun. It turns the horizon in front of us a deep mix of orange and purples. Scootching close enough to lean my head on Vinny's shoulder, his arm wraps around me and pulls me even tighter.

"Do you want to talk about why we're going wherever we're going?" Tilting my head up, our eyes meet at a glance before his return to the darkening road ahead. Vinny exhales a deep breath, a long moment of silence before he finally answers.

"My mother's a drug addict. Has been as long as I can remember." My heart tightens in my chest hearing his low spoken words, even though he's confirming what I already know. "Has a habit of getting herself into trouble. This time, it's with a dealer that doesn't screw around. Not a good guy."

"What are you going to do?" There's no disguising the worry in my voice, Vinny hears it too.

"Nothing. Don't worry. I just need to find the guy who got her into this mess and drag him back." His grip on my shoulder tightens. Realizing his words just aren't doing it, he's trying to assure me with his physical strength.

"Is he dangerous?"

"To himself. He's a dirtbag. A loser. That's who I was looking for the other night when I saw Krissy."

My body stiffens just hearing her name from his lips. Vinny notices. "I'm sorry about that too. She knows him, I asked her to reach out to him. Nothing more."

Inhaling a deep breath and exhaling slowly, I admit the truth, "I know."

"You knew nothing happened?" surprised, he responds.

"Deep down I knew you were telling me the truth."

"So why did you storm out?"

Unable to keep the truth from him when he's being so open and honest, sheepishly, I come to terms with full disclosure. "I was jealous."

"Jealous, huh?" I don't have to look to know he's smiling, but I glance up at him anyway.

"What are you smiling at?" I nudge him in the ribs playfully.

"You like me." His smile widens.

"You're just figuring that out now?"

"A lot."

Rolling my eyes, even though he can't see me with his eyes on the road, "You're full of yourself."

"Maybe. But you're hot for me anyway."

Isn't it the truth?

Hours later we pull into a parking lot of a small hotel. "He's staying here?"

"No."

"Do you need to rest?"

"No. I'm checking us in so you can stay safe while I go find him."

"I want to go with you." I loathe the sound that comes from my mouth, whiney and grating.

He parks near the main entrance and reaches into the back and grabs our bags. "You're staying here where I know you're safe."

"But…"

"Liv, these people are drug addicts and dirtbags. I can't be distracted with you there and keep us both safe while I find this loser."

"So I'm a distraction?" My voice rises higher.

Hooking his arm around my neck, he pulls me close to him. "You're a big fucking distraction," he says without remorse to my face.

Insulted, I try to pull back from his grip, but my effort is fruitless. "Not so fast." There's an edge to his voice. He waits until he catches my eyes before continuing. "I'm fucking crazy about you, so yeah, you're a big damn distraction. So how about you give me this one. Cut me some slack. Because the faster I find him, the faster I can be back and show you just how much you distract me."

A strong sense of feminine satisfaction rolls over me, making me forget what I was even fighting for. Everything that came after 'I'm fucking crazy about you' unnecessary, he already had me convinced.

CHAPTER 40

Vince

Slipping the baseball bat I keep tucked underneath the seat of my truck out, I'm careful to keep quiet as I walk around the perimeter of the boarded up house that Jason's supposed to be in, assessing my new surroundings. A rancid, plasticky smell wafts through the air and confirms I'm in the right place. The unmistakable smell of crack being smoked billows from a broken window, the only one not boarded up and covered in graffiti. Squatters den. A place that people wind up when they think they've hit rock bottom, only to find there's a whole new level down they didn't even know existed.

The door creeks as I try to slip inside undetected. It's not the drug addicts I worry about, it's the trigger happy dealers desperate to protect their stash. A few candles burn lighting the way, electricity likely turned off a long time ago. There's three or four people sitting around a table with some folding chairs in the kitchen, none of them give a shit I've come in.

Two women lie half-baked on a ratty couch in the living room. One's useless, eyes rolled back into her head, she couldn't find a door in a fucking fire. The other notices me, gives a halfhearted attempt at a come-hither look and props her head up in her hand.

"You looking for something, honey?" She's probably only in her late twenties, yet her teeth are rotted brown and it looks like she hasn't had an easy life. One too many times around the block.

"Jason Buttles. Supposed to hook up with him. You see him?" Scares me how I can drop back into this life, communicate so easily.

"He's gone. Left yesterday. Said something about a sister up north he was gonna stay with. Some scary dudes came looking for him this morning too. Guess he got out just in time."

Fuck. "You know where up north?"

"Didn't say. But if you see him, tell him he still owes Felicia a pack of smokes."

Yeah, that's what I'll do when I find him…deliver your message.

I rummage through the house anyway looking for Jason, learning early in life to never trust the word of a junkie. Unfortunately a few more losers confirm Felicia's story. Reaching the last closed door on the second floor, I use the flashlight on my cell phone to guide me through the darkness.

An electronic something illuminating in the corner of the bed takes me by surprise. A boy no older than ten looks up, grabbing a long pipe resting on the bed next to him. Holding up my hands in mock surrender, I quickly scope the room looking for any other signs of danger.

"Your mother live here?" I ask, seeing garbage bags in the corner with clothes spilling out all over the floor. Suitcase of the junkie.

Putting down the game he's playing, but not the pipe, he keeps his distance, but not his manners. "None of your fucking business," he scowls, foul language rolling from his tongue like it's an ordinary occurrence.

"I'm not looking for trouble. Was looking for a friend, but I can see he's not here."

"Who's your friend?"

"Jason."

"Guys a loser." The corners of my mouth twitch, he's a hundred percent right, but the kid's got balls saying it to me.

"You're right. He is. You live here?"

"For now."

"Your mother Felicia?" I hope she is, the other one's a bigger disaster.

"Nah, that's my Mom's friend."

Damn, poor kid. "You eat?"

He shrugs his shoulders. "I'm not going anywhere with you."

I smile, smart kid. "Good. You shouldn't. I'm not a bad guy. But you don't know me."

"My mom will probably bring me something to eat later."

Saw her on the couch, not much of a chance of that happening tonight. Probably not tomorrow either, "I'll get you something. Be back in a few minutes."

Returning fifteen minutes later, no one has moved from where they lie. Knocking quietly on the door, the kid doesn't answer, but I open it anyway. I toss the bag to him on the bed, careful not to get to close. I wait as he rummages through the bag, pulling out the sandwich and ripping the paper off in a fury. God knows when the last time he really ate was.

"There's fruit in there and vitamin water. Eat it, don't trade it. And a toothbrush and toothpaste. Use it. I put a fifty in the bottom of the bag. Hide it in the clothes you're wearing. Don't leave it in your stuff. They'll smell it and it'll disappear before you can buy your next meal. Use it for food only."

I don't know if he pays any attention to my instructions, but his voice stops me on the way out. "Thank you."

The entire drive back to the hotel, I think maybe it's time I say thank you to Nico.

CHAPTER 41

Liv

Pacing the room for the hundredth time, I hear a key slip into the door and freeze. Quietly, Vinny opens the door. "Hey. You're awake."

"Of course, I'm awake. Do you think I could rest waiting for you to come home from somewhere you might get hurt?"

Tossing his keys on the desk near the door, an amused grin on his face, one of his deep creviced dimples threatens to appear, "You do know what I do for a living, right?"

"That's different." Shaking my head, refocusing on the subject that brought us across the great state of Illinois, "Did you find him?"

His playful face changes to grim. "No."

"Was anyone at the address?"

"Yeah, a whole fucking treasure trove of losers, but no Jason. He left yesterday, went up north to a sister's or something."

One eyebrow shoots upward, "Treasure trove?"

He saunters over, a cocky smirk on his face. "I had a good English tutor."

"She must have been a very good teacher." Grinning, I wrap my arms around his waist.

"I might have had a crush on her. Hot little smart girl. If all my teachers looked like her, I might've stayed in school." Wrapping his hands around the nape of my neck, Vinny leans down and crushes his mouth to mine.

Both breathless, still standing just barely inside the doorway a few minutes later, I ask, "What are we going to do now?"

"I can think of a few things." Vinny smirks and raises a brow. Kissing me gruffly on the lips, he reaches down and effortlessly scoops me up into his arms. "Come on my little distraction…distract me."

He settles on the bed, surprising me by keeping me on top of him. Seeing the familiar look of desire in his eyes, I expected to be pinned beneath him, lost to his control within seconds of hitting the bed. But he seems to cede some control tonight. Sitting with his back to the headboard, he lifts my shirt, revealing a pink lacy bra. He groans. My nipples already swollen, he swipes a thumb over each, eliciting a low moan from my throat. He dips the lacy demi cups holding my overflowing breasts slightly, allowing the pink, hard, fleshy points to protrude freely as he leans forward, catching a taut nipple with the tip of his tongue.

Arching my back to allow him greater access, he tangles my hair in his long fingers, clenches them into a ball, and pulls my head back roughly. "You want me to suck on your pretty swollen nipple?"

Breathless, I respond, "Yes."

Drawing deeply, he sucks hard on my nipple, tugging and nipping with his teeth before releasing and turning his attention to the other waiting, needy breast. His hot mouth continues to suck as his teeth nibble slow, unhurried nips around my engorged breasts.

Feeling his hardened cock grow thicker beneath me, I grind down, desperate for friction. Another low moan begins to escape me, but Vinny's mouth finds mine and stifles it beneath his kiss. Moving his mouth to my neck, his tongue trails up and down, alternating between biting and sucking.

"Are you wet for me?" His velvety voice muffled against my neck, his words are my undoing. God I love it when he talks to me like that.

"Yes," the word tumbling from my quivering lips between pants.

"Ride me." His mouth at my ear, every breath, every word, sending shivers down my spine. There is nothing more I want to do.

Realizing what he's giving me is far greater than just what it seems on the surface, I slow, cupping his face in my hands. Kissing him with purpose, full of emotion. Sensual. Seductive…everything I could give in the moment. I want him to feel me. Need him to want me. Need me. As much as I need him.

Palming my ass in his hand, Vinny lifts me enough to remove the rest of our clothing without losing contact. Reaching down between us, I pump the length of him up and down a few times, although it's hardly necessary. He's already hard as stone.

Watching me intently, Vinny grips my waist and lifts me to my knees, allowing his wide rimmed cock to sit patiently at my opening. I feel his arms tremble as he reigns in his need to control. His offering to me far greater than the actual desire to take control, locking his eyes with mine, I return what he's just given me. "Take me. Please."

Closing his eyes, he breathes deep, exhaling and opening them again, a wicked smile on his face. Pulling me down onto him as his powerful hips thrusts upward, the length of him fills me deeply. He keeps me firmly seated, rooted within the depths of my body for a long moment, looking into my eyes, searching for something.

"Love being deep inside of you," he growls before he begins a relentless pounding into me from underneath. Thrusting hard and fast, furiously he lifts me, his biceps bulging as he pulls me down to meet each and every plunge. Each time he seats me further and further, until there's not another ounce of space remaining between us.

Frantically, together we race to orgasm, him in complete control of my body, even though I'm the one rising on top. Our bodies drenched in sweat, loudly slapping into each other, our mouths desperate to touch, needing every part of our bodies connected, he kisses me hard. My orgasm hits me powerfully, taking a strong hold of my emotions, tears stream down my face as I moan through rolling waves of pleasure pulsating through my body.

As I begin to fall asleep, my head tucked into the crook of his shoulder, his arms wrapped tightly around me, I find my hand resting on his dog tags, covering his heart. There's an ache in my chest I just can't ignore anymore. This complex man protects his mother, yet has no one to protect him.

CHAPTER 42

Vinny

Nico kicked my ass today. Brought new sparring partners in from a gym across town, ones that have no power to their punch, but their hands and feet work are so fast they made my head spin. Little fuckers didn't leave me bruised, yet I feel like I did a twelve-hour day of nonstop cardio.

"Out of breath?" Nico asks, grinning as I bend over, grabbing my knees to catch my breath after finishing my last spar of the day.

"You're a sadist."

"Nah. I only enjoy watching *you* get your ass kicked." He laughs as he throws me a towel.

"How's Elle and baby Nicholas?"

"Good." Nico smiles reflectively, chuckling to himself.

"What's so funny?"

"She burned the bottle."

"Burned the bottle? I'm surprised you even let her near the stove." It's been a running joke since Nico and Elle met, the woman is smart, beautiful, funny…but put her in the kitchen and she's like a nun at a sex toy shop, scared and totally at a loss at what to do with any of the equipment.

"It was two in the morning. I guess she didn't put enough water in the pot she was using to warm the bottle. Melted the plastic. Smoke alarms, fire department…the whole nine yards." Nico smiles, clearly amused instead of upset.

"She's never gonna live this one down."

"Nope."

Laughing, together we walk to the back room for water. "Can I ask you something?"

"Shoot."

"Why Elle?"

Nico furrows his brow, confused at my question. He's not sure where the question came from and oddly, neither am I. "You went out with a lot of women." I smirk. "A lot. Think half the reason I got to the gym so early in middle school was to see what you had coming out from the night before."

Tersely, Nico replies, "You got a point to this little walk down memory lane?" He folds his arms over his chest and leans against the counter, chugging half a water bottle down in one big gulp.

The amusement draining from my face, I'm in serious need of some advice, something I rarely ask from Nico. Not from anyone for that matter. "What made you know Elle was the right one?"

He's quiet for a minute, giving his response thought before he replies, "I started to think about the future. Before Elle, I lived in the moment, never thinking past today or tomorrow. But the day I met her, I started to think about down the road…and every thought, every plan I made in my head, she was standing by my side."

I nod. Thinking a few months ago I wasn't even sure what I was doing at night as I got on my bike to go out. Yet this morning, as my mind wandered, I realized my lease would be up in six months, and I found myself wondering if maybe it would be time to move. Find a nicer place, one that Liv would like, possibly even want to share with me.

Nico waits, watching as I give his words some thought, I see a knowing grin rising to the surface. "You running on the treadmill or lifting every time you find yourself thinking of the future with Liv?"

I chuckle to myself, he's so god damn right. "Running." I smile.

Tossing our water bottles in the garbage, Nico slaps one hand on my shoulder as we head toward the door, turning off the lights as we pass through each room. "Eventually, you'll be so exhausted from all the running, you'll just give in."

CHAPTER 43

Liv

The office I once loved walking into, with a feeling of pride and accomplishment consuming me, now relegated to Monday morning dread. My co-worker hates me, glares and sneers at me at every conceivable opportunity, my boss is a dreadful, leering sleezeball. All the honor and journalistic pride I felt starting this journey, crushed beneath the weight of the story I've been assigned.

"How's the story coming, Olivia?" Summer smiles at me. I'm not sure if she's grown ugly in the last two months, but I can no longer remember what I saw in her that I was jealous of when I first started. Her natural, glowing beauty disappeared, replaced by fake, stale, formulaic tricks to attract attention.

Ignoring her completely, I make my way into Sleezeball's office for our Monday morning team meeting. Our sorry excuse for a team is one with only two players and a coach whose sole purpose is to get in our pants, rather than mentor us to watch our careers grow and prosper.

"Ladies. How are we today?" he asks, but doesn't wait for a response. Mostly because he doesn't really care. He exhales loudly, feigning remiss. "I'm really going to miss our Monday mornings together. Just a few more weeks and our little trio will become a couple." Is this supposed to be motivation for winning the job? Because it's making me feel like losing might not be such a bad thing after all. A lesser job a thousand miles away in New York is starting to sound appealing.

"I need both of your final stories two weeks from today." Leaning back in his chair, he folds his arms over his chest and smiles at both of us, raising an eyebrow, almost daring us to complain.

"No problem, James. Mine will be ready. I had to scrap the fluff that was started, but my new research brought me a great new angle for the story. I think you'll be very happy with it." As she speaks, Summer slowly crosses and recrosses her legs, her barely professional length skirt hiking up a tiny bit more each time, a clearly calculated move. One that Sleezeball falls for, hook, line, and sinker. Of course.

"Wonderful, I'd expect nothing less from you, Summer," he leers. "You've really shown us what an asset you can be." Yeah, she's shown her assets alright.

Begrudgingly, Sleezeball turns his attention to me after a minute, but only because I'm speaking and he's forced to. "I'll have your story ready."

Almost salivating at the thought of the story I'll be bringing him, his smile makes my skin crawl. "I can't wait to sink my teeth into your story, Olivia. Can't wait."

Heart heavy in my chest, I spend the morning working on the background for my story. I pray I'll never need to hand it in, but I need to get words on paper nonetheless. I start with Senator Knight, still unable to bring myself to write anything at all about Vinny. Guilt consumes me. My mind wanders, looking back at the last month I wonder where I went wrong. How did I let myself grow so attached to a man that may soon hate me? Is this really what I worked for? The chance to write stories that will sell papers, at the cost of tearing apart lives? Have I just been naïve all along, putting my journalistic role models up on pedestals as noble, when they're really only ink slinging exploiters?

By lunchtime I'm in desperate need of fresh air, my brain clogged with questions for which I have no answers. Feeling everything I dreamed about my whole life might just be a sham, I feel lost. Like the weight of the world I built up in my head is coming down to crush my dreams.

Outside the gloomy, gray day seems fitting, as if the universe is in sync with my feelings. Caught up in my head, at first I'm startled as a strong arm grabs me from behind, pulling me into the alleyway just a half a block away from my intended lunch destination. But something familiar hits me, and for a few short seconds, I think it's Vinny being playful. Then my arm's wrenched back further, causing pain to shoot from my shoulder to my wrist, and I realize I'm wrong...Vinny would never hurt me.

One of the hands gripping me moves to cover my mouth and the other locks both my hands in one of his, using a shoulder to slam my back into a brick wall. Hard. The force knocks the wind right out of me.

"What kind of a game do you think you're playing, Miss Michaels?" My eyes widen to find Senator Knight's face inches from mine, scathing anger mars his normally perfectly refined features, his practiced smile nowhere to be found.

His hand tightly over my mouth, I couldn't respond if I wanted to, although it doesn't take long to realize he wasn't expecting a response.

"My life has value. Unlike that drug addict and her violent spawn. If you think you can just waltz in and destroy me, you're sadly mistaken. No one will give a shit if they were to be lost in a tragic accident. Do you understand me?" He increases the pressure on his hand covering my mouth.

I stare, frozen in place, unable or unsure if I'm expected to respond this time.

"Do you understand me?" he screams loudly, his eyes wild, our faces nose to nose. It's not the volume that scares me, it's the anger and desperation in his voice that makes me believe his words are more than just a threat. I shake my head as much as I can with his hand still pressed to my mouth, pinning me against and the wall.

"And this time, I won't show any mercy." His voice is so detached, there's no question in my mind that he's capable of what he promises. Senator Knight's hand at my mouth loosens slightly, "Kill the story. Or whatever happens is on *you*."

Releasing me from his grip, he stands tall, straightening his suit and running his hands through his hair to tame the few strands that dared fall out of place. The smile I'd met when I interviewed him slips back into position. An icy chill sweeps over my body at how easily this man can transform. Taking one step back, he smiles at me, every bit the perfect politician the world thinks he is. "Good day, Miss Michaels," he nods his head and turns.

I watch from the alley, still unable to move from where he held me against the wall, as a dark town car pulls up to the curb just as he exits the alleyway. Opening the back door, he gracefully steps in and never looks back. The entire two minute exchange is so surreal, it makes me wonder if I've just dreamt it.

CHAPTER 44

Liv

It's been two days since Senator Knight's visit, yet I still can't get his threats out of my head. Sometimes my heart tells me one thing, and my head tells me another, leaving me conflicted as to how I'm supposed to feel. Senator Knight's visit did not leave me feeling there was any room to wonder if his threats were serious. My heart and head both in agreement, his words were not a veiled threat. They were a promise. One I'm certain he would make good on and then go about his day as if whatever heinous acts he has committed, never even happened.

I need to take my mind off of work for a little while, the only problem is that my work and personal life have become so tightly entwined, it's difficult to know where one starts and the other ends. Two days without seeing Vinny leaves me feeling anxious and sad, I can't imagine what a lifetime would do to me.

Walking into the restaurant where I'm supposed to meet Ally for drinks before dinner with Vinny, I'm surprised to find her waiting with her brother Matthew.

"Hey," I smile and greet Matthew, who stands as I approach. "This is a nice surprise. Ally didn't tell me she was bringing her bodyguard." Matthew's five years older, he's always been our protector. Only now it's official, since he's a detective with the Chicago PD.

"Someone's gotta keep an eye on you ladies." Matthew leans

down and kisses me on the cheek. "Plus, she talked me into driving her here."

"Driving her here? It's only a six block walk," I question, as I shrug off my jacket, which Matthew is behind me to quietly take. Such a gentleman, he reminds me a lot of his dad. When I was little, I remember going places with the Landry's and always loving the way Mr. Landry jogged around the car to open Mrs. Landry's door for her. It's funny the things you take away from watching adults as a child that stick with you.

"I can't walk six blocks in these." Ally points down to her black open toe shoes. Silver buckles adorn the front, clasping the black leather material together from just above the toes to high on the ankle. The inside of the six inch heel is a bright girly pink, a stark contrast to the sleek, rockeresque shoe you see from the front.

"I don't get why she buys shoes she can't walk more than a few steps in," Matthew says, smiling and shaking his head. Turning his attention to the bartender pouring drinks at the other end of the long bar, he motions with a simple wave of his hand for her to come over. "Still drinking cheap wine?" He looks to me for confirmation and I nod and smile.

Leaning on her brother's shoulder, Ally responds to Matthew's earlier comment, "I wear them because they're hot."

"Creepy Al. My sister's shoes can never be hot. Nothing about my sister is hot."

"Bet you would think they were hot on Liv." She teases, something catching her attention from the other end of the bar, Ally waves to a guy with a goatee. "I'm gonna go say hi, he's in one of my classes. Watch as my shoes work their magic."

A full hour goes by and Ally never glances back in our direction... so much for happy hour drinks with my best friend. Although it gives Matthew and me a chance to catch up. It's been a long time since we've really talked. When Ally and I first moved in together, he helped us move and then even came by a few times with his girlfriend Brie.

"How's Brie?"

Matthew shrugs, "Over."

"What happened, she seemed really nice?"

"She was. Just wasn't there." His face sincere, almost saddened at the recollection, Matthew draws a long pull on his beer and sets it down on the bar. "Can't control it, although life would be a hell of a lot easier if you could."

"You can say that again." I finish my second glass of wine.

"Ally mentioned you were seeing someone. Not the one you would have picked for yourself?"

Vinny's familiar sexy voice startles me from behind, there's a hard edge to his words. "I'd like to hear the answer to that question too."

Swallowing hard, I turn in my bar stool to find Vinny standing less than a foot away, positioned in the middle of the two chairs that Matthew and I fill. He looks angry, hands turning to fists at his sides, torn between coming to me and tearing apart the man I'm sitting next to.

Matthew stands, his naturally authoritative posture firmly in place. The silent gesture serves only to challenge Vinny's already heated temper. Realizing the need to quickly diffuse whatever is beginning to brew, I stand and wave the white flag of surrender, turning my full attention to Vinny and laying my hands flat on his chest, brushing my lips softly over his.

"Hi."

Glancing at Matthew and back to me, Vinny asks, "Who's your friend?"

Stepping back, my kiss erasing some of the anger from his face, yet far from all, I introduce the two men. "This is Ally's brother, Matthew."

"Matthew, this is..."

"Vince Stone." Matthew finishes my sentence for me.

"You know him from watching fights?" My eyebrows draw together in confusion.

"Sort of."

What the hell kind of an answer is that? It's a yes or no kind of question. "Sort of?" I repeat back to him, waiting for a further explanation.

"Broke up a fight last year in a bar, almost arrested him for busting some loudmouth's nose."

Vinny's jaw clenches and his eyes close in reflection. He hadn't recognized Matthew. Opening his eyes, he nods to Matthew, "A lot's changed in a year."

"I hope so." Matthew looks between Vinny and me. "She's like a sister to me."

Raking his hands through his hair, Vinny turns to me, his jaw tight as he stares into my eyes. "Ready?"

Knowing I needed to tread lightly, I nod quietly and smile at Matthew, careful not to offer him an opening for our usual kiss goodbye. Something in Vinny's posture just tells me Matthew's lips on me wouldn't be a good idea. Vinny's hand grips my hip possessively and I thank Matthew for the drinks before moving to the restaurant for dinner.

"Are you upset with me?" Vinny's been quiet since we sat down, but that's not what stirs a knot in my belly, making it difficult for me to relax. It's the unspoken that speaks volumes to me, things that an outsider wouldn't even pick up on. He didn't order for me, or sit on my side of the table, not even a borderline inappropriate kiss to mark his normally visible territory.

"Should I be?" His eyes lock-on to mine.

"Of course not. Matthew's like my brother."

"I'm not worried about him."

"Then what is it?"

"What's the answer to his question, Liv?" There's no need to ask him to clarify the question he's referring to. He wants to know if my head is aligned with my heart. Would I have picked him for myself if my heart hadn't made up its mind? I wish I could hide my response, but he's good at reading me, sees my answer written on my face.

Closing his eyes, almost as if accepting a punishment he deserves, a small nod causes my heart to sink in my chest. Reaching for his hand, I finally respond with words, "I don't think it matters what we plan for ourselves. Some things in life are just too powerful to change."

Vinny's mood lifted slightly, we laugh as we walk back to his place. I'm tipsy from a third glass of wine with dinner, although Vinny's strong arm wrapped around me keeps me feeling steady. "Do you remember the afternoon we worked on Romeo and Juliet in the park and we took turns reading the parts?"

"Remember? How could I forget? I was sitting up against the tree, and your head was resting on my lap about three inches from my crotch. I had no idea what any of the words you were saying meant, but I liked looking down and watching you...the way your mouth moved. I kept having to shift to keep my dick from poking you in the eye," Vinny teases.

Stopping as we reach his building, I turn and face him, reaching up and wrapping my hands around his neck. The alcohol leaving me feeling bold, I press up on my tippy toes and bring my mouth to his ear. "I went home and touched myself that night. Masturbated for the first time, with a picture of you in my head as I closed my eyes," I whisper seductively into his ear.

With a growl, Vinny lifts me, tossing me over his shoulder like a sack of potatoes, and races up the stairs taking them two at a time.

Unlocking the door in a frenzy, he kicks the door shut with his foot, and carries me to his bedroom, gently setting me down at the foot of the bed.

He steps back, drinking me in in a way that makes my insides shudder with anticipation. The way he looks at me, hungry...ravenous with need, makes my blood course through my veins with fury and every sensor on my body goes on high alert, even though he hasn't even touched me.

"Show me," he commands, his sexy as sin voice low, guttural in a way that affects me way more than any sound ever should impact a person.

Looking up at him, I know what he wants, yet I look for confirmation anyway. "Show you?" I ask, my voice a whisper.

"Show me how you touched yourself that night." His voice is still raspy, but more demanding this time. He knows the command in his voice does something to me. Something I can't even explain. It creates a need to obey when he talks to me like that.

"Take off your clothes." I do, my hands shaky as I unzip my skirt, allowing it to pool at my feet. Removing my top, I stand in just my black lacy bra and panties, and look up at him under long, hooded lashes.

"The rest of it too." I slip out of the rest of my clothes, standing before him wearing only my earrings and a long white gold chain with a big heart locket that hangs between my breasts, coming down to dangle near my navel.

Slowly, Vinny's eyes rake over me, making me feel warm. Beautiful. Appreciated. His beautiful baby blues reach mine and hold my gaze as he speaks. "Sit at the top of the bed, back against the headboard."

I comply, feeling a bit hesitant with him still standing at the foot of the bed, fully dressed, but I force myself to do it anyway. The desire to please him becomes stronger with each spoken command.

"Spread your legs," he continues. I hesitate at the thought of sitting so completely bared to him. Looking up at him, he senses my need, "Do it."

Slowly, almost sheepishly, I open my legs, spread only a foot or so wide, yet enough to allow him to see me.

"Wider."

Taking a deep breath in, I glide my legs across the bed, as wide as I can manage without causing physical discomfort. The smile on his face tells me I've pleased him. It helps shed the feeling of being utterly exposed.

He takes a step closer, but still remains at the foot of the bed, "Show me, Beautiful. How did you touch yourself thinking of me that night?"

My eyes dart to his, his strong, unwavering desire fueling me, pushing me to give him what he wants. Slowly, I bring my hand up to my nipple. My fingernail trailing tentatively across the sensitive pink flesh makes my already swollen nipple harden more. I close my eyes, allowing myself to relax into the heady feeling that touching myself brings.

Raising my hand to my mouth, I wet my fingers before returning them to my nipple to rub small circles. The cool air meets with my wet arousal and a low, throaty moan escapes as my need ratchets up, fingers pinching my sensitive nipple hard until I feel a jolt straight down to my already swollen clit.

Opening my eyes, I find Vinny unmoved, his eyes hooded, glazed over with need as he watches my hands work myself intently. Making their way up to find me, his eyes dark and hot, they lock with mine. I take a deep breath, my courage fueled by the desire I find reflected back at me, slowly I let my hand glide smoothly over my body. I watch as Vinny's eyes follow, locked to my drifting hand. Watching him, unable to tear his eyes from my hand as I touch myself, is as much, if not more, of a turn on than the actual act of my touching.

My two fingers gently find my clit, applying pressure as they make slow rhythmic circles. Each turn transmits a small burst of electricity that shoots through my nerves, my body becoming electrified at my own touch.

My desire intensifying, I feel the unmistakable tightening at my core. I need more. Shutting my eyes again and pushing back hard on any feeling of inhibition and shyness still lurking in the corner of my brain, I drop my fingers lower, circling my wet entrance slowly. I gasp as I push two fingers into myself, my body slick, coated with my own juices.

Vinny growls, the sound making my body begin to contract and my orgasm begins to build. No longer hesitant, my fingers begin pumping into myself, wet and needy. Slow pumps turn quickly into deep plunging thrusts and I moan as my fingers slip in and out, in and out, desperate to feel filled, the way my body does only when Vinny's inside of me.

I'm vaguely aware of the sound of a zipper and movement, although I'm too intent on finding my own release for anything to really register.

"Open your eyes," Vinny says with a low, thick voice, but one that's still clear it's an order and not a request. I comply.

"I want to be inside you when you come. As much as I fucking love watching you touch yourself, I'm even jealous of *you* bringing yourself to orgasm instead of me." Possessively, he grabs my waist, dragging me down the bed, and positions himself over me. "Eyes open. You come with *me* inside of you," he coaxes as he spears into me, his cock thick and hard.

"Does it feel better when I'm inside you?" He groans as he sets a frenzied pace, pushing deeply into me and pulling out almost to the tip each time.

"Yes."

"Tell me, who makes you come?"

"You," I whimper, my body trembling as the power of my orgasm takes hold.

"So fucking beautiful." Vinny crushes his mouth to mine, as I moan his name over and over, my orgasm hitting me like a blow. Wave after wave of pulse pounding, uncontrollable spasms grip him inside of me. Still riding the last of the aftershocks, I feel the heat of Vinny's release spill into me as he pushes into me so deeply it leaves me feeling like he wants a piece of him to stay deep inside of me forever.

CHAPTER 45

Vince

I've never been a morning person, but waking up to Liv's naked ass might help change that. I'm just about to show her how much I enjoy the view, when my phone rings on the end table.

Reaching over, I'm ready to hit REJECT. Who gives a shit who it is, they can wait. Until I see the name and picture come up on my phone. It's worse than throwing a bucket of cold water over me. My mother. She never calls, especially at 8AM on a Saturday. I get the pang of unease in the core of my gut.

"What's up?"

"Can you stop over today so we can talk?"

"Yeah, everything okay?" She sounds sober, that alone sends up a red flag, oddly enough.

"I'm fine. I just need some help in figuring things out." Her voice cracks. "I'm sorry to bother you. I know I don't have any right to ask you for anything, but…" Her voice trembles as it trails off.

"I'll be there in an hour. We'll be fine. Don't worry."

Tossing the phone back on the table, I scrub my hands over my face and lie on my back, taking a deep cleansing breath to try to relax.

"You okay?" Liv's sweet voice whispers, I didn't realize she was awake. Planting a soft kiss on my pec, she rests her head on my chest and wraps her arm around my stomach, snuggling in tightly. I fucking love the way it feels. Used to hate women touching me, outside of sex. Didn't see the point of lying in bed with someone else unless we were working toward one of us, or both, getting off. Yet now I lie here wanting to do nothing else but run my fingers through her hair and feel the warmth of her cheek against my chest. Fuck, I'm becoming whipped. Turning into the same sap I watched Nico turn into, and made fun of every step of the way.

"My mother. She wants me to come by."

"She didn't say why?"

"Nope. But something's up. She doesn't call unless there's trouble."

"Can I come?"

"You want to come?"

"Sure, I'd love to meet your mom."

Why? I wish I could forget I ever met her. "If you want."

"I do."

"Then okay. Told her I'd be there in an hour…so we have about half an hour to kill." I flip her over on her back. She laughs and giggles as I toss her around. The sound makes me smile. So fucking whipped.

"Mom?" I'm surprised when I let myself into her apartment that she's not in her usual place…on the couch, in front of the TV

She comes out from the bedroom, not looking too bad. "Hi, Baby." She's too skinny, needs some color on her face, but at least she seems lucid this morning. And her clothes might even be clean. Is today a holiday and I forgot?

Taking Liv's hand, I bring her into the living room. It smells of stale cigarettes and a lifetime of spilled shit that rotted under the carpet because she was too wasted to clean it up.

My mother looks at Liv and then me, a look of confusion on her face. I'm not sure why…I've brought women to her house lots of time. A different one each month for the years seventeen through nineteen, before I finally moved out.

"This is Olivia."

Liv smiles and walks to greet my mother with her hand extended. Such a class act, I feel like an idiot for bringing her here. "Hi Mrs. Stonetti, it's really nice to meet you." Her smile is genuine, I can tell. Although I'm not sure why, seeing as I would much rather be anywhere but here at this moment.

"Nice to meet you too, Olivia." My mom smiles at Olivia and then back to me. I hadn't given it any thought until now, but it's been a very long time since I saw that smile. Too long.

The three of us sit, my mother taking her usual spot on the couch, Liv and I sitting together on the love seat across from her. "What's going on Mom?"

Pensively, she looks between me and Liv, not saying anything, clearly unsure if she should air her dirty laundry.

"It's fine, Liv knows what's going on," I reassure her.

"The two guys were back. Said they haven't been able to find Jason and I only have a few days left. I'm sorry for burdening you with this, all I ever do is cause you grief." Tears well in her eyes. "I just don't know what to do. I can't find him anywhere."

Exhaling loudly, I fill her in. "He's up north. Has a sister up there."

"How do you know?"

"Liv and I went on a road trip, had a lead on where to find him. He was gone by the time we got there. But the losers he was staying with said he went to hide out at his sister's. That's if you take the word of a bunch of lowlife drug addicts."

My mother winces. It's not nice, but it's the truth…that's what they are. Untrustworthy, crackhead, fucking losers. Liv's hand goes to my thigh and squeezes to get my attention. Turning to look at her, she gives me a look of admonishment.

"I'll go talk to them. See if we can get more time. Loser's bound to resurface when he burns his bridge with the sister. Shouldn't take too long for him to burn through all his support and snake his way back here."

A little while later, back in my truck, Liv's quiet. Until she's not. "Can't you be a little nicer? She's your mother?"

She's gotta be kidding me. "I've been the parent since I was old enough to carry her to bed at night, Liv. She doesn't get special consideration. This isn't the first time I've dragged her ass out from trouble, and it won't be the last."

"I know. It's just…"

"No. You don't know," I cut her off. "You grew up in your little perfect family, with your perfect grades and your nice life. You have no idea, so don't tell me you know anything."

CHAPTER 46

Liv

Vinny and I left off in an odd place yesterday. I'd given him time to cool off, thinking he'd come around and realize that, although he's probably right telling me I didn't understand his relationship with his mom, I was only trying to help. But I never heard from him last night, and this morning I knew he'd be at the gym early for the first half of his two-part workout.

My stomach growls, reminding me it's almost noon, although just the thought of walking to lunch alone makes me almost forget my appetite. The memory of Senator Knight grabbing me is still fresh in my head. The man scares me. Desperation makes good people do bad things. I don't even want to think what it does to bad people. I skipped dinner last night, my hunger waned as I reflected on my argument with Vinny, my own guilt always guiding my thoughts, spiraling my emotions out of control.

Walking through the glass turnstile on my way to lunch, I catch a glimpse of something that makes my heart stop. Parked at the curb, leaning against his motorcycle, ankles crossed casually, a big bouquet of brightly colored flowers held up in his hand, waits Vinny. Every female head turns at the sight of him, some of the males even stopping to stare too.

The man's just so damn ridiculously sexy. He's wearing nothing but a white t-shirt and jeans that hang perfectly on his narrow waist, his hair a natural mess that people pay big money just to look like a knock off of the real thing. Standing a few yards away from me *is* the real thing. The one that others try to copy. Day old scrub, a shit eating grin with playful, deep creviced dimples, complete with sparkling blue eyes that pin you in place.

"Looking for someone?" I ask. He grins cheekily as I approach.

"Yeah, my girlfriend. She's probably pissed at me for being an asshole. You seen her around?"

Pointing down the block, I play along. "I think she went that way."

Vinny grabs my extended arm and pulls me to him, taking both my hands in one of his and holding it behind my back. "Forgive me?" He kisses me sweetly on the lips.

Smiling wryly, I respond, "You think I'm easy. A sexy smile and some flowers?"

"You think my smile's sexy?" The dimples grow deeper.

Rolling my eyes, I reply, "You only hear the parts that you want to hear."

Pulling me closer, he arches his eyebrows. "I want to hear you moan my name when we have makeup sex," he says too loudly.

"Shhhhhh!" I look around and see a few heads turn.

"You don't like when I say *sex* in public?" He practically yells the word sex. The streets are filled in Downtown Chicago at lunchtime. I feel my skin blush as more people look on.

"Okay, okay. I forgive you. Now please be quiet."

He smiles triumphantly and pulls my hand to take me to lunch, carrying the flowers that gets him even more attention than usual the whole time.

Walking me to the entrance of my building after lunch, he makes me feel like a teenager being walked to the door of their house with her dad watching on after the end of a date. He kisses me, uncaring that the world goes on around us, likely gawking and feeling uncomfortable at the passionate private display made public. Handing me the flowers he's been carrying for the last hour, he smiles as he smacks me on the ass as I walk away.

"Hi Summer." Vinny winks at me as I turn back when I hear him greet her. At first I think he's kidding, but there's no mistaking the unhappy face that whips past me, flustered from his smile.

CHAPTER 47

Vinny

Never in my life have I thought about wanting to win a fight to impress a woman. Don't get me wrong, I know in the past winning was the foreplay to some of my hookups, but it was never *why* I wanted to win. Until now. My fight next week isn't just for me, I want Liv to be proud of who I am. Shit's changing for me. The way I feel, the way I look at things. Brings me new motivation, also scares the crap out of me at the same time.

I'm still at the gym an hour after my training ended. Running on the treadmill, doing extra cardio...shit I used to think was punishment. But I want to be ready. So I push a little harder, stay a little longer, think smarter.

Pushing the button to move from a run to a walk for my warm down, I wrap the towel around my neck and catch sight of a woman I don't expect to walk in. Sal, the guy at the door, points her in my direction with a dirty grin and a wiggle of his eyebrows, and I watch as she struts her way over to me. She's definitely used to men enjoying the show. But this show is a repeat, one I've watched way too often, and it bores me before she even comes to stand before me.

"Hi Vince," her voice purrs from beneath shimmering glossy lips.

"Summer." I nod curtly. I know the deal. To a girl like her, I'm a game, one she would like to play with to piss off the woman who sits next to her. *My* woman. Not gonna happen.

"Do you think we can talk a few minutes?" She tilts her head to the side in an attempt at coy.

"Kinda busy. What do you need, Summer?"

Looking from left to right before speaking, she leans in, lowering her voice, even though she just confirmed for herself that no one's within earshot. "I'm helping Olivia on her story. Just wanted to ask you a few things."

"Her story was already printed weeks ago. What could you be helping her with?" The alarm on the treadmill rings, signaling the end of my warm down. For a second, I consider setting it for a few more miles, just to make it more difficult for her to stay and talk at me. But I'm supposed to pick up Liv in an hour anyway, so I don't. Instead I jump off and fold my arms over my chest, showing my lack of interest and impatience in my posture.

"Oh, not the first story. The one she's working on now."

"I don't know what you're talking about Summer, but I'm in a rush to pick up Liv, so can you get to the point?" I'm not pretending to be impatient for effect, I am impatient. She needs to go.

"The story about," she pauses, and looks around. Again with the looking around to see if the coast is clear? What the fuck drama queen? And then she whispers, "you know, your real father."

An hour later, I'm at Liv's door. I pace for a few seconds before I knock, my mind racing. Liv would never use me. Would she? That boney ass bitch has to be making this shit up, probably pissed because I didn't give her the attention she wanted...trying to get even with Liv. Every ounce of my body wants to believe everything she said was a lie, yet the gnawing feeling in the pit of my stomach is screwing with my head. Big time.

Eventually I grow a pair and knock on the door. Liv answers and smiles, she looks genuinely happy to see me. Can I be that big of an idiot that I'm seeing what I want to see? Her smile disappears when she takes in my face.

"What's wrong?" Her voice is laced with concern.

"Can I come in?"

"Of course." She steps aside, and quietly closes the door behind me.

I can't even muster up small talk, I get right into it, not two feet inside her apartment. "Summer came to see me."

Liv's jaw tenses and I pray it's jealousy and not nervousness, but I can't tell. "Okaaaay." She draws the word out slowly.

"She said you're working on another story about me. Is it true?" I look right into her eyes as I speak. Her reaction tears me in two. It rips my heart out and stomps it on the god damn ground. She doesn't respond. I begin to lose my patience. And my ability to control myself.

"Answer me!" I yell loudly. She jumps, my angry voice taking her by surprise.

"It's not what you think," she whispers. Tears fill her eyes.

"Answer the fucking question, Liv." My eyes bore into hers. She stares blankly back at me, no response. "Answer the FUCKING QUESTION!"

"Yes...but..."

"Are you fucking kidding me?" I stop her before she finishes. The adrenaline pumps through my body, unclenching my balled up fists, I run my fingers anxiously through my hair. I feel like a lion in a cage, only there's no restraints holding me here, not physical ones anyway.

"I'm sorry." The waterworks turn on. "I never meant for you to find out this way. I was trying to protect you."

Years of letdowns leave my mind trained to jump to protective mode, my hurt turns to anger. "I don't need anyone to protect me." Breathing labored, I seethe at her. "I don't need *you* to protect me."

"You don't understand." She should be an actress, she's so god damn good at this. Her face looks pained and her body trembles as the tears roll down her face.

"No, Liv, that's where you're wrong. I finally *do* understand. You're just like the rest of them." My maniacal laugh scaring even me, I need to get the hell out of here before I do something I'll regret. I reach for the door, yank it open so hard it almost tears from the hinges, and turn back. "You could have just told me you wanted to take it out in trade. I probably would have agreed to it anyway, I wanted to fuck you so badly." I lean down, my face in hers, so close I hear her breaths as she silently sobs. "At least the other whores are up front when they use me." It takes every bit of willpower to walk out the door. But I do. And I don't look back.

So much for my dedication, I walk into the gym three hours late and hungover. Maybe even still a little drunk from the night before. Or was it this morning when I stopped drinking? I have no idea, since I smashed my clock. And my phone. And a whole bunch of other shit when I flipped my dresser in my last drunken tirade.

"Where the hell have you been?" Nico scolds the minute I get past the front desk.

"Out."

"You don't answer your phone?"

"It broke." When I threw it against the fucking wall.

"This have anything to do with the girl I saw come in last night?" Nico questions disapprovingly.

"Yeah, but it's not what you think."

"Listen to me." Nico stands before me, putting one hand on each shoulder. "You're too close to screw this up. Whatever's going on, deal with it quick or tap it down. There's no time for games."

"Got it," I growl through clenched teeth. "I was a little late, don't blow it up into something more." I push his hands off my shoulders.

Brows furrowed, eyes squinting, Nico assesses me. "Go do five miles, clear your head. Then we'll start."

Half an hour later, the remnants of last night's alcohol sweated out through my pores, my buzz has turned into the start of a rip-roaring headache. Although the pain feels good. I strap on my headgear and climb into the ring where Alex waits for me. He's one of my sparring partners, but he thinks he's better than he is and he doesn't know how to keep his mouth shut. Today I'm in no god damn mood for his mouth.

Jumping up and down a few times to get my blood pumping, I wait as Alex clasps his own headgear. "That your new woman I saw come in last night?"

"No." I answer shortly, hoping he'll take the hint. No such damn luck.

"You still seeing that other one? The writer?" I throw a one-two jab combination, which he catches, but barely.

"No." The simple one syllable word burns my throat as I speak it.

Alex grins, even his smile at my response pisses me off, although it's his words that send me over the edge. "If you're done, can I get her number? What an ass on that one."

Like a bull being taunted, I see red. My body full of testosterone and mind angry, nothing could stop me. I take him down in one punch he didn't even see coming. So full of rage, it takes me over, possessing me past the point of no return as I pound blow after forceful blow straight into his face while he's pinned to the mat. By the time the four guys trying to wrestle me off of him are successful, the poor asshole's face is a bloody mess.

The half full gym backs away from me, no one dares come within twenty feet. Except Nico. Fucker never did know when to keep his distance.

"You done? Hope you enjoyed yourself, because you aren't going to be able to lift your arms by the time I'm done putting you through the ringer today." He pauses, taking a step closer to me, standing nose to nose. "Get your ass to the bag. Twelve three-minute strike rounds. One minute between. Max."

Any normal fighter, even one in the most pristine shape, would be soaking in a hot tub after the intensity of the workout Nico ran me through today. But not me. Adrenaline still pumping wildly through my veins like a current through wire, I head back out on my bike after a quick shower. I need to stop thinking. Need to forget. Stop feeling for a little while. It's been a while since I went GIMP trolling, but not long enough to forget what I need to clear my head. A little power fucking till I can't see straight ought to do the trick.

Stopping at the light, I look up at the looming building towering over me as I settle my feet to the ground to wait. *Daily Sun Times*. The urge to run my bike through the plate glass window is so strong, I have to fight myself to stay in place. Something burns a hole in my front pocket, itching at me from the depths of my mind, till I dig in and pull out a card with an address scribbled on it. Summer Langley. I turn left instead of heading straight.

She answers the door with only a skimpy robe and a smile, and steps aside for me to enter. No words are exchanged, although I know the smile well. She may look classier, have more window dressing than the average GIMP down at Flannigan's, yet she's the same nonetheless. Has no idea who I am, doesn't even want to try to find out. Prefers the idea of me in her mind to the reality. Usually I'm more than happy to play the game. But tonight...tonight I'm here to get what I need.

Exhausted from lack of sleep, my body desperate for rest, I pry myself from the bed against the protest of every aching muscle in my arms and legs. I'm sure Nico thinks I'm gonna no-show today, be too weak to train after the rigor he put my body through yesterday, but I'm too stubborn to give him the satisfaction of thinking he's right. So I take an extra ten minutes in the shower, allowing the scalding hot water to run over my aches, before I head out early. I need to stop and check in on the only other woman that I've allowed to cause me real pain.

Grabbing for the door knob, it turns before I put the key in. Not a good sign. When she's wasted she's careless with her own self-preservation. I'm surprised to find her awake and alert, sitting on the couch, smoking a cigarette. A full ashtray in front of her. Not her usual two dirtbags sitting opposite her on the couch, the dynamic duo is back. These two look better than most, but looks can be deceiving. They're more trouble than anything she's ever gotten herself into before.

The shorter of the two, the one that does most of the talking, spots me first. He opens his jacket ever so slightly, silently reminding me of who's in charge before I can even open my mouth.

"What's going on, Ma?" The room is so quiet, I hear the draw she takes on the cigarette. She's smoked it so low she's inhaling the filter, not far off from burning her fingers.

Closing her eyes, she smiles at me. It's a face that apologizes at the same time it tells me she's glad I'm here. "They found Jason."

Exhaling a deep breath, I feel a small sense of relief. Although it doesn't last long.

"Dead. Overdose," the gun carrying drug dealer says to me stoically.

Great, just fucking great. I hang on for dear life, desperately needing someone...anyone...to catch the lifeline I'm throwing out. "The drugs or cash happen to turn up next to the body?"

Slowly, he shakes his head back and forth in silence.

Of course not, what was I thinking? This is my life, land of the 'I don't fucking believe this shit' for the last twenty odd years. "So what now? You're out 200 K." I look to my mom who watches me and I see her wince at my next words. "You kill her, you're still out 200 K. Gets you nothing, except now you gotta watch over your shoulder every minute of every day. Because I'll snap your neck when you least expect it." I stare unwavering into the eyes of a man that has killed before.

It's a funny thing that happens when you feel like you have nothing else to lose. Everything that you say cuts right to the chase. No more taking time to deliberate, think about how to cushion your words. Because you don't give a flying fuck what someone thinks anymore.

Eyes locked, me and the drug dealing boss stare at each other for long minutes, neither one of us cracking, not a flinch between us. Then he stands and what looks like a real smile crosses his face and he chuckles while he shakes his head. "I really like you kid. You're either crazier than I thought you were, or you got balls made of titanium." He slips the sunglasses from where they are hooked on his shirt and positions them over his eyes. "Think it might be a little of both." He pauses. "So here's what I'm gonna do. I'm not gonna kill your mother. I give you my word on that." His smile widens. "But I'm gonna cut off a few fingers, maybe even some toes just for the fun of it. Then I'm gonna blind her. And fuck her up so badly that she'll *wish* she was dead. But she won't be. She'll live. And the burden for taking care of the mess that remains every day for the rest of her life...that'll be on you."

My hands ball into fists at my sides and I watch his eyes drop to see I'm just about to blow. The taller guy stands and moves to his side, a silent declaration of support. "But like I said kid, I like you. And I don't want that to happen. So here's what we're gonna do. We're gonna place some big bets. And you're gonna lose that fight next week." He nods his head. "Then we'll call it even."

One hand on his waistband, holding what's beneath his shirt, he walks to me and places a hand on my shoulder. "Got that?"

And then they're gone.

CHAPTER 48

Liv

I don't want to cry anymore. Sitting on the couch with Ally, I rehash everything in my head for the thousandth time, only this time I speak my thoughts aloud. Finally. Two days curled up in the fetal position alternating between crying and sleeping scared her. Scared me. I feel bad for making her worry. Never in my wildest dreams would I have thought losing a man would affect me so profoundly. Although Vinny's not any man, and the loss affects me deeply. I finally own up to why.

"I'm in love with him, Ally." A trail of dried tears stains my face, my eyes puffy and nose Rudolph red against my pale skin. Perhaps the well has run dry, I'm ready to talk now, words without tears.

"It really took you this long to figure that out?" she questions, half joking. I guess deep down I knew it all along, only I was afraid to admit it. Afraid I would get hurt again if I gave him my heart. Irony is a funny thing.

"I'm not even sure where I went wrong. It started off innocently enough. I admit, at first the thought of trading his story for my dream job was tempting. May have even thought I could do it, I wanted the job so damn badly. But the more time I spent with him, the harder I fell. Then I talked myself into things to avoid dealing with it. For a while there, I actually had myself believing it wasn't true. That I could be the superhero, prove the truth to the paper, kill the story, and get the guy in the end."

I laugh at how ridiculous it sounds to even say the words aloud. "By the time I finally admitted to myself that the story was true, I couldn't bring myself to crush him by telling him what I was assigned to do. Every day it just got harder to come clean, yet I fell deeper at the same time."

"You need to tell him, Liv."

I smile at my best friend. She's always there for me, I appreciate she's trying to help. But she didn't see him. That ship has sailed. "I wish it was that easy, Ally."

"So what are you going to do, sit here and let him walk out of your life? Again."

"I don't know, Al, I'm not sure there is anything I can do at this point to change things. You didn't see him."

After another restless night of sleep, I wake feeling like a freight train ran me over. Then backed up. And ran me over again. Physical ailing aside, at least morning brings me some semblance of clarity.

"Morning, sunshine." Ally smiles at me as she retrieves her toast from the toaster, burning her finger in the process. Bringing her finger to her mouth, her usual first aid treatment, she asks, "How are you feeling?"

"Like crap."

She smiles. "You look like crap too."

Leave it to Ally to make me laugh. "Thanks, friend."

"No problem." She grabs out a plate and tosses her half burnt toast in the general vicinity. "Want me to make you toast?"

"Ummm…no thanks. I'll get something on my way."

She arches her eyebrows in surprise. "You're going out?"

"I'm going to see Delilah."

"Vince's mother?"

"Yep."

"Why?"

Pouring my morning coffee into a to go cup, I head toward the door. "I have no idea. I just need to talk to her."

I manage to find my way back to Delilah's, which is a feat, considering I've only been there once and my propensity for getting lost. She looks exhausted and stressed, although after hearing Vinny talk about her, I'm grateful that she seems to be sober.

"Can I come in?"

"Of course, is everything okay?" Stepping aside, Delilah looks past me, expecting someone to be with me.

"Everything's fine. Well, no. That's not true. Everything isn't fine. Vinny is fine. Well, I mean he isn't hurt or anything," I stammer. Nice job playing it cool, Olivia, real cool. I mentally roll my eyes at myself.

"I know what you mean." Her shoulders slump in defeat. "He was here earlier."

Jesus, I hadn't even thought of that. What if I'd come by and he was here, or walked in while I was sitting talking to his mother? I'm not even sure why I've come…there's no way I could have explained myself to him. Surely he'd think I was working, trying to glam more for my story.

"Is he upset?"

"Angry. He's very angry." Tears well up in her eyes. "All I've ever done to that boy was let him down. I just know I'm going to lose him for what I've gotten him into this time."

"I'm afraid I've lost him already." I look at his frail mother. Time has not been kind. She looks older than her years, not healthy, way too thin. We come from different places, yet the two of us have a bond in the moment. Two women, loving and hurting the same man. A lone tear falls, I don't have the energy to even try to stop it. I'm just so emotionally drained.

"Oh no. I'm sorry honey, I didn't realize you two were having trouble." Reaching over, she gently takes my hand into hers, "I saw the way he looked at you. Whatever happened, I'm sure you can fix it."

"I'm not sure he can forgive me."

"Forgive you? What could you possibly have done?"

I guess he didn't tell her that I was the reason he found out in such an awful way the truth about his father. "It's a long story." I exhale loudly. "But I was the writer assigned to write the story about his real father."

"His what?" Her already pasty face goes stark white, every bit of color disappearing almost instantly.

I spend the next hour telling her everything. Spilling my heart out. The Senator, Jax, the fight, the newspaper. All of it. I leave no stone unturned in my confession. I'd thought she just didn't know about my role in the story, but it turned out, she didn't know any part of the story. After the shock of her dark past comes to light, she looks sad, yet something in her also screams relief. Carrying around such a big secret for twenty-five years had to have been difficult.

"But I'm confused, if you didn't know about the secret coming out, why were you so concerned about losing Vinny?"

"I dragged him into something horrible. There was this guy I trusted. I introduced him to some bad people..." She trails off.

"Jason?"

She nods and does her best attempt at a smile. "Well, they found him."

"That's great." Might be the first piece of good news I've heard in days.

"Not exactly."

For the next hour, it's her turn. She fills me in on what they've been through the last two days. I feel sick thinking of the choice before

Vinny. As if what I've done to him isn't bad enough. He's now forced to give up the one thing that he probably feels like he can control. The thing he has worked so hard for all these years. My heart that I thought was already broken beyond repair shatters into a million little pieces.

Leaving even more drained and tired than I felt when I arrived hours earlier, I stop as I get to the door, remembering one more unanswered question. "Whose dog tags does he wear every day? He thinks they're his father's."

Not thinking it could get any worse, her answer betrays even me, sorrow oozing from her voice. Her face. Her every being. "Bought them from a used bin at the Salvation Army."

I drive downtown and walk for hours. Getting nowhere, aimlessly thinking in circles. Finding myself in front of Nico's gym, I decide I'm more afraid of the consequences of my inaction than the reaction I might receive. Trembling inside, I will myself steady and open the door. The guy at the front door has a face full of cuts, bruises, and bandages, and turns away quicker than I can get my voice out to speak.

But I don't need for him to tell me if Vinny's here, because I know. I feel it in my bones, in my blood…the crackle in the air, the unmistakable tension that tells me he's near. Scanning the room, I turn…it doesn't take me very long to find him. He's found me across the room, before my eyes find his. Staring daggers, he takes long strides to make his way to me. Seeing the look in his eyes, my brain tells me to flee, yet my heart has me frozen in place.

"What do you want?" he asks, his words scathing through gritted teeth.

"I wanted to see if you were okay."

"I'm fine. Is that it?" He folds his arms across his chest, feigning indifference, although I know better. He's hurt and in protective mode.

"I'm sorry, Vinny."

"You've said that. Anything else?"

"I never meant to hurt you."

"You didn't."

I lower my head. I feel ashamed for what I've done, but I have no shame in telling him how I feel. I need him to know. "I love you." A tear runs down my face.

"If you're done, you can get the hell out, Liv." He turns his back and storms away angrily.

CHAPTER 49

Liv

Whoever said that time heals all wounds obviously never met Vince Stone. I didn't expect him to call me, certainly not come running to tell me he forgives me. Yet I also didn't expect it to end this way either. My heart keeps beating, but with each beat it withers just a little more, forlornly unhappy.

"When are you telling Sleezeball?" Ally leans over the back of the couch, her arms dangling as she talks to me while I pack things up from the kitchen.

"The article is due Friday. So I figured I'd see him then. Don't want to give them any time to do any of their own digging. The story was supposed to run in the paper the day after the fight."

"What about your trip to D.C.?"

"Flying down Friday night. If all goes well, I'll be back to Chicago by Saturday afternoon." I sigh. "I really do want to see his fight. I know he doesn't want me there, but I want to be there anyway."

Picking up the vase of dried wild flowers I'd set on the counter the afternoon Vinny brought them to me, I pick one out and dump the rest in the garbage. I'm just not ready to let go of everything yet.

I've been packing for a week. My job in New York starts in seven days. I couldn't save Vinny from being hurt, the least I could do is leave him and his mother to struggle through everything privately. Give them the dignity and respect they deserve to work it out without being in the public eye. Not surprisingly, the results of the DNA test proved positive. Senator Knight is Vinny's father, but no one will ever know it. Ally and I burned the results and Senator Knight will be happy I've decided to keep quiet. He's so arrogant, he'll probably even think I did it for him. That his threats scared me into submission.

"What am I going to do without you?" Ally sprawls onto the couch in an overzealous display of drama, one arm thrown across her face theatrically.

"You mean who's going to drive you places?" I tease.

Sitting upright, her response reminds me just how much I'm going to miss her. "Well, with you in New York, at least now I'll be bicoastal!"

"You do know Chicago isn't on a coast, right?"

"Whatever." She waves her hand at me like the details are just not important.

Friday morning, Summer smiles at me as I come out from Sleezeball's office. Actually, it's less of a smile and more of a gloat. Oddly, I feel a sense of relief telling the paper that I wasn't able to connect Senator Knight with Vinny. It's like closing a door behind heartbreak and pain. I only hope that Vinny and his mother find a way to heal, to get through the agony that years of lies and deceit have caused.

While I pack up the few personal belongings I kept at my desk, Summer sits back in her chair, smiling like a Cheshire cat. She's won, yet I can't help feel pity on her for what she had to resort to in order to get to the finish line.

"You know Olivia, you shouldn't feel too badly. If it wasn't the story, it would have been something else." She pauses and I pretend I don't hear her as I clear out the rest of my drawers. Getting a last rise out of me is just what she wants. "That man is just way too much man for you to handle."

The need to defend him wins out, even though he's not mine to defend anymore. "You don't know a thing about Vinny."

"Maybe that was true, but I know he came to *my* apartment a few nights ago. And not *yours*."

I take a deep breath, digging deep to quell my rising anger. Closing my eyes, I try desperately to rise above it. But I'm a writer, and closing my eyes just brings the visual of the words to life in my head. And it's more than I can bear to witness. Unable to stop myself, I take the two steps to walk around my desk to where she's standing and pull back and smack her square across the face. Her head flails to the side with the power behind my angry slap.

Hand stinging, box in hand, head held high, I don't look back as I walk out of the *Daily Sun Times*.

CHAPTER 50

Vince

Underneath the arena, less than an hour to go until the biggest fight of my life, and I'm fucking miserable. Finding it difficult to pretend to be psyched up for a fight that I know I can't win, I'm glad for the chaos in the locker room that surrounds a championship fight. Otherwise I'd have to deal with Nico one on one. The fucked up part is I feel worse for doing this to Nico than I do for myself.

Over on the other side of the room, I see him talking to a reporter. He talks about the years that we've worked together with pride. He's a pain in the ass, always has his nose in my business, yet I don't know where I'd be without him. In more ways than one.

Half an hour before we have to go up for announcements, Nico kicks everyone out of the room. Wrapping my hands, he starts with the pep talk I knew was bound to come.

"You're better than this guy."

"I know."

"Don't let it go to your head."

"Watch for when he drops his left…"

"I know."

"And don't let him take you to the ground."

"I know."

"Well if you know everything, what the hell do you need me here for?" Nico jokes, giving me a playful smack across the face.

"Listen, Nico," I pause, not sure of my words, not wanting to come out all sappy, sounding like a pussy…so I go for simple. "Thank you."

"I'm your trainer, you don't have to thank me. I get a cut, remember?" He smiles.

"I meant for everything."

Finishing the tape, Nico stills and looks up at me. A nod that says more than words ever could. He slaps one arm around my shoulder. "Come on, let's go kick some ass."

Standing at the back of the arena behind closed doors, I wait as the crowd cheers after the announcer calls my opponent into the ring. Head bowed, I close my eyes, taking in the electricity of the moment. A moment that should be mine. Ten years in the making, and I'm finally here. The doubters never thought I'd make it. Thinking back, neither did I most days. I spent my life swimming upstream, but sometimes… sometimes, it just got to be too much. So I'd stop swimming and just let the current take me for a ride, never knowing where I was going to land.

Nico clasps his hand to my shoulder as the door opens and I look down the familiar dark aisle toward the center where all the lights shine. "You ready to do this?" he yells to me over the sound of the crowd leaking out through the open door.

"As I'll ever be."

CHAPTER 51

Liv

The plane circles in the air for what seems like the hundredth time and I sit fidgeting in my seat. I'm not going to make it. They need to land this damn plane. A voice breaks into my thoughts, coming from a speaker above me. "Ladies and gentlemen we're just going to be a little while longer here. We're backed up and they've got us in a holding pattern. It seems our delay out of D.C. has made us miss our ground time here in Chicago and now we need to wait our turn in line."

A hand covers mine, stilling it, ending my mindless tapping with worry on the armrest. "Relax, we have time. We'll make it." Elle's smile comforts me. A little anyway. There are no words to describe how much Elle making the trip means to me. She did so much more than prepare the legal documents, I'm not sure I could've gone through with it without her. Standing by my side the whole time gave me the confidence I needed to know I was doing the right thing. Well, technically, what we were doing wasn't the *right* thing, I'm not even sure it was really legal, but sometimes it takes a series of wrongs to come out in the right place in the end.

"Thank you so much for doing this with me," I say, turning to the beautiful woman sitting beside me. "I know how hard it must have been for you to leave the baby all day. And I'm sure Nico is going to have a whole lot to say when he finds out the real reason you went out of town." Half teasing with my last comment, I attempt a playful smile, although it comes out what it really is...a sorry excuse at covering my frayed nerves.

"You've thanked me a hundred times, Liv." She smiles. "I'm glad I could help, but really, Vinny's family. I'd do anything for that boy." Turning in her chair to face me more directly, her eyes filled with sincerity, she says, "I know you don't think so now, but everything is going to work itself out. I just feel it. He loves you, Liv. He wouldn't be so angry and miserable if he didn't."

I know she's trying to help, yet hearing that I've made Vinny angry and miserable just tugs at my heart. Seeing my face falter, she continues, "It hurts. I know. But you're sacrificing a lot to make it right for him and someday, when his hot temper cools down, he'll see it."

Finally we pull up to the front of the arena. The cab barely stopped, I throw money in the front seat and rip open the car door. It's quiet outside as we make our way to the entrance. Everyone is already inside. Not a good sign. Elle needs to get to him before it's too late.

We pass through security quickly and shove our tickets in the hands of the man collecting them and take off running down the hall before he even has a chance to rip them in half and give us our stubs.

"This way." Elle yells over the sound of cheers coming from the inside of the arena. Grabbing the door to the first entrance we find, the announcer's voice comes over the loud speaker, filling the air over the sound of the cheering from the crowd.

"Ladies and Gentlemen, in the red corner, standing six-feet tall, weighing in at one hundred eighty-three pounds, the contender for the middleweight champion of the world, with a record of 12-0, looking to make it lucky number thirteen tonight, the ladies love him, the men fear him...I give you Vince 'The Invinnnnnnciiiible' Stone!"

My heart thuds in my chest, beating rapidly in sync with the sound of the crowd cheering wildly and I watch frozen in place as he steps into the center of the ring. As my foot passes over the doorway threshold, barely on the carpet that covers the inner venue, I see Vinny turn, his eyes scanning the crowd, almost looking for someone. Snapping me out of my stupor, Elle grabs my arm and the security guard points us in the direction of our assigned seats. We make it to the front, finding our two empty seats, just three rows back from the cage.

"Sit, let me try to get to him." Elle yells over the crowd and I do as instructed, my eyes still fixated on the back of the man now standing in his corner. Horrified, I sit frozen in my seat as I catch Elle arguing with yet another oversized security guard. He repeatedly shakes his head no, denying Elle passage as the two men meet in the middle of the ring and bump fists while the referee goes through the rules.

We're running out of time. Running out of time. I silently plead with God, trying to make a deal to get him to help me. Please, please, just let her through. Let her get to him in time and I'll do anything. Anything. And then the bell dings...

Eyes glued to the cage, I watch in horror as the two men begin to jump around. Vinny's opponent striking first, he lands an early shot to Vinny's right shoulder, but Vinny keeps moving right through it. Landing a few quick snap jabs to the face, Vinny turns slightly to the left, following up with an elbow that crashes into his opponent's cheekbone, his skin tears at the point of impact.

The two back off a few seconds, both jumping around, looking for an opening of some kind. Finding one, Lamaro lowers his shoulder and charges, plowing Vinny into the cage, in what looks like a failed attempt to bring him down to the ground. But now Vinny's backed into the corner, and his opponent throws punches at him at a feverish pace. Somehow he's able to avoid many of them, although not all, as some connect while he tries to break free.

Vinny finally manages to push his opponent back and regroup. But before he can get his left arm back up, Lamaro lands a powerful roundhouse kick that connects directly with Vinny's face and I watch in horror as his head sails to the side from the sheer momentum of the strike. He's still standing, but the hit leaves Vinny wobbly on his feet, and his opponent sees an opportunity and lunges in, taking Vinny to the ground, his back connecting with the mat in a loud thud that makes me cringe. It takes my breath away from the impact of the fall and I'm not even the one in the cage.

The two men go at it on the ground, rolling and alternating powerful knees crashing on each other's torso for what seems like forever, yet in reality is probably less than a minute. And then Lamaro maneuvers swiftly and winds up on top, Vinny's face to the mat, arm stretched in what looks like a painstaking hold behind him. And I think it's all about to end, my prayer's unanswered, Vinny's going to lose...when the bell dings ending the round.

The crowd goes crazy and two young fans run toward the cage, momentarily distracting the monster sized security guard from Elle's never-ending pleading. She ducks under his left arm at the moment he tries to catch the two charging fans with his right, and darts to the cage. Nico enters the cage and meets Vinny in the corner, just as Elle reaches them, yelling frantically from the other side of the metal patchwork cage.

The security guard grabs Elle's arm from behind, just as Nico looks up, catching sight of the grip the hulking guard has on his wife. Looking at Nico's face, for a second I think there might be an even more brutal fight about to occur as he barks something at the guard who quickly complies, throwing his hands up in surrender.

Anger still rooted in his face, Nico listens as his wife unloads the information she needs him to pass on to Vinny. Shaking his head, I can almost see the steam coming from Nico's ears. He looks between Elle and Vinny and quickly turns his attention to Vinny, an angry tirade unloading all over his prized fighter.

Seconds tick by and I watch on the edge of my seat, unsure what I'm waiting for to happen. Vinny's jaw clenches as he listens, then he lifts his gaze and catches sight of me. Neither of us moves, not a blink, not a swallow, not a flinch…and I try to tell him everything without words, will him to trust me, know it's okay to listen to what he's hearing. But why should he? He trusted me once, and look what I did when he gave me the gift he offers so few.

The bell dings, forcing us to disconnect. Eyes and body refocused on the task at hand, I watch as the two men quickly go at it again.

"Alright, well he knows now. All we can do is hope he believes us." Elle collapses into her seat next to me.

"Oh my god, Elle. Nico looks so pissed."

"Yeah, me and Vinny are going to have to go into hiding somewhere for at least three or four decades to give him time to cool down over this one." She grins, trying her best to make light of the situation. But seriously, she's going home to one angry man, regardless of how the fight ends.

The first kick catches both of our attention, our focus back inside the cage. We can worry about the fallout later. Vinny pursues his opponent, throwing a rapid series of punches, closing the distance between them as he backs Lamaro into the corner of the cage. Not about to back down, Lamaro lifts his leg, using the cage behind him as leverage and slams his foot into Vinny's ribs, sending him backward three steps, hindering his approach.

Vinny recovers fast, stepping in with one foot as his opponent comes at him and landing a powerful round house kick to the side of Lamaro's chest. Recovering swiftly, the two men spend the next minute going blow for blow, literally beating each other to a pulp. Each successive strike coming faster and harder than the last, it's amazing that either of them is even still standing.

Finally, both unable to keep up the pace of the excruciating battle in the center of the ring, they both appear to back off, putting distance between them. Catching sight of the time clock at the corner of my eye, I watch the seconds tick down, twenty, nineteen, eighteen…

The two men circle slowly, their chests heaving wildly up and down, both struggling to catch their breath before the other. Fourteen, thirteen...

Unable to sit anymore, I jump from my seat, anxiety getting the best of me. "Come on Vinny...you can do it!" I hear myself scream, but it's like an outer body experience. Everything is in slow motion as I watch it all play out in front of me. Ten, nine...

Hearing anyone over the roaring crowd would be impossible, but yet, as I jump at my seat, one hand on each side of my mouth to direct the sound coming from within me, I could swear I catch Vinny's eye... just for a split second.

Eight, seven...

Vinny fakes to the right, Lamaro falls for it, dropping his hands just slightly on the left and then Vinny goes for it, hitting him with a powerful right that's too much for his opponent's battered body to absorb.

Five, four...

His opponent staggers, a last ditch effort to remain on his feet, but his body can take no more. Collapsing to the mat in slow motion that ends with a thud as the arena goes quiet, Lamaro's body sprawls across the mat on his back.

The crowd cheers as medical personnel rush into the cage. They run something under Lamaro's nose and he comes through, his eyes darting open. For a second, it looks like he might attempt to get up, but then his head falls back and he realizes he can't continue. It's over.

Two, one...

The referee raises Vinny's arm in the air and the crowd goes crazy. The decibel's rising to painful levels, people jump out of their seats, screaming and shouting. Everyone loves to see the underdog win, especially one from their home town.

The cage starts to fill, and I watch with tears of joy in my eyes as Nico rushes to Vinny, lifting him in the air in celebration. Elle nudges me, "Come on." She wants me to go with her to the cage to see them, help them celebrate the win. More than anything, I wish I could. Wish I could rewrite the story of my life to bring us both a happy ending. But I can't and I want more than anything for Vinny to have his moment. "You go. Help them celebrate. I want him to be happy."

Sadness in her eyes, she smiles at me, pulling me close for a hug. I watch as she tries to make her way to the ever filling, chaotic cage, but I can't bear to let him pass me when he exits. So I leave, never turning back as I make my way out of the arena.

CHAPTER 52

Vince

The celebration at Nico's gym is in full swing before we even arrive. Two hours of interviews and photos leaves me feeling restless, but also pissed off at myself. I won the fucking championship. I should be reveling in every minute of the attention, god knows in this business it sometimes doesn't last long. There's always someone bigger and better.

With every interview and every photo, I find myself looking at the door, wondering where she is. I still have no idea how she pulled off the shit she did. Liv doesn't have the kind of money to buy them off, I'm not even sure how the hell she knew what I was up to.

Grabbing a beer from the makeshift bar set up behind the practice ring, I try to make my way over to Elle, but I'm stopped with every step by someone offering me congratulations. Nico's brothers alone take up almost an hour. Great guys, but sure as shit can talk your ear off.

It's after midnight by the time I've made the rounds, and the GIMPs have started to trickle in. Word spreads quickly when a gym party pops up, the groupies know it will be filled with fighters. Avoiding passing by two aggressive women that have no qualms letting me know their plans for the evening entails them sharing, I find myself standing off to the side with Nico.

Raising his beer to clink with mine, he smiles, "Tonight, we celebrate." Drawing a long swig, he nods his head to me, "tomorrow, we talk about what the hell almost happened out there."

Fuck. I nod my head. He must be happy, normally he'd be in my shit, never giving me space. "Where's Elle?"

"Babysitter needed to go. She went up."

Shit. "I really need to talk to her."

Pushing off from the wall he's casually leaning against, Nico chugs the rest of his beer. Slapping me on the back, he smiles. "She said you wouldn't rest till you had answers."

I wait, hoping she's given him some to pass along to me. Help me make sense out of the last few hours.

"She said to tell you to go talk to your mother."

"Really?" My mother has the answers? She's usually the question.

Nico walks away and then stops, looking back at me pointedly and smirks. "Oh yeah, she said to tell you when you're done with that, pull your head out of your ass and go get your girl before it's too late."

Seven in the morning is not usually a time my mother is awake, unless it's from the night before. I quietly enter her apartment and I'm surprised to find her standing in the kitchen, pouring a cup of coffee. She smiles at me and pulls down a second cup.

"I watched on TV." She hands me a full cup of steaming black coffee, not letting go, forcing my eyes to hers. "I'm so proud of you." Searching my mother's tired, weary eyes, I'm surprised to find sober staring me back. I nod, accepting the compliment.

She sits at the kitchen table and sips her coffee, motioning for me to sit as she begins, "That woman loves you."

My jaw clenches, she sees the anger in my face, it's difficult to hide. She's cut me deep.

"This is all my fault. You shouldn't blame her. My lies got us here. I know it will be hard for you to understand, but she was only trying to protect you. Keep *my* lies from hurting you."

"Start from the beginning, Mom. I don't need protecting, I need answers now."

Two hours later, and a bucket load of tears from both of us shed, I have my answers. It reads like a fucking tabloid story. One that Liv was supposed to write. But instead she lied, trading keeping my secrets for the job she's dreamed about since she was a kid. And then sells her keeping that secret to my rich scumbag of a father, only to pay off my drug addict mother's debt so that I can take a shot at *my* dream. Only in my life does shit like this happen.

Kissing my mother on the forehead before I leave, she reaches for my arm. "I have no right to give you advice. I've been a shitty mother to you. But if you love her, find a way to figure it out, because you're a good man and you deserve to be happy."

"Where's your boss?" Skinny ass Summer turns at the sound of my voice.

"She's already gone."

"Did I ask where Liv is? I'm looking for your boss." Her mouth hanging open, she points to a nearby closed door. I knock once and let myself in without waiting for his response.

CHAPTER 53

Liv

Ally drops me off at the airport. "Be nice to my car. I'm coming back soon to check on it."

"You better." She smirks. We've been best friends a long time, she knows I don't care about the car...I'll be back to check on her.

"I'll drive it back Labor Day when I come to visit for the long weekend."

"If you change your mind..." Ally hugs me hard and then pulls back to look at me, concern evident on her face. "Our door is always open."

Still another hour before my flight, I stop at the coffee bar before going through security, waiting in the long line, staring blankly at the television monitor behind the cashier's head. Lost in thought, it takes a few seconds for the words my brain reads as they scroll on the bottom of the screen to register. *Breaking News - A Daily Sun Times Exclusive - Senator Preston Knight has a love child.* I watch in horror as seconds later a photo of Vinny flashes on the screen.

Numb, I stare at the TV, a real wave of nausea rolling over me. Cold sweat percolates from within, sheathing my body, while dread and sadness consume me. How? I'd destroyed the evidence and the only people that knew had everything to lose and nothing to gain by leaking the story.

Shock still keeping my feet firmly planted, my brain finally reignites and begins to fire on all cylinders. I need to get to Vinny. Warn him. Tell him it wasn't me. Make him believe me. I'm not sure why it's so important, I only know I need to do it. Now. Grabbing my bags, I turn and take two steps back toward the exit, stopping in my tracks at the vision a few feet before me. Vinny.

Bags falling from my shoulder, I stare, confused, feeling nervous and anxious to see him, yet relieved at the same time. Four feet of empty space between us, my words barely loud enough to make their way to him, I whisper with emotion blanketing my face, "I didn't leak the story."

Hesitantly, Vinny takes one step closer. "I know."

"You know?" Confusion clear on my face.

Another step closer. "I did."

Eyes wide, I hear his words but don't understand. "Why?"

One more step, he closes the distance between us. Every hair on my body stands at attention, my body inexplicably drawn to him like every other time before. Nothing quells my desire for this man. Not anger, not sorrow, not years of separation.

"Traded the story for your job back." Gently, Vinny reaches for me, brushing his warm hand softly over my cheek.

"But why?"

"You and Elle run off to D.C. to sell your silence to pay off my mother's debt, seemed like the least I could do." He pauses. "Although I should also put you over my knee for putting yourself in danger like that." The corner of his mouth twitches.

A small smile bubbles to the surface, although it's quickly extinguished when my heart reminds me of how I've hurt him. How he hurt me. Again. Thoughts of Vince with Summer cause physical pain in my chest. Looking down, I draw a deep breath in, stealing a few precious seconds to compose myself. The words pass through my lips tasting like bile, "You and Summer?" Head still bowed, I steady myself for his response. But nothing comes. Without words or seeing him, I feel the intensity of his stare burning into me.

"Look at me, Liv." His tone firm, but words soft, I take a deep breath in. Hesitantly, I lift my eyes and find his. Our gaze locked, he's quiet for a moment before he speaks. Eyes searching mine, I find my own sorrow and sadness reflected back at me. "Nothing happened with Summer."

"But Summer said…"

His voice is low and calm, yet his tone is firmer, more commanding. "Nothing happened, Liv."

I want so badly to believe him…my body aches to trust his words. He sees my internal struggle on my face.

"You need me to tell you the details?" The words sound cruel, but he's offering them to me because he knows how I am. Even if I told him I believed him, visions of the two of them would consume me, subconscious doubt never allowing me to fully forget. I need the full story, so my imagination doesn't make up its own.

I nod.

Vinny closes his eyes for a moment, reaching for strength. When he reopens them, I see torment and it breaks my heart. So badly, I want to reach out and hold him, make it better, take his pain away, but I can't. I need to hear what he has to tell me. Pain in his words when he speaks makes tears sting my eyes, but I fight to keep them back. "Summer came to see me. Told me about the story you were writing. I told her to get out, I didn't want to believe her. She left me her card, with her home address written on the back."

Vinny pauses. The hope I had felt hearing him say nothing happened with Summer begins to flee.

"I was pissed, Liv. Angry. I wanted to hurt you back. I just couldn't shake it, no matter how hard I hit the bag or how fast I ran. So I headed out to find some random woman to help me forget. And somehow I wound up at Summer's." I flinch at his words. Releasing me from his gaze, Vinny bows his head. His expression one of shame, he continues,

"It's what I've always done, Liv."

Unable to hold it all back any longer, a lone tear falls from my eyes, just in time for Vinny to look up at me and gently wipe it from my cheek. His hands cup my face and pull me closer to him. "Nothing happened. I went there and she let me in smiling. It would have been so easy." He shakes his head, thinking back, remembering. "But I couldn't do it. And her big gloating smile, just made me more pissed. She was enjoying hurting you. So I left. Didn't lay a finger on her. Think I might've put a hole in the wall behind her door, I flung it open so fast to get the hell out of there."

Vinny leans down to me, his face so close I can feel his warm breath on my cheek. "I didn't touch her, Liv." His thumb brushes my cheek tenderly. "Do you believe me?"

I nod my head, because I do. It's the honesty in his eyes that makes me believe him.

Closing his eyes with a look of relief, he leans his forehead against mine for a long moment. There's less tension and anxiety in his face when he pulls his head back, but some of it's still there, lurking in the shadows of tranquility. "Why didn't you just tell me about the story, Liv?"

I wish there was an easy answer. One that would take away the pain I see in the depths of his eyes. Pain that I put there. He trusted me and I let him down. Seeing the hurt on his face, knowing I put it there, hurts me even more than I ached thinking he was with Summer. But I know I need to be honest with him, give him what he just gave me, if there's any chance of us ever getting past it all. So I start with the truth, because it's where I should have started all along.

"At the beginning, I talked myself into that it wasn't true. I think I thought I could prove it and I'd get both things I wanted...the job and you." I pause, thinking back to the minute I realized I was only fooling myself. "Then I met Senator Knight. And Jax."

Vinny's jaw clenches. I'm not sure if it's the mention of his father or if he's remembering meeting Jax at the exhibition fight. "He put his hands on you, Mom told me." He searches my face, fists clenching in an innate response, his protective instinct taking hold of him at even the thought of someone laying their hands on me.

"By the time I realized it was true, I couldn't bring myself to tell you. I didn't want to hurt you. You've always been proud of your father's memory. Sometimes I felt like you *needed* it. I just didn't want to take that away from you."

"So you never used me for a story?" His voice is desperate, full of agony at even having to ask the question. He needs to know that it was real. Needs to understand I could never betray him like that.

"I wanted to protect you. I never meant to hurt you."

"I. Protect. You. Liv. I don't need you to protect me. That's how it works," he says, his voice rising, eyes stern and serious. He waits for me to accede.

"No." My response spoken with conviction, it surprises him.

Squinting, he studies me for a moment, not saying a word. I suppose his look could be labeled menacing, yet it doesn't make me waver in the slightest. Instead, I stand taller.

One eyebrow cocked, he questions. "No?" I can't tell if he's amused or annoyed.

"No. *We* protect each other. *That's* how it works."

Both eyebrows pop this time. Although I catch a hint of an upward tilt on the left side of his mouth before he's able to hide it. He's amused, but doesn't want to let me in on the secret.

"Okay," he finally responds.

"Okay?" I question. Feeling bold, I push further. "Why was that so easy?"

Vinny laughs, his face and whole body shedding the last of the anger, diving head first into happiness. He wraps his arms around my waist and pulls me flush against him. Eyes sparkling, it warms my heart knowing I had something to do with putting the smile back on his face. "You're a pain in the ass."

Pretending to be offended, I feign trying to escape from his death grip. But the truth of the matter is there's no place I'd rather be.

A few minutes later, Vinny picks up my bags and reaches for my hand. "You ready to get out of here? I'm pretty sure you owe me a shitload of makeup sex." He grins at me.

Although even the thought of this man naked sends a shiver down my spine, there's more I need to say. "Wait." Vinny stops after taking only one step forward and turns back to me. "There's more I need to tell you."

He nods once and waits, cautiousness in his stance. Closing the small distance between us, I reach up to the beautiful face that still takes my breath away, even after all these years. Draping my arms around his neck, I pull him closer so our bodies are touching, yet he can still see my face as I speak. My voice barely audible as my eyes finds his, I tell him what I feel in every ounce of my being, "I love you."

He smiles, cupping my face in both his hands. "Love you too, Liv. Think a part of me always has." Softly, Vinny's lips cover mine as he seals a kiss on words I've waited almost a decade to hear.

EPILOGUE

Liv

Walking into the steam filled bathroom, I marvel at the sight of the gloriously naked body stepping from the shower. It's been months, yet it never gets old.

Vinny grabs a towel and wraps it around his waist. Lucky towel.

"Morning." He leans down and kisses my lips, uncaring that water is dripping everywhere, a playful, devilish grin on his handsome face.

"Good morning." I smile.

"It could be." Taking the towel from his waist, he purposefully lifts it to his shoulders to dry off, leaving his very aroused bottom half delightfully naked, standing firmly at attention. The confident, knowing smile tells me it's a calculated move and has nothing to do with needing to dry off. He wiggles his eyebrows suggestively when he catches me staring.

"You're insatiable." I laugh.

Wrapping his hand firmly around the back of my head, he tilts my head toward him. "You know I get turned on when you use SAT words." Another hot, wet kiss planted chastely on my lips.

"Insatiable is definitely not on the SAT."

"Whatever. Keep talking." Allowing the towel to drop to the

ground, he reaches down under my knees, scooping me up into his arms.

"Existential, exculpate, ebullient, evanescent, ephemeral."

Reaching the bed, Vinny quirks one eyebrow. "Ephemeral?"

"Short lived. Fleeting."

"Yeah, what I'm about to give you isn't going to be ephemeral."

Lying in bed sated, my ear pressed to his chest, I listen as Vinny's heart beats steadily. The sound soothes me, leaving me feeling replete, a feeling I've come to cherish after so many months of chaos swirling around us. Thinking back, things could have gone so differently. The press had a field day with Vinny's admission. Months of nonstop badgering from reporters could have taken its toll, but instead, somehow, it bound us even tighter. Me and Vinny against the world.

After giving the exclusive story to the *Daily Sun Times* in exchange for my job, we hung low for a while. Vinny needed to recover physically from his fight and mentally from the toll the last 25 years had taken on him. Preach, Nico's old trainer, loaned us his lake house, a serene, picturesque hideaway where we could escape the hordes of reporters and photographers vying for a piece of Vinny.

Like Vinny, Senator Knight eventually gave the media his side of the story, falling far short of full disclosure, although finally admitting to a one night drunken affair. Mrs. Knight stood dutifully by his side the entire time, a plastered smile on her perfectly made up face. I noticed Jax was suspiciously missing from all of the family photos aimed at restoring the Senator's public image, but I kept my thoughts to myself.

"I have to get up soon." Vinny strokes my head as he speaks.

"I know. But I'm so comfy." I snuggle closer to him, his warm body feeling incredible flush against mine. My body uncaring that it just spent the last hour greedily consuming his, the desire for more of him is just never quelled. Selfishly, I want to stay in bed all day, forget the ride they have planned, and keep him all to myself. I'm worried that today will be hard on him. Nico, on the other hand, thinks it will be good for Vinny. Help him get past the sour memory of his lost father by riding in the Veteran's fundraising motorcycle run again this year. I'm not so sure. The loss to Vinny, of a father that never really was, came harder than anything else. He grieved the loss of a man he honored from the time he was a child. A veteran that he clung to for purpose in his darkest hours.

As Vinny gets dressed, I'm still undecided on giving him what I've planned. For five weeks, I've tossed the idea back and forth, one day thinking it was a great idea, the next wondering if I was crazy for even considering giving it to him.

Eventually, we both begin to get dressed. "You okay?" I sit on the bed next to Vinny. He's been quiet since he got back out of bed.

He nods silently, seemingly lost in thought. "There's lots of Veterans out there that should be honored. I keep telling myself it's not about me. But it's hard not to be reminded." He pauses. "I don't know, I feel like I lost someone, yet I never really had them to lose."

My decision finally made for me, I walk to my purse and pull out an envelope. Removing a single page I'd written and balled up so many times, I offer it to the man I love as comfort. Vinny takes it and begins reading.

Staff Sargent Charles Fisher, Jr.

3/30/1960–1/19/1988.

Survived by his parents, Charles Fisher, Sr. and Laura Cantly Fisher, Staff Sargent Charles Fisher, Jr. was laid to rest on January nineteenth, nineteen hundred and eighty-eight.

A dedicated, two tour military hero, Sgt. Fisher was killed in the line of duty in Helmand Province, Afghanistan. Three days before the end of his second tour, Sgt. Fisher was passing through Helmand in route to the US Embassy, when he came upon a bus exploded by the detonation of a suicide bomber.

Acting quickly, and without regard for his own safety, Sgt. Fisher dragged seven children from the burning vehicle while under enemy fire. As he removed the final child, insurgents moved in closer, finding a new target for their hostile fire, hitting Sgt. Fisher five times. All victims were rushed to a nearby military hospital. Miraculously, all seven children survived. Sgt. Fisher was pronounced dead on arrival.

A look of confusion on Vinny's face, I remove the dog tags he'd ripped off his neck the day he found out the truth about his father.

"These dog tags belong to a hero. I researched the ID number. The man you've honored by wearing them may not be your father, but I thought you would be proud to wear them today anyway."

Vinny closes his eyes for a minute and I watch as his throat works to swallow. Eyes opening to a window of emotion, pain that was only just recently in the forefront being overshadowed by caring and love, he leans down and lowers his head. Gently, I slip the worn tags around his neck, softly kissing his cheek.

Vinny pulls me against his chest for a hug, wrapping his arms around me tightly. "You rewrote the ending of my story with the truth."

I smile against his chest. I hadn't thought about it that way, but I guess I did. Releasing his grip on me, Vinny pulls his head back enough to look into my eyes. His baby blues shoot an arrow straight through my heart, "I'm rewriting the ending to our story, Liv. I'm giving you your happily ever after. I promise."

Finally, more than seven years in the making, I have no doubt that he will.

Dear Readers,

*If you liked Vince & Liv, then please check out Jax & Lily this Spring. Growing up the privileged son of a wealthy Senator, Jax Knight followed the path he was expected to follow. But after realizing everything he grew up believing was a lie, he decides it's time to forge his own way. And for the first time in his life, things don't come easy. Especially love. The MMA Fighter series concludes in **Worth Forgiving**, the story of Jax & Lily.*

OTHER BOOKS BY VI KEELAND

Life on Stage series (2 standalone books)
Beat
Throb

MMA Fighter series (3 standalone books)
Worth the Fight
Worth Forgiving

The Cole Series (2 book serial)
Belong to You
Made for You

Standalone novels
Cocky Bastard (Co-written with Penelope Ward)
Left Behind (A Young Adult Novel)
First Thing I See

AUTHOR LINKS

Facebook: https://www.facebook.com/pages/Author-Vi-Keeland/435952616513958

Website: http://www.vikeeland.com

Twitter: https://twitter.com/ViKeeland

Instagram: http://instagram.com/Vi_Keeland/

Pinterest: http://www.pinterest.com/vikeeland/pins/

Goodreads: http://www.goodreads.com/author/show/6887119.Vi_Keeland

Amazon Author Page: http://www.amazon.com/Vi-Keeland/e/B00AZJ8TT0/

Mailing List Signup: http://eepurl.com/brAPo9

ACKNOWLEDGEMENTS

To Andrea, how did I make it through the day before you? I'm not even sure where to begin. Thank you for beta reading (the same book a dozen times), midnight stalking, 5AM chats, and your constant support and guidance. I can't believe it took us so long to find our friendship when it was clearly meant to be.

To some very special women, Carmen, Jen, Dallison, & Nita, thank you, thank you, thank you! For beta reading, editing, honesty, support and friendship.

Thank you so much to all of the bloggers that generously give their time to read and support Indie Authors! Without your support, our stories would not be read by so many!

Finally, thank you so much to all the readers. It is so much fun to create stories when you have amazing readers to love your characters. Keep your notes coming, I truly love hearing from you!

All my best,
Vi

CPSIA information can be obtained
at www.ICGtesting.com
Printed in the USA
LVOW10s1649300318
571778LV00010B/610/P